The GreenGlow
HAWK'S ARRIVAL

The GreenGlow

HAWK'S ARRIVAL

Gustavo Flores

The GreenGlow
HAWK'S ARRIVAL

ISBN-13: 978-0-615-55715-1

Logo Design and Cover Illustration
recreated by Jude Nielson
Artwrist
jude@artwrist.com

Editing Services by Lisa Rojany Buccieri
Editorial Services of Los Angeles
EditorialServicesLA@gmail.com

Book design by Maureen Cutajar
www.gopublished.com

In Collaboration with
{DvT} Hex

*You'll never realize the dream if you can't find the courage
and strength to take the first step.*

*This book is dedicated to everyone willing to try,
fail, and try again...*

Acknowledgements

Everyone should be so lucky. I'm fortunate to have been surrounded by a great group of people who, through their own approach and at what seemed to be perfect timing, assisted along the way.

Peter H., {DvT}Hex, thank you. Thank you for taking this journey with me, for being there every step of the way, for continually dropping hints, ideas, and occasionally adding your own flair. Although we had some ups and downs along the way, I couldn't think of anyone else I would have rather worked with on this project.

Thank you, Jon C., for creating and allowing the use of the Deviant logo. To my fellow Deviants, thank you for the inspiration.

Aaron W., in the early stages and Claire P. later on, thank you both for your honest feedback as the book progressed.

Tamara R., I appreciate your taking the time to perform the early edits.

To my son, Abelardo (Falcon), I truly appreciate your willingness to keep reading draft after draft. Your excitement and feedback about the story were an incredible help.

Kerri G., if you hadn't come along when you did, this story may still be sitting, waiting for my return. Thank you for asking the right questions, nudging me along, and believing in me.

To Stacey, Nina, Cassie, and all the girls at Starbucks for allowing me to sit in the store for hours, coffee in hand, to work through the additions and edits.

And last, but certainly not least, thank you, the reader, for taking a chance on an unknown. I hope you enjoy reading this story as much as I enjoyed writing it.

Prologue

The thief had never seen a knife with such workmanship, such detail. The handle was tightly wound in fine leather. Solidly embedded in the center was a pure, deep-green emerald with a band of solid gold surrounding the stone, locking it in place. And the double blade! Just the look of it told him the balance was true. It was only by chance he saw the contents of the pack that the man carried earlier in the day at the market square. The man seemed to be preparing for a long trip, but in this weather he would have to wait before getting started. Neither the weather nor the stranger's plans, made any difference; he had to have that knife.

Thankful now for the days of constant rain, the thief observed no one on the streets—thereby mostly eliminating the possibility of witnesses. The only ones out were at the bar and far into inebriation long before the thief entered the tavern. Even the barkeep was deep in his well.

Laughter and loud drunken conversation dominated the room. It took a moment for the thief's eyes to adjust to his surroundings. The bar was dimly lit with candles on tables and sconces sparsely lining the walls. The flickering light from the candles caused waves of shadows to dance off the patrons sitting in the bar. The occupied tables were arranged in clusters, cluttered with empty ale glasses as barmaids struggled to keep up. No one paid attention as the thief made his entrance from the cold and rain.

Looking about the bar, the thief spotted the man across the room. The pouch carrying his prize was resting on the man's back. The thief took a moment to plot his approach and departure in an attempt to prevent any unexpected bumps or contact with anyone other than his target. He wanted to make as little disturbance as possible. Interference would be disastrous.

His course plotted, the thief saw that approaching the stranger would be easy, for his back was turned. He was facing the bar, focused on the contents in the glass in front of him. *And with no small bit of acting,* the thief thought. The act was almost routine. Almost. As the thief moved toward the stranger from behind, he began to rock like a man having had his fill. His advance was expertly timed. The swaying back and forth allowed the thief to stagger himself into the stranger's back with enough force to push him into the bar. The initial contact allowed for the thief to open the pack and remove the prize unnoticed. Mumbling something drunkenly unintelligible, the thief expertly weaved his way through the tables, intentionally avoiding the larger pockets of men, and quickly made his way out of the bar.

But the man was not as drunk as the thief had thought. The stranger gathered his wits about him and pulled open the pack. Noticing that his knife was missing, he looked about the room just in time to see the double swing of the closing doors. The stranger stumbled through a more direct path toward the door, pushing his way past the men and their drink and exited the tavern, looking out into the pouring rain. Turning his head left revealed nothing, only the sound of the rain pattering loudly on the Rusted Lantern's porch awning. But turning right, he noticed the shadow of a man disappearing into the building's side alley. The man staggered to the corner of the porch when movement caught his eye.

Under a lamp illuminated in the alleyway, the now unsuspecting thief had paused just long enough to admire the dual blade. Standing in the pouring rain, holding the handle in his right palm with the blades resting in his left hand, the thief could not believe his great fortune...when a hard thump landed on his back. The stranger's arm then swung around from behind him, tangling the thief in his grip. The response from the stranger at the bar had not been expected and the fight in the man caught the thief completely off guard. The stranger was strong. But the thief had the advantage: He had not had a drink all night.

The thief fought to wrangle loose as the man went for the knife. The stranger reached over the thief's back, grabbing him by his right wrist in an attempt to wrestle the blade from his hand. Instinctively, the thief doubled over to pull away but in doing so caused the blade to stab his lower left side just above the hip. Bending over caused the dual blades to roll on the bone, cutting into the thief's flesh, but not penetrating deep enough to pierce any vital organs. The sudden sting of the cut angered the thief enough to turn suddenly toward the stranger and thrust his arm forward.

The other man stood there, stunned.

The look on the stranger's face told the thief his strike was true. As the thief pulled back the knife, the stranger doubled over and sank to the ground. The pool of dark blood, quickly clouding the puddles of rain, instantly told the thief that the stranger's shredded liver would drain away his life in a minute...or less.

The thief ran. His heart pounded. His lungs begged. His side burned, but that did not slow him down. Moving as quickly as his body would allow, the thief made his way into the forest and away from The Rusted Lantern.

The thief had never taken a life before. Not until now. And though the image of the dying man at his feet would last, remorse was not part of his emotional disposition. The thief's life, or rather his outlook on life, had changed.

He had the knife! And though a price had been paid, it was worth it. His left side had been grazed in the fight, but his guts had not been struck. The thief stanched the blood of the nasty cut, fashioned a bandage, and rested for a while before continuing.

A thief by trade, he had been roaming for years. He wandered from town to town, picking up small and precious items from the local townsfolk, always making sure never to lift enough to create suspicion. Occasionally, when the well-worn satchel he carried was full or contained enough to make the trip worthwhile, he would head south to the town of Falkenwrath to pawn his wares. The town was far enough away to prevent anyone from recognizing their possessions outright, properly displayed in a storefront window or mysteriously appearing in someone else's possession. Plus the shop owner there knew the materials the thief would inevitably arrive with were stolen but did not seem to mind—their return value was always worth the expense. Considering the thief had never before taken anything from anyone in Falkenwrath, pawning this particular possession could pose a problem. But the thief had no intention of giving up this prize.

Chapter One

And So the Tale Begins. . . .

The day had progressed with increasingly angry skies. As darkness fell, Hawk prepared a site at the base of a mountain, high enough in case rains came during the night. The ground was hard and cold as he lay down his head for what he hoped would be his last night in the dense forest of Shallow Rock. The snow was melting now, and spring was just starting to make its presence known, but the bitterness of winter remained. Somehow he knew that not too much farther he would finally reach the castle known as Deviant Stronghold. The journey had been a long one. Many lonely nights had been spent under blankets of frigid stars and waves of angry clouds dumping their wares as he traveled, but he persisted in making his way.

Hawk knew many before him had attempted the same journey but failed. Some returned to tell the tales that over time became legend, most did not. Hawk would not allow that to happen to him. He had heard of the legend of Deviant Stronghold years before and was determined to discover the truth for himself. Buried deep within the walls of the castle existed the entity known only as Sapient6. No one had ever seen this great power, and legend said only those deemed worthy were provided safe passage into the dense forest and allowed to locate the castle.

Hawk had been traveling endlessly, tirelessly. Much time had passed, and he knew he was now close. He could feel it deep within his very being as a controlling power, not his own, guided him to his destiny. It was as if his destination came closer to him with every step he took regardless of the direction his feet traveled. Eventually sleep overcame him as his mind eased away from his journey, and his body relaxed in the cold.

The new morning started like every other: early and rushed. Hawk gazed upon the sky as its deep purple slowly turned red. *The storms, they're close,* he thought as he gathered and rolled his fur bedding, carefully placing it in his sack to prevent it from getting wet should the skies open up. Hawk pulled a strip of jerky from one of the small pouches tied to his belt and munching thoughtlessly, started up the mountain. He wore a light-brown cotton shirt with the sleeves rolled up to the elbows under a leather coat. His pants were a dark shade of gray that disappeared into a pair of long boots, perfect for protecting his shins from missed branches and shrubs, perfect for traveling. Hawk used his sack to store gear for trapping and fishing along with the furs. Tied to his side was a large knife sharpened to a fine edge. Hawk's hair was dark and long, tied back by a piece of string given to him by a fair lady who had stolen his heart many years before.

With the use of a staff he maneuvered, careful to avoid holes or loose rock. The woods became thicker as he climbed and the smells of the forest dense. As Hawk reached the plateau of the mountain, a strong gust of wind hit him as if to knock him over. Catching his step and bracing himself for the brunt of the force before him, Hawk moved to the cover of a misshapen oak. *What is an oak doing here among the pines?* The thought had barely crossed his mind when down before him, beyond the valley, Hawk saw it.

There at the far end of the valley stood a large fortress, storm clouds raging high above the walls. Tightening his sack against him, Hawk continued down the mountainside toward the castle. With every step he took, the sky became darker, the air denser, the colors around him changing to a deeper green. The sun's light slowly disappeared as the canopy of trees became a filter, allowing only the smallest of rays to reach the ground below. Hawk became more and more tired with every step.

Hawk came upon a brook and stopped for a drink and to refill his water skins. As he stood over the water, Hawk could sense he was not alone. Remaining as still as possible, Hawk listened for movement. His eyes darted back and forth as his mind rang out the warning. From the corner of his eye he saw it. Turning slightly to get a better look, he saw a green glow behind the trees beyond a large stone that jutted from the side of the mountain from the opposite side.

"Face me!" Hawk shouted toward the shadows to no response. "Present yourself, and face me!"

Leaping over the brook, Hawk removed the sack from his back and dropped it alongside the staff to shed the extra weight and free himself to maneuver. He reached for the sheath tied to his leg and removed the blade while closing the distance between himself and the green glow—when suddenly it disappeared.

"Face me!" He stood at the ready.

"All that is kept is gained in peace. What is lost in war shall be no more," a voice declared from behind him.

Hawk turned. The green glow hovered over his rucksack. A blink and the glow above his sack disappeared, the staff vanishing along with it. He ran toward the spot where his belongings once lay, but it was too late. The entity was gone and left no tracks for him to follow. The wind ceased as if a door had been closed; the forest quieted. Replacing his blade in its sheath with frustration, Hawk started out again, this time looking for his rucksack and evidence that he was not losing his mind.

Deeper into the forest, the foliage was so thick that making any progress became an incredible burden. Hacking away with his knife, Hawk pushed further and further into the dense brush. Upon reaching a clearing, he stopped to rest. The image of the glow persisted in tormenting him, and the loss of his sack was a major blow. Much of the day had passed, and it seemed that darkness would once again fall upon him and he would need his fur skins. He began scanning the surrounding landscape for shelter as his priorities shifted from seeking the fortress to survival.

The broken logs and branches Hawk had collected for firewood were damp, causing much smoke at first, but after the wood fired up, the smoke cleared. Sitting by the fire, Hawk took note that along with the staff, his bedding, nets for fishing the rivers, rope, and the small traps he carried to catch food were also gone. All that was left to eat was two days' ration's of jerky. He would need to find a way to trap food soon. *Maybe I can fashion a bow in the morning. I hate making arrows. That will waste half a day. At least I still have my knife.* Taking a look around, Hawk cleared an area for his bed. He would need to sleep closer to the fire now that he was short his furs. The chore of setting camp complete, Hawk made his way over a small hill to gather more wood and familiarize himself with the surroundings. He eventually made his way back to the campsite for the night, settling in close. The warmth of the small fire and glow of the embers beneath it were comforting.

Through the darkness came the snap of a twig. Hawk awoke from his sleep at the sound and stared into the blackness. Another crack. Hawk quietly reached for his blade and waited. He watched for movement, but could see none. The thought of the glow that swallowed his pack chilled him. Slowly Hawk's eyes adjusted to the darkness as sleep left his head. From a short distance away, an image of someone appeared, but Hawk was still unsure.

"Do you always leave your camp after setting your fire?" the image said, a woman's voice.

"I gathered wood. Who are you?" Hawk replied, his head still waking.

"I saw the smoke from before. I came to see what caused it," she said, avoiding the question. The woman approached Hawk as he lay on the ground. The light of the burning embers was orange and dark, too faint to make a difference in the darkness. The small campfire illuminated her only slightly. Hawk stared at this woman in her long cloak but could not make out her face.

"Where did you come from? How long have you been there, watching me?"

The woman placed a stick into the embers and allowed for the tip to ignite.

"From below, not far from here. Come, smother the fire and follow me."

Hawk noticed she had no provisions so certainly she had not traveled far.

"Where are you taking me?" he asked.

"Come, follow me," she repeated. Lighting a candle lamp with the burning stick, she turned to leave.

Hawk watched her back as she slowly disappeared into the forest, unsure of what to make of this unusual happenstance. *What does this woman want from me?*

She paused about ten paces forward and turned. "Come, you're safe."

Hawk rose, gathering what was left of his belongings. After tying the sheath straps to his leg, he kicked dirt upon the burning embers of his campfire, dousing the flames and killing the light they provided. Hawk followed behind her into the dark night.

She had obviously traversed the path many times before since she had no problems making her way in the dark. She led him down the mountainside but not quite to the valley floor where, tucked away from view, a small cottage revealed itself. It was not a long trip from where they had started. Opening the door, she led him in and closed it behind them.

Hawk studied the home. It was warm and comfortable. A small table and chairs sat just off the center of the room, not far from the fireplace where a fire was burning. A cast iron pot hung on a hook over the flames. There was a small cot covered in blankets resting in the corner under a window. Hawk stared at the bed for a moment. *I sure miss my bed.* On the opposite wall was another window with shelves on each side that lined the walls, filled with pots, cookware, and other normal necessities of living. Below that window was a chest of drawers and trunks. Alongside the fireplace a corner served as the kitchen in the small home. The smell of the contents of the pot permeated the small cabin, waking Hawk's hunger.

He turned to see that she had removed her cloak and hung it by the door. Her back was facing him, revealing a long, beautiful mane of softly curled, golden brown hair. When she turned to him, he saw for the first time how lovely she really was. Her eyes were a captivating deep blue. Her skin looked soft and toned with full lips that, when parted, revealed a beautiful smile.

Stretching out her hand she said, "Give me your things. I'll place them by the door." Hawk did not move. "Please, you have nothing to worry about here."

Hawk removed the sheath, handing over only the small pouches that he carried tied to his belt, keeping the knife nearby. The warmth of the fireplace enveloped him. Much time had passed since he enjoyed the luxury of such provisions.

"Are you hungry? You must be. Come, sit at the table, and I'll set you a place."

"Who are you? And why are you helping me?" Hawk asked.

"I'm Deborah," she responded while serving a portion of beef and vegetables. "I come from a town not far from here to the west of the valley."

"My name is Hawk." Looking around for signs of a man but not seeing any, he added, "You have no husband? No children?"

"I did," she said, looking down with saddened eyes. "I'm widowed."

Hawk sensed her pain shoot right through him and instantly felt regret for having asked. He knew the feeling of losing someone you love. He did not pursue it any further. It did not matter anyway…not to him.

"We had no children."

Conversation ended there. Hawk ate his meal and was very thankful for it. Deborah prepared him a place to sleep by pulling some blankets off the bed and placing them on the floor where he would be warmed by the fire.

Hawk sat on a chair as he removed his boots and slackened his belt. He paused and looked at Deborah. She smiled and nodded her head. Hawk pulled his shirt over his head and placed it on the floor beside the blankets. Deborah watched as he crawled under the blankets and made himself comfortable.

After setting Hawk's bed, Deborah seemed embarrassed as she began preparing herself for the night. She asked if Hawk would look away as she readied herself. Hawk turned and lay facing the fire, propped on his elbow, his back toward her.

"You'll be comfortable here," she said. Turning down her blankets, she crawled into bed, her back toward Hawk.

Only a few moments passed, but Hawk could hear Deborah's breathing becoming heavy. *Was she asleep already?*

"I come from a town several valleys' distance from here. Thank you for your kindness," Hawk said, but receiving no response, he laid his head down, murmuring, "I must remember to ask if she has a sharpening stone," and fell right to sleep.

Deborah heard his fading words. She felt a strange sense of calm. Here she had a complete stranger in her home, the first man she'd ever invited in, and yet she felt no danger from him. Oddly, she felt comfortable, safe. Deborah smiled as she closed her eyes and drifted off to sleep.

As the hours of the night passed, Hawk slept comfortably, deeply. The weeks of travel had taken their toll. This night no overlooked pebble prodded his back, no whisper of the wilderness intruded upon his instincts. He dreamed. No visions of the past or of the future, but the deep slumber of a resting mind. When he would awaken, Hawk would know of this trance, but it would not be one he would be able to recount, for there was no tale here, only green. Even as his mind recorded this enigmatic perception, it did not trouble his sleep; it merely enveloped and comforted his psyche, as did the furs that Deborah had provided for his bedding.

*   *   *

It was Deborah who woke first. The call of the rooster roused her from sleep. She gazed upon the still sleeping stranger in her home. Slowly, carefully, as to not wake her guest, she lifted herself out of bed and moved toward her robe. The sun was reaching over the mountain as it made its way above the valley, and her figure was exposed as she passed through the morning light entering the window.

Hawk had been awakened by her movements but lay there silently, enjoying the remaining vestiges of a deep slumber. He witnessed her beauty as she passed by the window and reached for her robe. The exposed curves of her body through the sheer fabric of her gown caused an immediate stir deep within him. It had been a while since Hawk had held a woman. It had been even longer since he had seen one as beautiful as Deborah.

Deborah had not noticed Hawk's attention as she made her way outside to the henhouse for eggs. When she returned, Hawk was sitting in a chair beside the small table in front of the fireplace, wrapped in a blanket to the shoulders.

"Oh!" she said, startled. "I hadn't expected you to wake so early. I'm sorry if I woke you. Good morning, Hawk."

"You didn't wake me, Deborah. My mornings always start early. I wanted to thank you again for your kindness. I won't intrude on you much longer. You said you are from a town west of here?"

"Yes, Falkenwrath, about a half day's distance from here by foot. But please don't go, stay awhile," she said.

Hawk desperately needed supplies. He also had to find materials for a bow and begin making arrows—a chore he was not fond of by any means, but that was necessary all the same. "Do you have a sharpening stone?" he asked.

"Of course, and I have a leather strop as well. You are welcome to them but only after breakfast," Deborah said, concealing a smile.

Hawk really was not ready to leave. There was something familiar about this woman that reminded him of a love once lost. Stripped really, forced apart by circumstances out of his control, only to lose her forever. "I must make a bow and carve arrows as well. Many arrows...it may take some time."

"You are welcome to stay for as long as you would like, but you don't have to make a bow," she said. "After we eat, I'll show you."

Breakfast consisted of fresh eggs and bread from dough she had prepared the day before. As Deborah cooked, Hawk watched her move. She was graceful in a way that made him aware he was staring. Deborah could feel his eyes upon her but did not say a word.

Hawk rose up and placed the blanket on the cot then wormed back into his shirt. He tightened his belt and pulled on his boots.

Afterward, Hawk thanked her for breakfast and made his way outside to stretch and look around. The cabin was surrounded behind a wall of trees. Hawk could tell some trees had been removed to extend a natural clearing to make room for the home. It was in a perfect location where it would be difficult for any traveler to stumble upon the cabin had they been passing by this area. Walking around, he saw a small shed behind the cottage but did not venture toward it. There were hens pecking all around as his feet stirred up dirt while he walked. The sun was warm on his face, and there was a slightly cold breeze blowing, reminding him of the snow that remained on the mountainside. Deborah followed him outside shortly afterward. She came upon him as silently as she had the night before, startling Hawk.

"Come," Deborah said as she headed toward the shed, which she opened to reveal its contents. It was very dusty inside as if she had not visited it in some time. As Deborah cleared a path, she moved toward a wall where two bows were wrapped in cloth. One was noticeably smaller than the other. Alongside them were three old quivers, but only one had a few arrows in it. There, sitting beside a sack of grain, was a sharpening stone. She pulled an old leather strop off a nail and handed it to Hawk. "You said you needed this? For your blade, right?" she said, pointing to the stone.

"Yes, I used it coming through the woods and dulled the edge. Thank you," he said, taking the strop and picking up the stone. "Your bows...one is smaller than the other."

"That one is mine. I only use it when I need to hunt venison. Normally, I travel to town and pick up my supplies but sometimes, well…" Her words trailed off.

"And the other?" Hawk asked.

"That one belonged to my husband. It's not been used since he passed. The bow is strong and should serve you well," she said. "You are welcome to it. I have no need for it anymore."

Hawk removed the cloth cover and inspected it. The bowstring was taunt and well maintained. Deborah handed him the quiver containing the arrows.

"Try it," she said.

Hawk walked to the side of the shed, nocked an arrow, and drew back steadily. *Swoosh!* The arrow embedded itself into the center of a tree. He gazed at the bow in approval.

"It's a fine gift. I shall repay you someday," Hawk said.

Deborah removed the other smaller bow from its cover and strung an arrow. Pulling its bowstring back, she let the arrow fly. The arrow plunged into the same tree not an inch from where Hawk's arrow was buried. "Yes, you will," she said, smiling.

Hawk spent most of the remaining hours of the day honing his knife and tying sharpened stones to the ends of arrows he had created. His hands were tired and his back ached from being bent over, but his efforts yielded enough arrows to fill all three quivers. He filled one quiver with all it could hold and tied the remaining arrows together into two bunches.

As dusk settled across the valley, Hawk knew the time had come for him to bid farewell. He would leave at dawn. During supper there was little conversation.

Deborah also sensed that it would not be long. Hawk would leave soon, too soon. Having spent the day working in her kitchen, she packed a bag of fresh biscuits and separated it from the rest, placing it by the door with Hawk's things.

After supper, Hawk sat by the fire taking in every last bit of the comfort it provided. Deborah sat in the same seat that Hawk had used earlier that morning. "Must you leave so soon?" she asked.

Hawk nodded. "I must. Tell me, how do I reach the town of Falkenwrath?"

Deborah explained in detail the directions that Hawk must travel. While she dictated the route, her mind was elsewhere. She had heard the legend of Deviant Stronghold. She had heard of the mysteries that dwelled within its walls. She also knew the horrible price some had paid in trying to discover its secrets.

She, too, had paid a price to this unseen power. *There was no other reason*, she surmised, *as to why this man before me would come from so far. Should I warn him of the danger?* Giving advice, unasked for, to this self-assured stranger? *No, not now....*

She rose from the chair and said simply, "There is a man there. He is a bearded man with dark eyes. He is tall and wears a tattered coat, but no hat. You will find him in the tavern across from the church. The Rusted Lantern it's called. He answers to the name of Ehrig. Find him. Mention my name, and he will look after your needs while you are there in the town."

Night fell once again. And again the comforts of home enveloped Hawk. The night was quiet except for the crickets that took to song. Sleep did not come easy to the occupants of the cabin. Deborah prepared for the night.

She spread the furs for Hawk as she had the night before. Turning down the covers of her own bed, she looked at Hawk. Her eyes were filled with emotion.

Without her asking, Hawk turned his head as she crawled into bed. The image of her body in the morning light came to him, flooding his memory. He lay his head down, but the warmth of the bed did not embrace him as it had the night before. Hawk had to force himself to purge the picture of Deborah from his mind. Finally, sleep overcame him.

Deborah also struggled. She tossed and turned for a bit before finally getting comfortable.

The embers burning in the fireplace were faint but provided just enough light to see the figure resting on the floor of the cottage. As Hawk slept, Deborah watched. Images of her husband came flooding back to her, reflections of days past where her happiness could not be questioned. She longed for him, for his touch, his embrace. Many nights had passed since she had wanted a man as much. She closed her eyes and prayed for a dream.

Sleep came upon her slowly as she lay with her eyes closed, her arms crossed over her breasts. Behind her eyelids, she tried to conjure a dream, her mind darting between memories of her husband and of imagined images of Hawk making his way through the broad forested valley, ever closer to that castle. Where the imagining left off and the dreaming began she would never discern. Tonight her mind was random, but not chaotic; dreams of the happy days with her husband dissolved into scenes of walking through the forest as a child, which faded to Hawk encountering mythical beings from the fairy tales of her youth, then snapped to the pleasures of her husband's bed, and back again to the forest.

Again the forest, this time seeing with eyes that were not her own. The rays of sunlight filtering through the branches of the trees glowed green, not golden, through these eyes. Even in her sleep, her mind tried to make sense of this—*Sunlight is not green*—but failed.

"Face ME!" intruded a voice. "Face me! Show yourself!" The casual passage among the trees that these eyes were seeing neither slowed nor hurried, but as the voice continued to shout, it seemed to recede as if being outdistanced by a galloping horse.

The darting of the dream between the familiar scenes of her life and the forest trail had ceased. For what may have been minutes or days, the view through these strange eyes continued in the trees, making its way without hesitation. Suddenly a break in the trees showed the Hold called Deviance in the distance—but much closer than she had ever dared, or cared, to approach. From across the valley it had appeared to be just another castle: large stone buildings rising above the tall gray walls. Here, it was huge. And green. Not merely tinted green, as her mind tried to tell her the sunbeams were when viewed by these eyes, it glowed green. The green engulfed her and became one with the dream.

Chapter Two

Hawk woke earlier than Deborah. Quietly, he rose from under the furs and prepared himself to enter the cold morning air. Taking his time, trying to be careful so as to not wake Deborah, Hawk slowly dressed himself and gathered his things. He found the bag of biscuits beside his pouch as he prepared to leave. He turned and looked at Deborah, still sleeping. *She is beautiful,* Hawk thought as he passed through the door, closing it quietly behind him. Hawk stepped off the front porch, tied his pouch and extra arrows to his belt, laced the sheath of the blade to his leg, and slung the bow and quiver across his back. He walked a few paces forward and turned to face the door. Then, looking around the clearing, memorizing the view, he disappeared into the forest.

Deborah woke to the morning sun, and when she looked to the floor, the stranger was gone. Hawk had left. She rose from her bed feeling the emptiness of his absence and began gathering up the furs and placing them in the corner when a thought came to her. *It will be a half day before he arrives. If he has trouble finding the river crossing, it could take longer....* Deborah finished putting things away, found her cloak, and went outside to gather sticks.

Hawk made his way deeper into the woods, leaving the cottage behind. The woods slowly began to thin out as Hawk pressed down the mountain. The further away from the cottage he moved, the easier the terrain became to traverse, making his passage seem quick. Heading further down the mountain, Hawk took the time to look around at the beautiful valley below. The trees were deep green and filled with sounds of life. Hawk could hear the birds calling from far away and the chatter of the squirrels as he passed. Rustling in the underbrush told him deer were nearby, but he decided against seeking them. Deborah had indicated that Falkenwrath was not far, and he did not feel like hauling a deer down the mountain, nor did he have the time to track, hunt, and clean the deer. And though the thought of another skin pleased him, there would be food in town.

The thought of food wakened the morning hunger in Hawk's belly. He reached for the biscuits that Deborah had packed for him as he continued walking through the forest toward the valley floor.

There seemed to be an unusual calm surrounding him today. Hawk's mind occasionally wandered back to the cottage and the woman who lived inside it. The location of her home was perfect. Tucked away and covered by thick trees. As the sun continued its morning race across the sky, he reached the valley floor. The slope of the mountain eased into the valley. Hawk's steps were lighter now, having had something to eat, and after the initial trouble of becoming comfortable, having rested soundly the night before. Hawk continued his trek into the flatlands. Time slipped past as the distance that separated him from the cottage grew.

Hawk's path eventually led to large fields filled with winter wheat in various stages of growth. In the distance, he could see the river that fed the crops over the lazy descent into the valley. He could hear the sounds of rushing water from beyond the field of grain as the wind blew in the sound in waves across the open land.

His thoughts returned to a lazy time in the wheat fields back at his hometown of Rothersbucke, a sleepy little town where the farmers would gather when the sun went down and talk about the issues of the day. The markets there were always filled with people, fresh fruits, and vegetables. Hawk missed those sounds, those smells, and the people of that fair town.

Hawk had always been grateful that his father had hunted rather than farmed. Game was plentiful in the meadows and woods surrounding the crops. There had been times when he had actually felt guilty upon returning after a successful day in the woods. Even with his father on the other end of the pole, carrying a deer or boar back to town was hard work, but it was nothing like the mind-numbing labor some of his friends had to endure while helping their fathers outwit a particularly stubborn clod of dirt or remove a large stone in the fields.

Hawk felt a pang of that guilt now as the thought of him as a child teasing and taunting his friends crossed his mind. *"Being smarter than a rock" hardly would have prepared me for this journey.* Hawk smiled at the thought of his childhood. Then his smile faded. Not all his memories were so pleasant.

Hawk gazed up to the sky and saw that, in fact, he had been traveling for some time now. The sun was no longer sitting low in the sky but high above him. Reaching for his water skin, Hawk took a long drink. Making his way, careful to not crush the stalks of wheat, he searched for the river's crossing as Deborah had described. Hawk walked along the river's bank, following the curving path that seemed to lead nowhere, but the bridge was not to be found. *It must be further along than I'd thought.*

The search for the bridge was proving fruitless. Deborah never mentioned there being a bend in the river that snaked toward the right. Hawk could have sworn that he would have found the crossing by now. He paused for a moment, looking back along the path he had taken to see if perhaps he had missed it. Scanning the river forward along the horizon, up ahead in the distance in what looked like the middle of a field, he spotted a large tree. Hawk could barely make out the silhouette of a man stomping about underneath it. Hawk decided he would ask the man if he knew the location of the bridge and left the river's edge, once again coursing his way through the wheat fields. As he drew closer to the tree, Hawk could hear the faint sound of metal being pounded along with the man's loud cursing. As he approached, the sounds of the metal grew louder, the cursing even louder still.

"Damn! It's not right! It's not hot enough…need more…Damn!" An old man hollered at the top of his lungs to no one but certainly directed at someone.

Hawk slowed to watch the man at his work, trying not to disturb him, and even considered walking around the tree to avoid the old man altogether.

"Can't you see?" the old man yelled at himself.

"What are you doing?" he responded to no one, frustrated.

"How in the hell do you expect that to work if you can't get the fire hot enough? Damn you!" the old man continued, turning as if to yell at no one in particular when he saw Hawk walking toward him.

The man stopped. He looked at Hawk approaching, away, then back at Hawk again, trying to figure if his mind was playing even more games with him or if there was, in fact, a person coming his way. "Shut up. Let me do the talking," he said, "because YOU are an IDIOT! That is why, because!"

"What do you want?" the man called out as Hawk drew within shouting distance. "Why are you here bothering us? We've done nothing wrong."

"I need directions," Hawk replied as he approached, looking around and seeing no one else but the old man.

"Directions? Directions to where? Where are you going? SHUT UP!" he yelled over his shoulder.

"I am searching for a crossing over the river. I am heading toward a town. Falkenwrath it's called. West of here," Hawk said in a normal tone, having reached where the old man stood. He looked curiously behind the old man but still did not see anyone else.

Hawk studied the old man. The man stood slightly bent. His clothes were tattered and dirty. Hawk could tell the cloth of his shirt was once white, but no more. Now the shirt was a dingy brown, the kind of brown that comes from wear and sweat that rarely sees a brush and soap. The pallor of the man's skin was no different. His hair was long and unkempt, well on the way to gray. The pants legs the man was wearing were shorter than the man himself, the fabric worn and thin. Hawk could see the sandals on the old man's feet were well traveled.

"Falkenwrath! What business do you have in Falkenwrath?" he yelled. The man began pounding on a metal plate and stoking the fire below it, trying in vain to increase the heat. "I don't know of the crossing that you seek. Damn this fire...need more heat!" he said, waving Hawk away and returning to the task at hand.

"Sir. Sir?" Hawk repeated. "Sir!"

"What! What in the hell do you want?" the old man bellowed. "Leave us alone!"

"I need directions. I will pay you."

The man dropped his hammer, hitting his foot. "Arghhhhh! See what you have done!" He paused. "How will you pay?" He fell, more than sat, upon the ground and began rubbing his foot through the sandal.

"I will give one silver coin. And another if you lead me to it," Hawk replied.

"One! Only one silver coin! I cannot possibly take you for one! In advance?"

"I will give you one now and one after we have come to the crossing," Hawk answered.

The old man looked puzzled. "What about the fire? We can't leave the fire! It will go out, and then what would we do? Quiet! We can always come back to the fire. The fire will remain," he argued with himself. "Yes, but only one coin is not worth the fire going out!" The man thought for a moment and realized that the voice in his head was right. The rekindling of this troublesome fire would require more than two coins of silver.

"Three! Make it three coins! And I will lead you right away to the crossing you seek."

"Done, old man. Lead me to it," said Hawk.

"First you must keep your promise!" said the man, holding out his open hand. Hawk placed a coin in his palm, fully expecting to see it swiftly disappear. Instead, the man stared at the round piece of metal, biting and inspecting its authenticity, before fumbling with the pouch on his belt. The coin finally dropped in without a clink.

Then, staring up and holding out both arms toward Hawk, exposing numerous scars upon his arms as his sleeves hiked up with the motion, he said, "Well? Damn it. Help an old man up!"

Hawk pulled him to his feet. The old man hopped once as he put weight on his still sore foot. "Damn!" With that, he abruptly turned from his tools and began walking in the direction from which Hawk had just come, talking to himself. "We'll be back before too long. Don't you worry."

Hawk was surprised at the strength in the old man's grip. Even for a blacksmith, his grip was extremely firm.

Hawk had not seen a crossing nearby and wondered how he had missed it. Watching this old man was amusing, but Hawk did not wish to spend any more time than was necessary with him. As he began following behind, he said, "Sir, I just passed this part of the river. I've come as far as the foot of the mountain and through the wheat fields. I did not see a crossing."

"He didn't see the crossing!" The old man snorted with glee. "No one 'sees' the crossing," he snickered. "The crossing is there but no one 'sees' the crossing," He was mocking Hawk. Stopping suddenly, the old man turned and faced Hawk. "Just because you didn't see it does not mean it does not exist. Come…not much further," he said, pressing further up the river. "He didn't see it! Hehehe."

The old man made his way across the wheat field that Hawk had just crossed without so much as a care for the crops below him. Plowing through with complete disregard as to where he placed his feet, the old man continued his verbal assault. "I suppose you would have 'seen' it if you were actually looking!"

Hawk followed without responding. He did not know where he was being lead, but the man did seem to know where he was going, and at this point Hawk needed this man's help more than not.

They had not walked very far from where the tree stood in the open. Coming to the bend in the river the old man pointed toward the water and shouted, "There! Do you see it? Do you see it now?"

Hawk stared up the bend and across but saw nothing except a strong current sweeping past.

The old man stopped suddenly, turned into Hawk, and grabbed his shirt. Pulling Hawk to his level, the old man growled, "You must see with more than just your eyes!" Then he pointed again in the direction of the river.

Hawk studied the riverbend more closely. Suddenly out of nowhere there was a shining below the river's edge. Hawk leaned in and with closer observation of the clear moving water could see a small path that cut across the river bottom from where he stood to the bank on the far side.

"Do you see? Do you see the crossing now?" the old man, his knees bending up and down, his hands silently clapping, asked excitedly.

He did. Hawk reached into his pouch and pulled out two more silver coins. The man eagerly reached for them, his eyes crazed. Slowly, Hawk dropped a coin into the man's outstretched hands. The man looked at the single coin in his hand and searched for the second but did not find it. He looked up at Hawk in disbelief and demanded, "You must give another coin! You promised another coin!"

"And you shall have it," Hawk replied. "But first, what is your name, old man? How can I refer to you?"

The old man turned about and stomped his feet, feeling the pain shoot once again through the foot that had suffered the hammer's blow. "Damn!" he yelled, falling to the ground for a second time. "Why must he know our name? Why should he care anyway?" he muttered, debating with himself. "It is of little consequence what he asks. I see no harm in it." The old man sat on the ground rubbing his foot. Rocking back and forth, pondering the question, he turned his head over his shoulder and whispered, "Timothy. I am Timothy...oh shut up! Up Yours!"

Hawk was taken aback slightly by the outburst. He reached down to hand Timothy the remaining coin to settle the debt. Timothy snatched away the third coin, holding one coin in each palm.

"There, now. We are even," Hawk said.

"Well? Damn it, help an old man up!" The man extended both hands, again revealing the scars upon his arms. Hawk eyed them but did not stare as he pulled the man back to his feet. Both coins found their way into the pouch on his belt. The old man turned and started walking away, back to his tools, back to his place under the tree.

"Thank you, Timothy, for your help!" Hawk called out as he stood there, watching him leave.

"Up Yours! Up Yours!" Timothy screamed with his back turned, slowly limping away. "Would you shut up? Up Yours!" The man walked off, still disputing with himself.

Hawk stared at the crossing. The path's shimmering reflection slightly unnerved him. This was not the same crossing as described by Deborah, but it was a crossing still.

Carefully his feet left the safety of the riverbank and entered the cold, rushing water. He could see the flow racing past him but did not feel the force with which it passed. Holding the bow and his pouches of food above his head, he steadied himself as he made his way forward. Hawk fully expected to lose his footing and get swept away by the current, but he slowly progressed across the river without incident. Reaching the other side Hawk looked back in amazement. He could feel the water brushing against him, but it was as if a barrier was set between him and the current. Not once did he slip. Making his way up the far side of the riverbank, Hawk looked back at the old man disappearing in the distance, heading in the direction of his tree on the other side of the river.

While the passage across the river had not required that much exertion, Hawk was tired. The early afternoon sun was bearing down, the water had been cold, and save the upper portion of his shirt, he was dripping wet. Hawk made his way along the riverbank until he came upon large stones resting near the edge. Dropping the bow, quiver, and pouches, he stripped off his clothes, spread his pants across a large boulder, and hung his shirt on the bushes to dry. Wet already, he walked back into the river and quickly bathed himself. Hawk left the water shivering. Shaking out his hair, he opened the sack containing the food and took out a biscuit and a strip of jerky, lay on his back in the cool grass, and munched while he and his clothing dried in the warm afternoon sun.

When he finished his early lunch, he rolled onto his side and using his right arm pushed himself to his feet. "Damn, that hurt," he said out loud, rubbing his forearm. Only then did he notice the five, finger-shaped bruises just above his wrist. His left forearm was similarly bruised. *There's more to that crazy codger.* The thought brought him to a stop. Nothing had been "normal" since his knapsack had simply disappeared three days earlier. *No, it didn't "just" disappear, the green gl— the green...what the hell was that thing?* Though the loss of his possessions was a major blow, he'd never seen anything like the green apparition that had hovered over his sack before.

In his mind, Hawk wrestled with the events that had occurred since his arrival on this side of the mountain. *What the hell is going on?* There were no answers to his question. Nothing Hawk could think of would offer any explanation as to what had happened as he crossed over the Shallow Rock mountain range. *Deborah was a miracle*, he thought. She had trusted him in her home, going so far as to give shelter and a valuable bow. She was also very kind to have left him the food by his pouch, but how could he have missed the bridge? She had explained its location clearly enough. He had recognized all the landmarks—the wheat fields, the river—and followed them just as she had described. It was only by chance that he stumbled into that old man tinkering under the tree. Hawk felt fortunate to have encountered the two of them.

Hawk tried to put the last few days out of his mind. With nothing else to do but wait, Hawk leaned back against the stone where his pants were drying. His mind began to wander, and soon he began to recollect about Rothersbucke and his childhood and the games he and his friends would play.

Often Hawk and the other children would take to play fighting with sticks meant as swords and use wooden boards fastened with a leather handle as shields in their mock battles.

Born with natural agility and quickness, Hawk often found himself victorious over the other boys. Most times the ease with which he won brought frustration to the other children, but in spite of his competitive spirit, he was an easygoing playmate, and they always soon got over it. As he grew, his hunting skills also advanced. His ability to track, trap, and capture food for the town was surpassed only by his father's.

Then Hawk's thoughts wandered to how this journey started and why he now found himself so far from home. Hawk's first vision had come to him as a boy. In a dream long ago, Hawk found himself cloaked in a warm blanket of green. When he woke the following morning, he felt rested, but remembered the odd feeling as he lay there in bed. There was nothing more he could recall but the dream had never faded. The bed felt as if it had fallen out from under him. He could remember feeling as if he were being pulled lower and lower into the darkness of sleep. But the darkness was not black…it was green like the blanket.

As he lay there engulfed in green, Hawk had a vision: a cemetery. It was as brief as a flash, but clear. The image startled him out of his slumber.

As he got older, his dreams—or nightmares as he began to call them—increased in frequency. They also began to change. Sometimes Hawk heard loud explosions, explosions so close they shook him from his sleep. Then there were times when he would see others but could never make them out. Flashes, his dreams were always flashes. *They were so real,* he thought. Hawk often came to his father bothered by the visions in his mind. Clouded by distorted facts and often mixed or incomplete details, Hawk could find no way to link or rationalize his dreams into something more concrete. It was around his fourteenth birthday, after Hawk's being awakened by another nightmare, that his father sat with him while he lay in bed.

Trying to calm him, Hawk's father began telling a story in hopes of settling his son's mind. The stories he told were of the legends he was told by his own father. The tales of the power of Sapient6 and of the legend Deviant Stronghold, along with accounts of fierce battles, heroic deeds, magic, and weapons undreamed of filled Hawk's imagination. It was not his father's intention to create increased havoc in Hawk's mind but to send him into slumber with stories of valiant men and battles and heroes.

The following weeks were calm after his father began the storytelling. Hawk could rest, but his days were filled with thoughts of the stories his father would tell. He wondered just how much fiction was webbed into the stories and how much of these captivating details were twined with fact. It was said that all legends were based in truth and that somewhere in the past, as the story was told and told again, the truth became fiction based in fact giving birth to legends. Thinking back, Hawk could recall when he first heard those words.

The idea of finding the truth behind the legend had first been put into Hawk's head by a drifter who had passed through town shortly after his father had started telling the bedtime tales. He called himself Eth, and during the few days he had lingered performing odd jobs or chores for food and coins, had entertained the children in town with similar, though less detailed stories. Hawk was intimidated by his size, as were all the children, but his demeanor and kindness balanced the giant. It was his eyes Hawk feared most about Eth. They seemed distant and cold.

One day, Hawk approached while Eth was working on a sharpening stone for Hawk's father. He told Eth of his father's bedtime tales and asked if the stories Eth told were one and the same. Hawk wanted to know if Deviant Stronghold actually existed and if it did, where was this mysterious place? Hawk recognized the unease and evasiveness in which Eth answered his questions. It was then Eth replied with the remark about the intertwining of facts with fiction and how legends were born—and that Hawk would be better off asking his father.

Every night Hawk would beg his father for another piece of the puzzle. Every night his father would oblige his son with another story, and Hawk would sleep soundly. When confronted with Eth's words, his father dismissed the comment by saying simply, "These are only stories. Sleep now."

Still, from time to time, the nightmares would return and continue to plague Hawk. *Ah, the mysteries of childhood...*

By then, several hours had passed. Hawk checked his clothes. Though still slightly damp, they were not near the soaked pieces of fabric they were before. Donning his garments and checking his gear, Hawk continued his trek to the town of Falkenwrath. If he recalled correctly, it would not be long before he found the tavern. And he wanted to arrive before nightfall.

Chapter Three

Deborah spent the morning hours gathering sticks. Apparently Hawk had found all those surrounding the cottage worthy of turning into arrows and so Deborah was forced to search a wider area. Having sufficient numbers to begin, she returned to the cottage and started on her task of manufacturing arrows. The day passed slowly and as she progressed, so, too, did questions in her mind, the same questions that haunted her ever since the news of her husband's death had come to her two years before. Seeing her husband covered by earth and stone nearly broke her will to continue living, but she managed to get through that horrible period in her life. Now time had passed, and although his place in her heart would never be completely filled, she knew she needed to move on. To Deborah, there was only one way she would be able to do that, to move on, and that was to finally get the answers she needed about Robert's death.

Hawk was heading in the same direction that her husband had taken so long ago. If she was to find out what it was that took her husband's life and finally put this chapter to rest, then she must do now what she should have done then: Follow.

She worked all day fashioning the arrows and, having almost completed her task, ran out of stones for arrowheads. She got up and exited the cottage to the small shed in the back. Slightly annoyed, she mumbled to herself, "I probably have enough. Let's see." Opening up the doors, she reached for her quiver, removing it from the nail on the wall and turning to leave when she saw beside a grain sack a neatly tied bundle of arrows. Hawk had left her this. She picked them up and looked out into the forest, smiling for the first time since Hawk had left. *In the morning*, she thought, *in the morning I'll leave at first light.* Kneading an extra portion of dough, she made bread for the trip at the same time she prepared her supper. She knew the market owner in town and would pick up the remaining supplies from him then.

*   *   *

The afternoon sun was leaning into the sky and seemed as if it would slip off its mount at any moment. Hawk left the riverbank and made his way through the wooded valley where he came upon a dirt road that wound through the trees. Stopping to recall the directions that Deborah had dictated earlier, he gazed up at the sky to gather his bearings and turned right onto the carved path. Nothing seemed the same as Deborah had described. Hawk decided to follow his instinct and made his way down the winding lane when he came upon a sign with one word written on it: FALKENWRATH. Not much further, the dirt turned to cobblestone leading to urban streets. Hawk entered on the southern end of town. He walked along the busy streets, looking for the steeple of the church. The Rusted Lantern would be across the way.

*   *   *

Deborah was preparing for the days to come. She did not know how long it was going to take or when she would be back—or if she would be back, for that matter. She was familiar with being out in the woods for long periods of time with little or no provisions while hunting venison, so she prepared accordingly.

Mentally, Deborah checked over the items then packed them neatly into her bag. She took her bow and rechecked the tension of the bowstring. With practiced skill she made a minor adjustment. She was restless and could feel the anticipation of the trip start to work its way into her body. She was nervous.

Deborah settled in for the evening. Her satchel was packed and her bow and quiver, filled with arrows, sat by the door. She would leave for Falkenwrath at first light. Her supper was light since she could not seem to find her appetite. Her thoughts turned to Hawk. She wondered if he made it safely and whether or not he found Ehrig. Then she smiled. *He couldn't just accept the hospitality and the gift.* But he had saved her from a few more hours of work.

*   *   *

To the townsfolk, Hawk from the looks of him was just another wandering hunter coming in from the woods to have a much-needed bath and restock supplies. As Hawk wove his way through the cobblestone paths, he eventually saw the church steeple, which led him to the tavern. He entered unnoticed by the few patrons who sat at the bar.

Hawk looked around and found a table toward the rear

of the establishment. Taking a chair, he sat with his back against the wall, ensuring a full view of all the other people within the four walls of the room. It was a habit Hawk had formed after being clobbered once from behind for having been misidentified by a drunk who thought Hawk had stepped off with his girl. Hawk was able to fend off the attack and eventually convinced the man he was not the person being sought. The man was even more convinced after Hawk bought him another pint of ale so he might continue drowning his sorrows. Now sitting in the dark tavern, Hawk waited to find the man described by Deborah as tall and bearded with dark eyes and wearing a tattered coat.

Night had fallen upon the town of Falkenwrath, and the bar had filled quickly. There were men everywhere, and the wenches were filling their drinks and marking their tabs, sometimes marking an extra pint or quart to the tally at the owner's approving wink. Most wore tattered coats, and none had on their hats, a formality not allowed within the establishment. All but a few were drunk. Those who were not were well on their way.

As the night passed into the morning hours the long day began to take a toll on Hawk. Perhaps it was too much to expect that he could just walk into a tavern and find a man he had never met. Deborah had made it sound as if recognizing this man Ehrig would be easy. Hawk had measured his own ale as he waited, but the dim lighting of the candles burning along the walls and tables were soothing; passing out from fatigue and drink would not have served his purpose.

He rose from his seat, slugged down the remaining quarter of a pint in his mug, and gathered his things. Dropping two copper coins on the table for the girl, he walked to the bar and asked the barman about the possibility of a private room for the night. Tonight he was in no mood for sharing a dormitory style room with smelly, snoring drunks.

The barman looked up from his wiping of glasses. "Aye, I can accommodate you this night. One piece of silver." Winking he added, "If you'd like a 'semi-private' room, for an extra three coins," thumbing toward the waitress, "the wench seemed to like you."

Hawk laughed. "I'm sure she's worth five, but not tonight, my friend. The day has been long, and I'm afraid I would not do her justice." Hawk pulled out the necessary coin as the barman stood there and waited.

Putting the coin on the counter, Hawk was instructed to take the room behind the fourth door to the left at the top of a set of stairs. The barman shouted to a waitress serving drinks and held up four fingers. She nodded. The barman smiled at Hawk approvingly. "In just a moment, sir," he said.

A few seconds later, Hawk made his way slowly up the stairs and opened the door.

The room was bright. There was a candle burning on a nightstand and drawer next to a single bed in the corner opposite the doorway. The bed was covered in light blankets and a pillow. Next to the nightstand was a window facing a side street, a small chest of drawers sat along the same wall opposite the nightstand. Along the center of the wall across from the bed was a water basin and towel rack with a single towel. A mirror hung on the wall just above it. Another, taller, chest cabinet was next to the door that had another lamp burning at full wick. A small piece of carpet was resting near the foot of the bed along with a small runner along the side. A square table and a chair sat in the only corner remaining. The room was small but comfortable.

Hawk settled his bow and quiver in the corner along the wall behind the door from which he entered. He removed his pouches and other belongings and placed them on the tabletop. Hawk forced off a boot from where he stood beside the runner alongside the bed and the table. Turning, he moved and sat on the bed for a moment. He was sitting on the bed gathering the strength to pull his second boot from his foot when a soft knock rapped the door. "Damn it. One boot off, and he sent her anyway," Hawk growled to himself. "Just a minute!" Hawk quickly pulled the first boot back on his foot, loosened his knife in its sheath just in case, and went to the door. "Who is it?"

"A friend."

The male voice on the other side of the door caused the hair on the nape of his neck to rise slightly. There was a familiarity about the voice, but Hawk could not place it. Putting his hand on the hilt of his knife, he allowed his curiosity to win and slowly opened the door. Hawk did not see anyone in the dimly lit hallway as the door opened. As he widened it further a figure slipped past him into the room. Startled, Hawk turned, shutting the door behind him without meaning to do so, while reaching for his blade. Everything came back in an instant when their eyes met. "E—?" he started to say.

"—hrig" the man finished for him. "I understand you've been waiting for me." Ehrig shrugged off his dark, forest green cloak to reveal a tattered coat underneath, a wench embraced in his left arm, and three mugs of ale in his right hand. "It's been a long time, my young friend." The laughing voice disarmed him. When he had turned and the door had closed, Hawk's blade had started out of its sheath. His mouth dropped open as the blade fell back into its place of rest. A puzzled look came upon Hawk's face. *How the hell did he get through the door and past me with his arms full of ale and a girl?*

"Abby, get these mugs out of my hand. Give one to Hawk. I believe he could use it. Sit down, stay quiet, and don't guzzle yours," he said sternly, turning to smile at Hawk. "She'll drink me out of every coin if I let her!" The girl did as she was told, but instead of sitting, she lay down on the bed, winked at Hawk, blew Ehrig a kiss, and said not a word.

Hawk could not believe who he was looking at. This was the same man who wandered through his hometown so many years ago. The same man who had played with the children and told the tales so similar to those his father had told. *The tales! Then he would know! This man could possibly have some answers, and this time I am not the young boy of so long ago.*

Hawk was extremely tired from the long day and had had enough beer for the night, but these events caused him to come alive, so he drank anyway.

Ehrig could tell there were thoughts running through Hawk's mind and that the young man was having trouble understanding. *I've befuddled him a bit. Well, that was to be expected,* he thought. "I can see you are a bit confused and still searching for understanding. Well, worry not, the matter is well at hand," he said, taking a long pull from his mug. "I've kept watch...Would you stop with your wrestling, wench!" His attention turned to Abby tossing around on the bed.

"I am just getting comfortable!" she returned.

"It's not your bed to be getting comfortable in!" argued Ehrig. "Now come, sit in the chair as I told you before."

Abby got out of the bed and sat in the lone chair beside the table. Her eyes were on Hawk the entire time. She smiled and continued to drink her ale, holding her mug with both hands.

"I will not be in town for very long. I must be moving on, you know. Constantly moving, constantly moving. But that is the nature of my beast if you will." Ehrig smiled, slowly waving his free arm about for emphasis. "And you must be tired from your travels, so I will be off for the moment. I still have business to attend to this night," he said, glancing in Abby's direction. "I will be back tomorrow, find me at The Griffin, the pub at the other end of town, about midday's time."

Hawk stood there, still dumbfounded by the events of the last few minutes. He looked at his glass; it was still over half full as Ehrig was emptying his that very moment. Abby was not far behind in finishing hers. "I was to mention Deborah's name," Hawk said.

"Come, Abby, let us give this man his space," Ehrig said, cutting him off and with that, picked up his cloak, wrapped it over his shoulders, and enveloped Abby in his left arm. As he pulled the cloak over her, she disappeared; if he hadn't seen her, Hawk would have never known she was there. They moved to the door. Glided was more like it, and as smoothly as had been the entrance, so was the exit.

Hawk stood there, still. He looked at his beer, walked over to the table and chair recently vacated by Abby, finished the contents, and put down the mug. Moving over to the window, he looked out to see if he could spot Ehrig and Abby walking, but there was no sign of them; all he saw were the trees blowing in the wind. Turning his attention to the bed, Hawk found the burst of adrenaline had served its purpose. Again he sat, and again Hawk mustered the strength to pull the boots off his feet. He was tired no doubt. The sheets were disheveled from the tossing Abby had given the bed, but that was the least of his worries. Crawling under the covers, Hawk last thought of the drifter who told stories in his childhood.

*   *   *

Deborah closed the door behind her, ensuring the lock was in place. Stepping off the porch, she headed in the same direction that Hawk had the day before. Bow in hand and quiver strapped across her back along with her sack of biscuits for the trip, she made her pace casual but steady. It had been some time since her last visit to Falkenwrath, but she knew the path well.

The day was clear and the breeze was gentle. Making her way through the dense woods that hid her home, Deborah's thoughts were reaching out in front of her. She hoped Hawk would be able to arrive safely and locate Ehrig in town with no trouble. Discerning her husband's fate was the purpose of this journey, but she was not ready to dwell on this now. Turning to the more immediate future, she thought maybe Hawk had gotten caught up in the entertainments of the town. If he did, perhaps she would see him again. If he found Ehrig, that possibility was quite likely. She smiled to herself. Deborah fancied Hawk, but she also told herself that she would not distract him from his quest—nor allow him to interfere with her own.

*   *   *

Hawk woke to a commotion outside his window. Two men were arguing, and their voices were loud. Apparently, the issue of a horse and his shoes was what brought the two together and jolted Hawk from his slumber. That did not matter at this point, he just wished for them to take the discussion elsewhere. Leaving the comfort of his bed, he raised the window and shouted, "Shut the hell up with your damn horse! Take your leave!" One of them yelled an improbable response, but the men did lower their voices and Hawk likewise the window after checking the position of the sun in the sky.

The sun was sitting at the lower quarter of the eastern sky. He had time for bathing but preferred to lie a while longer. Resting on the bed lasted but for a moment when he heard a knock. Forcing himself up for the second time, Hawk went to the door. "Who is it?"

It was another barmaid with water for the washbasin and black tea. Hawk pulled on his pants, then returned and opened the door for her. After putting the tea tray on the table, the barmaid turned to the basin and started pouring from the jug. "Hot water!" Hawk exclaimed as steam rose above the bowl. At best, most taverns provided wash water at room temperature; cold from the pump was the norm.

"Classy place, this." She giggled. "We even have a bathing room downstairs."

She was much more attractive than the maidservants from the evening past, and Hawk was quick to take notice of her figure.

She could feel him watching her as he drank the tea and she tended to her chores.

"Do you like the tea?" she asked as she straightened the bed. "It's brought from the East, I'm told. I've never had it. It's too expensive."

"It is different…excellent…but I didn't order hot water or exotic drink," Hawk replied. "Does it come with the room?"

"No. I was told to bring them to you. The fee has been collected. Nothing further is required."

Ehrig? It had to be. But why? Putting the thought aside for the moment, Hawk returned to his tea and girl watching.

"A bathing room, you said?" Hawk broke the silence. "With hot water?"

"Oh yes. You won't believe the tub, either. It's big enough to stretch out all the way. I hate bathing in a bucket. Don't you?" She smiled shyly.

"How much?"

"Four coppers for the tub, soap, and towel. Uh, hot water requires a silver coin."

Hawk had not expected a large tub of hot water to come cheap. He found the girl's hesitation about the extra cost appealing. "A silver coin then. Have them stoke the fire for the water."

"I will. I'll go immediately," she said, turning.

"Where is the bathing room?" Hawk asked before she could get away.

"It's down the stairway and to the left."

Hawk watched as she turned and gazed upon her as she closed the door behind her. He finished the tea and cleaned his face. *No point letting these go to waste.*

Hawk finished dressing and strapped his blade to his waist. He wanted to explore the town a bit and perhaps pick up a few provisions at the market. It would take some time to heat the water for his bath if the tub was indeed as large as the girl claimed.

Locking the door behind him, Hawk proceeded down the stairs and turned to his left. *I should check with the attendant. I don't want to be gone so long that the water gets cold again.*

He found his way down the corridor and pushed open the door. This room was larger than his personal room though not nearly as furnished. The basics necessary for bathing were available. In the center of the wide room was a tub large enough to fit two men comfortably, already filled to near capacity, soapsuds floating on top. Directly next to the tub was a stand holding a large towel, a washcloth draped over the rim. A larger mirror with an equal water basin below it stood with a towel rack along its side as well. No towels were draped across any of the pegs. A chair and small table were along a window that had its curtains drawn, already closed for privacy. Hawk was pleasantly surprised at how tranquil the room made him feel. A burly young man entered the space and added another bucket of hot water into the tub as steam played over the top of the water.

"Your bath is almost ready, sir," said the lad. "One more bucket, if you please."

"Already?" Hawk said incredulously. "I'll go pay for it now and return momentarily."

"I was told your friend paid for it upon leaving last night. Even left a token for me. Most generous he was, too!" The young man scurried out and back again carrying the final bucket for the tub. He poured the water into the tub and smiled. "That should be all, sir," he said and left, leaving the door slightly ajar.

Ehrig! Why is he putting me in his debt? Hawk tried to scowl, but the water was too inviting. He had not noticed the door was still cracked open.

Coming closer to the tub, Hawk reached out and placed his hands in the steam, scraping the layer of suds. "Pleasures fit for a king," he muttered as he began shedding his clothes. Draping his shirt over the chair, Hawk loosened the straps of the sheath and placed the knife on the table. He released the clasp of his belt, resting it and the pouches next to the blade. Boots and socks removed, Hawk approached the waiting tub. Slowly lifting his legs over the rim, and sliding down the curve of the basin, allowing the heat of the blanket of water to envelop him.

True to her word, the barmaid had approached the tavern keeper with Hawk's request for a bath and had been told that it was already being prepared. As she headed back toward the stairs, she heard Hawk's voice coming from the bathing room. She passed an early drunk sitting alone at a table holding an empty glass and waving it in her direction. The barmaid reached for his empty mug, taking it along with a coin, refilled his glass, and brought it to him. She then left the barroom, filled another jug with hot water, and moved to the bathing room with the intention of topping off the tub and checking the temperature.

When she came to the door of the bathing room, she found it ajar. The barmaid peered in quietly, catching Hawk as he was preparing for his bath, his clothes half off his body. Her heartbeat pounded in her chest as she watched Hawk slip out of his pants and step into the curve of the bath, slowly allowing himself to slide into the water. Only then did the barmaid knock lightly on the door, making her presence known.

She approached Hawk. "How do you like the bath?"

"One can only wish for this every day," he replied, soaping himself. He slid under the water, wetting his hair before coming back up to the top.

"I brought this jug of water. I was to fill the tub and check the temperature. How is it?" she said, her eyes not leaving Hawk's.

"Check for yourself," Hawk said, returning her stare.

Taking the dare, the barmaid reached for the water and as she did, Hawk gently touched her arm. She did not pull away. As they looked at each other, she slowly stood. Backing up, she hung a sign on the door and closed it behind her, then moved in toward Hawk. The barmaid reached above her shoulders and untied the strings holding her apron, dropping it to the floor. She turned her back toward him as she loosened her dress.

Hawk watched intently as the clothes slowly melted off, exposing her back and shoulders, then the curves of her buttocks and legs under the sheer cloth of her slip. Facing him with only her undergarments remaining, she released the slip, revealing the firm breasts and curves of her young body. She lifted her arms to set free her long, dark blonde hair, her chest rising as she did so. As her locks fell from their bondage, her soft curls came to rest over her shoulders, caressing her breasts. She moved closer to the tub and sat on the edge. Leaning over, she kissed Hawk deeply. Not taking her eyes off him, she lifted her legs slowly over the bathtub's ledge and slipped into Hawk's arms. Knowing time was short the barmaid pressed her lips against Hawk's mouth as she mounted him, suppressing their mutual sounds of pleasure. Hawk could not help appreciating her aggressiveness as they soon climaxed together under a blanket of suds.

The heat of the morning sun was increasing. Hawk and the barmaid had spent nearly an hour in each other's arms. "Shilah!" a voice rang out from the distance.

"I must be going!" She quickly climbed out of the bath and gathered her clothes. She used the towel intended for Hawk but he did not care. Just watching her incredible figure as the soap ran down the small of her back and over the curve of her spine more than made up for a wet towel.

"I will return with another," she said, smiling, and kissed him again before leaving. Hawk was not ready for her to go.

Hawk lay relaxing when another barmaid scooted in. She bashfully placed a fresh towel over the chair and moved it closer to the tub. "There you are, sir," she said and made her leave, the door closing behind her.

A glance toward the window informed Hawk the day was passing quickly; the curtains were much brighter now. He dunked under the water to rinse his hair once more. He was soon dressed and on his way back to the room.

Hawk packed his things. Reaching for his bow, he made his way down the stairs to inquire about directions to The Griffin on the other side of town.

Seeing him approach, the barman pulled up a tab. "That'll be one silver coin for the bath. How was it?"

Hawk hesitated a moment, reached into his pouch, put two coins on the bar, and smiled. "That was the best bath I have had in quite a while, my friend," he said. "The second coin is for tonight. I don't yet know that I shall require the room, but be sure it is available should I return. If I do not, keep the coin for holding the room for me. If I don't return this evening, I will have to make sure I come this way again. The hospitality is beyond reproach...but next time,"

Hawk's tone dropped, "when the bath is paid, do not double charge for it." As Hawk said the words his face moved from a smile to a scowl to a broad grin.

The tavern owner moved back a step. "You can't really blame a man for trying, can you?" he asked nervously, stepping forward again and pushing both coins toward Hawk. "The room will be waiting for you tonight…without charge…whether you use it or not," he said with a slight stutter.

Hawk pushed the coins back. "If I were offended, I would have charged you before the constable. Keep both coins. As I said, the hospitality was more than I had hoped."

"Well, that's what I like to hear! I will look forward to seeing you again, my friend," the barman said. "Shilah!" he called, "come and clean these tables! And when you are done, clean the gentleman's room again. He will be our guest once more!" His voice was clearly less tense.

"I'll be right there!" Shilah came out and smiled at Hawk. Fully dressed in a different smock, her hair back up in place, she smiled at him and lowered her head, embarrassed. Hawk smiled back and turned to leave.

"My daughter," the owner told Hawk.

"A beautiful girl," he said, smiling.

Exiting the front entrance, Hawk paused for a moment and took a deep breath, turned and headed toward the center of town when, from around the corner of the tavern, Shilah grabbed him and pulled him into the alley. Hawk found himself held and pressed upon a long kiss goodbye before she let him go and watched him take his leave.

Chapter Four

The center of town was only a few blocks away. Entering the market, Hawk observed that the sun was past the halfway point to midsky. He still had time before he was due to meet Ehrig. *Ehrig!* How many times had that name come to his thoughts this morning in the form of a question? *I knew the man only a few days, many years ago. I only really spoke with him once. Why is he traveling under an assumed name? Or was the name then assumed? How did he know to seek me when I was seeking him? And why did he pay my bills? This day I shall require more answers of him than the brush-off he gave the boy I was,* Hawk thought as he walked the streets of Falkenwrath. He made his way through the marketplace for a look at the wares and to pick up a replacement sack large enough to carry supplies.

*   *   *

Deborah had come upon the winter wheat where Hawk had passed the day before. Instead of crossing as Hawk had done, she continued along the trees that lined the crops. Making her way down the end of the fields, she stopped for a rest under the shade of the forest. She ate a biscuit and took small sips of her water. Deborah knew she was making good time. It would not be long before she came to the bridge.

* * *

Hawk could tell he was coming upon the center of town. The noise in the streets was increasing with the activity of the people around him. This place was completely different from Rothersbucke. Falkenwrath was quaint and central with the homes and business buildings nestled closer to each other, unlike back home where the crops forced separation.

Hawk followed the sounds, allowing the people of Falkenwrath to lead the way. Along the way, he noticed a familiar look to the houses. Though none were exactly the same, most were single storied and small, and all seemed to have a yard surrounded by flowers of some sort, trees lining the front. The colors of the homes were warm and inviting, unlike the plainer hues of the houses in Rothersbucke. Even the roads of Falkenwrath were carved out and well maintained. Hawk could easily see why the people of this town would enjoy calling it home.

One complete central street block was lined with pubs, men already populating the establishments. Various shops and smithies along the opposing sides completed the square. Hawk noticed the children running through the streets and playing in the center park. Seeing the kids play reminded him of his carefree days, when responsibility and worry did not exist.

Crossing the street into the park, Hawk moved through the playground and headed toward a leather shop across the way in search of a new bag. Entering the shop, Hawk did not take long to find one suitable for the task at hand. Hawk paid the storekeeper his asking price and left. Needing a new stone for sharpening his blade, Hawk sought out a blacksmith. Walking along the perimeter of the square he came upon a general store that sold odd wares and necessities. Hawk entered the store.

"I need a sharpening stone."

The clerk looked over Hawk and assuming he was a drifter because of the bow said, "It'll cost you two coppers. You have the money for it?"

"I do. Do you have the stone?"

"Ahem, well, can I see the coppers beforehand?"

Hawk produced two copper coins from his pouch and held them up before the store clerk. The clerk lifted his head and squinted, looking at the coins as if to validate their authenticity. Hawk found the man's actions amusing and chuckled. This caught the attention of the clerk, who quickly turned his concentration back toward Hawk and with diffident measure, left for the back of the store and returned with a box of sharpening stones.

Handing Hawk a stone, the man reached for the coins. Hawk pulled back his hands and carefully studied the stone, mocking the store clerk. With a smirk and laugh, Hawk flipped the coins into the air, caught them, and slammed them onto the counter. "There you are, my good man. A pleasure doing business with you."

"Yes, indeed," the clerk said carefully.

"Can you tell me the direction to The Griffin?" asked Hawk.

"That way...past the end of the square. When you reach the end, turn right and follow that road. You'll see it not far from there," he responded, pointing in the direction that Hawk was heading.

Hawk placed the stone in the pack and left the store amused. The day seemed very bright, and he stepped lightly as he strolled. *It has been a good day so far. I hope this keeps up.* Making his way to the marketplace, he glanced at the sky and marked the sun's position. *Hmmm, should be about time.* Hawk arrived at the market, gathered fruits and dried figs for the trip, paid for the items with little conversation, then headed out of the center of Falkenwrath to make his meeting with Ehrig.

Along the way, Hawk came across a sign for the butcher shop. Without thinking, he changed direction and walked through the door. After only a few moments of talking to the butcher, Hawk was back on the streets of Falkenwrath, turning the corner as directed by the shopkeeper at the general store, and coming upon The Griffin.

True to his word, Ehrig was there, glass in hand. Hawk approached him and slid onto the neighboring stool.

"So there you are, my young friend. I trust you had no problems locating it?" Ehrig said.

"None at all," replied Hawk. "It's a quaint little town."

"That it is. That it is. Are you prepared for travel?" asked Ehrig.

"Not quite. I was planning to pick up some replacement supplies of things I lost along the way. I have no fur skins for bedding and need to replenish my jerky. I thought I would get some fresh biscuits as well."

Deborah came to mind as he said those words. He wondered how she was doing back at the cottage. Keeping herself busy, he supposed.

"Ah, right, well then, let's finish our beer and then head out, we have a little bit of a walk in front of us," Ehrig said.

"I don't have a beer at the moment," Hawk replied.

Ehrig looked down at the bar in surprise. "Well, we can fix *that* now, can't we?" he said with a laugh. "Barkeep! A beer for my friend," he said slightly louder than necessary, considering the barkeep stood only two steps from them.

As the brew was being drawn, Hawk turned to his companion and said, "We? You plan to accompany me?"

"Aye. This day's journey is not long. We have time enough both for a drink and your shopping."

"I really was not planning on leaving until tomorrow," Hawk replied. "As I passed the butcher's stall on my way to meet you, it occurred to me that I have spent more than I had intended this early in my journey. I spoke to the butcher. He agreed to a fair price should I bring him a boar for his shop."

As he finished speaking, the beer was placed in front of him. "A boar? In a single afternoon's hunt? Alone? An ambitious endeavor indeed!" the bartender exclaimed, wiping the countertop as he did so.

"My friend is one of the best," Ehrig replied, annoyed at the intrusion. "Now attend to your business, and allow us our privacy, if you please." The bartender moved further down the bar.

"'Ambitious' was well spoken," he said in a lowered tone, turning back to Hawk. "You intend to bag, bleed, gut, and return with a boar in a single afternoon?"

"Not exactly," Hawk explained. "Depending upon the luck of the hunt, my mind was to do just that, or, should I find the hour and distance to be too far from town, I would simply abandon the hunt and continue on my way. My funds are not *that* depleted. Now what is this about you traveling with me?" Hawk asked.

Ignoring the question, Ehrig exclaimed, "A boar it is then! Pig hunting is dangerous work. Sounds like fun." Lowering his voice, he added, "Besides we don't want you too exhausted for your wench!" He winked.

Ehrig continued without giving Hawk a chance to open his mouth. "Make your way back to your inn now. Pick up the supplies you mentioned on the way, and don't dawdle. I shall meet you there. After hunting pig you will want a good night's sleep…and another bath. I'll arrange and pay for it. Two in one day! Hehe. Some woodsman you are!" Ehrig laughed heartily, slugged down the last of his ale, and was gone.

Hawk sat there for a moment. The man moved with the grace of the wind and as quickly, it seemed. He picked up his as yet untouched draft, chugged half of it, and stood up. Only then did he notice the coins on the counter that Ehrig had left. Turning, he made his way back to the market. Having taken his time during the first trip through the square, Hawk knew where he needed to stop on the way back to the inn. Picking up three ears of corn and other necessary supplies, he made the purchases without fuss, and he quickly found himself approaching the inn across from the church.

Ehrig and the water boy were waiting at the front steps. Hawk was vaguely disappointed Shilah was not with them.

"Hail, mighty hunter!" Ehrig called as he approached. "Give your items to the boy, and let us be off. I smell pig in the wind," he said, crinkling his nose with a look of determination.

Hawk laughed as he passed his purchases to the youth and stepped off the porch. Removing his bow from his back, he checked the tension of the string and made a small adjustment. He kept it in his hand.

Ehrig, too, stepped from porch and without another word headed down the street away from the direction Hawk had just come, bearing back toward the woods. A few quick steps and Hawk was at his left, walking at a comfortable, brisk pace.

"Your weapon?" he asked.

Without slowing his step, Ehrig drew back the dark green cloak, which, Hawk now noticed, would make him all but invisible in the forest. The blade on the man's hip was too long to call a dagger yet not quite as long as a sword.

"My 'pig' sticker." Ehrig chuckled. The way he said "pig" left Hawk with the unmistakable impression that there was more to the word than pork on the hoof.

"Ah," Hawk said, wondering how many "pigs" had met the business end of that blade.

*   *   *

Deborah had started walking again. The sun was nearing its peak, and she wanted to make the town before too long. Leaving the fields behind her, she walked another stretch before coming to the bridge. She never really liked this crossing. The wood of the bridge was old and always creaked horribly when she tried to pass on it, as if it were going to give way any moment. The thought of being swept away by the raging current always frightened her. Still the only other natural crossing was much farther down where the river widened and rocks provided a path across. Deborah knew she did not want to travel that far out of her way to get to the other side.

Almost daring herself into motion, Deborah started across, leaving the sanctuary of solid ground behind her.

Her heart was picking up speed as the adrenaline in her body started to play havoc with her nerves. The bridge swayed a bit and made its unnerving sounds but held with each step she took. Deborah grasped the rope railings tightly as step by step she made her way across. She tried to avoid looking down as the river swept by quickly beneath her feet. Finally reaching the other side, she composed herself as if she were being watched, looking around to be sure no one was there to witness her moment of weakness.

Deborah pressed her way through the remaining path she had traveled many times before, the hardest part behind her. Though Timothy's river crossing had afforded Hawk a somewhat shorter northern path, it was not long before she entered the eastern entrance of the town. She walked through the town and headed to her parents' home. She would stay there before moving on.

*   *   *

Hawk and Ehrig came to the southern entrance of town where Hawk had arrived the previous day and followed the road for a small distance before leaving the path and disappearing into the woods. Along the way, talk was sparse as they walked up the road and away from the town. Ehrig seemed to be concentrating on much more than the mission at hand, almost lost in a trance. Hawk on the other hand was already putting into practice his experience of hunting boar.

Unlike hunting deer, boar were much harder to track but could be predicted if you knew what to look for. Deer tended to stay in an area, or territory, no matter how spooked they became or what threat they perceived as imminent. Boars were completely different, claiming no real territory, leaving upon the slightest hint of danger never to return to a part of the territory deemed hazardous. This, coupled with their generally foul disposition, made them dangerous prey, adding value to their meat. Hawk was well aware of this when he negotiated the price of a successful hunt with the butcher.

In spite of their ready willingness to abandon an area, Hawk knew that feral pigs were also creatures of habit. They would cut a path in a meadow through constant use and not veer away from it, using it over and over again. Other telltale signs were their wallowing in the mud by ponds, riverbanks, or streams, and indications of rooting where the boar would search for fresh shoots of tender grass and roots.

Looking at the sky, Hawk mentioned that the day was slipping away when both men left the road and pushed deeper into the forest, heading in the direction of the river. Hawk searched for signs of thick underbrush and fallen logs that could serve as a den for the boar.

Ehrig seemed to be enjoying his walk through the woods. Although just as quiet as Hawk while traversing the woods, he was very much at ease with himself, stopping now and again to take notice of a flower or rare shrub.

Though the sun was sloping downward, enough of the day remained for Hawk to search for signs of his prize. Hawk hoped to find a part of the trail by the river that led to indicators of the presence of the pigs. There he would set a trap for the hogs using the corn he purchased earlier in the day. As the sun slowly left the top of its perch and slid down the western sky, Ehrig and Hawk were approaching a clearing. Hawk paused to scan the scene causing

Ehrig to take notice and come up alongside him. Both men stood scanning across the pasture.

There were thick brush clumps in places low to the ground in several areas lining the woods, any one of which could hide a path used by the pigs. Hawk circled slowly along a ring of the trees that formed the barrier between the opening of the clearing and the woods. Every step he took was planned. Every movement he made was predetermined as he approached a thicket of shrubs. Bending low to see below the branches, Hawk searched. He studied the signs of the meadow until he found what he was looking for. There! He saw it! From the bottom of a patch of thickets and shrubs he saw a small opening to a path very low to the ground.

Both men pushed the opening a man's length apart. Then with Ehrig leading as if knowing, both broke off and headed in separate directions without a sound. Quietly. Hawk walked out into the field about thirty paces and looked around for the rest of the track. Locating the trail, he followed it up to where the feral pigs had left their marks in the mud by covering themselves as protection from insect bites and ticks.

Backtracking slightly, Hawk pulled the corn from his sack and dug a deep hole about twenty paces from the riverbank. Burying an ear of corn with loose soil, he planted a second ear above it, layering and covering just as he did before. With the hole all filled up with dirt, he broke the kernels off the last ear and spread them around the ground then made his way back to the treeline.

Ehrig circled around the treeline, making his way behind Hawk and leaving a small distance between the two. Having set the trap, Hawk backed off to the right and squatted, placing two arrows in front of him on the ground. He did not want to make noise as he pulled the arrows and spook the pig into turning and running.

The sun continued its slide across the sky. Dusk was settling in. Neither Hawk nor Ehrig had moved since the bait was set. Hawk was beginning to think that maybe tonight would not produce a pig when their patience finally paid off. Ehrig heard it first and motioned to Hawk with a slight movement of his head. Hawk glanced in the direction of the thicket he had spotted as they entered the pasture. From under the brush emerged the pig. It was huge!

Hawk could not immediately tell if it was a male or female since both grew large, sharp tusks as they matured. Both Hawk and Ehrig waited. Fortunately for Hawk, a feral pig's eyesight is horrible, giving the hunter the advantage if he knows to stay still. Unfortunately, the sun was low in the western sky, and with the light fading the battle was slowly balancing in favor of the pigs. Hawk did not want to shoot and miss, or worse, shoot and wound. The last thing he wanted was a pissed off boar bearing down on him.

The boar made its way slowly out of the thicket and into the pasture, following the well-worn path. Its body stood out in the tall grass as it stopped to root around the area where Hawk had placed the kernels of corn. Both could hear the pig snorting and digging at the dirt. Hawk could make out the shape of the pig but had to approximate the shot below the grass blanket covering the sweet spot for a clean kill. Slowly Hawk picked up an arrow off the ground where he had laid it before and rested it on the bow's shelf. Coming to his feet and pulling the bowstring back in the same motion, he released the tension and let the arrow fly.

The boar was struck just a bit low of the desired mark. The strike was killing, but just enough off that it would take a few minutes. Not good. The pig quickly identified Hawk as his attacker and immediately launched a counter-attack. As the boar raced in his direction, Hawk's adrenaline reached an all-new high. Instinctively, he hurdled into the air as the hog passed directly below him, just brushing his leg. Landing, Hawk turned while pulling his blade for what he was certain would be another pass from the boar.

As the animal wheeled for the second attack, Ehrig's cloaked figure appeared from out of the trees, pig sticker in hand, closing the distance between boar and Hawk. The doomed hog had started back at Hawk when it found Ehrig's blade embedded in its neck, piercing deeply and cutting its windpipe, severing arteries, cartilage, and veins. The hog collapsed, bleeding to death as blood poured through the gaping wound. Ehrig grasped the shaft of the arrow for additional leverage and with a deft movement pulled back the head, exposing the throat wide. He stood above it looking pleased with their work.

Withdrawing his blade from the mortally wounded animal, Ehrig kneeled and while wiping it in the grass, looked around in the fading light. "Ahhhh," he said, disgusted, "in this light we'll never find a pole strong enough to carry him back." The awkward blade disappeared under his cloak. His cloak was unmarked with blood.

Hawk laughed nervously, his body still metabolizing what remained of the adrenaline that coursed his veins. That was close, too close for his liking, but Ehrig's position had been perfect. *So this is his idea of fun?* Hawk wondered. Hawk walked over to the hog on the ground and eyed the tusks protruding from its mouth. Reaching down, he retrieved the arrow from the hog's side, cleaned it with grass, checked its capacity for future service, and slid it into the quiver.

Ehrig made his way back through the treeline and into the forest, looking for a pole strong enough to withstand the weight of the hog. With no further regard for noise, Ehrig took hold of the trunk of a moosewood tree. With his large knife, he hacked at its base, finally felling the tree. Stripping it of its foliage, he walked back to the clearing, dragging the moosewood trunk behind him.

While Ehrig had retreated in search of a log, Hawk went to his sack, pulled out a length of rope, tied it around the boar's hind legs, and threw it over a stout branch of the closest tree. Firmly grasping the line and putting his back into the effort, he dragged the dead animal until it was directly under the branch. Ehrig returned with the pole as Hawk was catching his breath from the exertion.

"Yes, this just might do it," Hawk opined.

"It had better. Finding another will have to wait until morning," Ehrig replied.

"Give me a hand. This damned thing is heavy," Hawk responded. "We still need to hang it to bleed, in spite of the fact that you opened its throat like a coin pouch to pay for a wench at a tavern."

Ehrig roared in laughter as he grabbed the rope. "Right you are! Heave!"

The boar was as heavy as they had anticipated, but after a bit of effort, they had it suspended from the branch.

"It will be full dark by the time this pig has bled dry," Hawk observed. "This has taken just long enough to make the task difficult. What do you think? Should we camp or carry this beast back to town in the dark?"

"I believe we will have a enough light tonight—or close enough. The moon will rise shortly," Ehrig said, looking to the eastern sky. No moon was visible, nor was the horizon through the trees. "We walked for only a small part of the day and are not that deep in the woods."

"I suppose. Do you think the tavern will be able to store this thing until morning? The butcher will surely have closed for the day by the time we return."

"Hah! The butcher will accept this prize regardless of the hour. I know his house. We will go there straight away. Besides, it's his wife I am afraid of!" Ehrig laughed. He looked again at the hanging boar. "What do you think? We can lighten the load if we decapitate it and remove the weight of his head." Ehrig started to move his hand under the cloak.

"No!" Hawk answered quickly. "The rich tend to appreciate the spectacle of the hog's head with an apple in its mouth, even if they do not purchase the entire carcass. The head is of value to the butcher and hence of value to us."

"You're right on that mark." Ehrig's reply came with a twinkle. "But I have yet to see a coil of pig guts on a platter! Apples be damned!" Ehrig drew his blade, stepped to the hanging hog, and with a single stroke opened it from crotch to breastbone. "I could care less whether the butcher has use for hog tripe," Ehrig declared. "I have no intention to burden my back with pig shit. We can leave the organs in place, but the guts stay here. The scavengers of the forest must eat, too."

With this he severed the intestines just below the stomach, and again just above the rectum. Hawk winced as they fell to the earth, not happy about the thought of the contents draining to the ground beneath the hanging pig and the difficulty of keeping from stepping in the mess. As Ehrig turn to face him again and stepped away from his work, Hawk could see that the man knew what he was doing. There was no spillage. Ehrig had somehow securely tied off the intestines, two places at each end, in the manner that a midwife ties the cord of a newborn, before cutting them from the body between the ties.

Hawk turned to his pack and as he bent opening it, he continued, "I had a good feeling about this hunt. I brought a small flask of spirits to celebrate. Will you join me?" he asked as the intestines unfolded to the ground.

"Such a small flask? I shall try to save you some!" Ehrig reached for the container and tilted it to his lips.

Hawk sat down next to his gear. In the dim light he could not tell whether the innards had been nicked, but he figured not. *Well*, he thought, *that pretty much settles that issue.* Hawk could not bring himself to object to the now lightened burden they faced; hog guts were heavy and this boar was big to begin with.

"You have skill, young man. It was a fine shot you took," Ehrig said, as if reading Hawk's mind while handing him back the flask. "Without a full view at that! A fine shot indeed." Taking another quick pull, Ehrig handed Hawk the flask and sat beside him.

Hawk knew that if Ehrig had not stepped in, the hog could have fought on for some time. Eventually it would have fallen, sooner more than likely, but there was no telling the kind of damage he could have sustained during the fight. "Well, I have never seen someone move as quickly as you. It was as if your feet were above the ground."

Ehrig looked over and grinned. "A gift."

Hawk smiled a crooked smile at his remark but did not respond; instead he went back to his thoughts. They both sat on the ground not far from the hanging carcass. At this point, there was nothing left to do but wait.

When it was clear that the blood had drained, the daylight was all but gone. Along with these signs, the odor of pig guts urged them to move on. Ehrig dragged the intestines from under the boar to the other side of the tree. Untying the rope from the tree trunk, he lowered the animal to the ground, not gently, but without aid, even as Hawk moved to his feet to assist. Moonlight began filtering through the trees.

Hawk gathered dry moss that had fallen to the foot of a nearby tree; conveniently a broken branch lay there as well. Ehrig stepped up to him, pulling a length of twine from somewhere beneath his cloak, took the torch materials in his hand, and bound the moss to the branch. Hawk struck a flame to ignite it. The moon was still very low in the sky, below the treetops; the extra light would help while binding their catch to the pole.

Securing the hog's legs together to form an inverted V on each end, Ehrig fed the moosewood trunk through the centers to Hawk. Grabbing the pole, Hawk at the rear, Ehrig leading, the two started back to Falkenwrath.

"This damn hog weighs as much as a fat man passed out on the floor!" Ehrig complained after a short walk back through the woods. "I have half a mind to deny the rich of their head!"

Hawk chuckled under the strain of the downward force brought by the dead pig's weight. The thought had crossed his mind as well. But he knew the value of the head was worth the trouble of carrying the pig back whole. The guts were not that big a loss, but the price Hawk and the butcher had agreed upon implicitly included the head. Ehrig's grumbling stopped when Hawk mentioned this.

The torch lit a small space before them as they made their way through the woods. The moon provided most of the light as its silver rays shimmered through the trees, but up ahead seemed odd to Hawk. As the moon continued its upward climb, the atmosphere almost imperceptibly changed. The light seemed to become tinged. The forest was not heavy here, and the moon would be expected to help illuminate their way as it rose higher in the sky, but that was not what Hawk perceived. He felt something was different... not wrong, just different.

"Put it down," Hawk said. "A break won't hurt, and I want to adjust the load on my shoulder." They halted and unloaded their burden to the ground. The pig hit with a thud but did not seem to mind. Ehrig sat down where he had stopped and rubbed his shoulder.

"This is too much like work," Ehrig resumed his grumbling. "My mind always seems to conveniently forget this part of the hunt beforehand."

Hawk heard the complaint. "I can't say it is my favorite aspect either, but it is part of the job," he replied. Changing the subject, he continued, "Have you noticed anything different about the forest as we have walked?"

"Such as?"

"I am not sure that I have the words. The woods somehow seem different, too green in the moonlight," Hawk said, looking around in all directions. He stretched to loosen the kink in his neck, then sat as well.

"Too green? I hadn't noticed." Ehrig looked at the treetops then the ground. Right then left.

"I am not sure I worded it well, but that is the best I can do."

Ehrig furrowed his brow and was silent for a long moment.

With a heavy breath he said, "It would seem that my complaining is annoying more than just you. I believe we may have some help on the way."

"Someone is coming?" Hawk replied curiously. "I haven't heard the sounds of someone approaching, only the forest."

"We won't encounter anyone before town," was the reply.

Hawk stood up. "More enigmas?" he said, too loudly. "You have been a boon to me, and I have no cause to complain of your treatment of me…save one."

"And what might that be?" Ehrig asked mildly, looking up at the young man.

"You. You have been much too helpful to one who is practically a stranger!" Hawk exclaimed. "I—"

Ehrig interrupted. "You wish to know why. You want to know how I seem to know things about you. How I seem to anticipate you."

"Yes," Hawk said, more subdued.

"This night is not the time to speak of these things. All will be made available to you, if." Ehrig stopped the sentence cold. It was clear to Hawk that the word "if" had not been left dangling as to invite a further questioning. Hawk stood there with questions on his face, but did not say a word. Ehrig sat silent for several moments and rose to a squatting position. "Grab the pole. We should be moving on." It was almost a command.

As he hefted his end of the burden, Hawk took note that it was noticeably lighter, by as much as a quarter. They walked in silence for a distance. As they did so, the pig seemed to become lighter still until it was almost as if the pole were resting on his shoulder rather than digging into it.

Ehrig's previous abruptness had the desired effect. Hawk held his tongue as they moved quickly toward town.

Hawk's mind churned over his questions, but there was little concrete to grasp.

As Ehrig had observed earlier, they were not deep in the forest, and under their lightened load the lights of town could soon be seen peeking through the trees. *Lights.* As the word went through his brain, it brought his earlier perception of the forest into focus. As they had traveled and the load had lightened, the green feeling that he had felt had almost resolved into a glow. Now, even the hog had a green tinge. *Glow.* Again his mind grasped at a single word. *My pack. My staff…everything. A green "something" had hovered over his things as they disappeared.*

This thought overcame his reluctance to speak. He opened his mouth and started to say, "Do you not see the green—"

"—of the forest?" Ehrig finished for him. "As I said, not this night. We will be in Falkenwrath very soon. You have business with the butcher when we get there. Hopefully the bath I purchased for you will still be hot."

Less than half an hour later they entered the town, and Ehrig quickly guided Hawk and the boar to the porch of the butcher's home. As they lowered the pig to the deck, the missing weight seemed to return in an instant, and Hawk almost dropped his end.

Ehrig turned to Hawk and said quietly, "Conclude your business here. Do not allow the man, or his wife, to cheat you of your full measure. The guts may be missing, but the boar is more massive than he expected. At the least you have earned the agreed upon price. If you are the businessman I believe you to be, you very may well extract a bit more from him." Continuing, he advised Hawk, "I'll be at the west gate of town at one hour after sunrise. It is only mid-evening now, and you have time to bathe and get a full sleep…if you occupy your bed alone," Ehrig added. "One turn following sunrise," Ehrig emphasized. "Do not be late. I shall not wait for you."

Ending his speech, Ehrig pounded loudly on the butcher's door, stepped off the porch, and disappeared onto the sparsely populated street.

*   *   *

Deborah spent the day with her mother assisting her with the chores around the house and preparation for dinner. Her father, a carpenter, was away all day at his shop in the square and returned home just before sundown. It was a surprise for him when he arrived home to find his daughter in the kitchen.

"Deborah! How are you, sweetheart?" her father asked.

"I'm fine."

"What brought you down from the mountain?"

Deborah's mother glanced up from her kneading, but did not stop. She knew the question would be asked eventually.

"I just thought it would be good to come down and visit. It's been over a month up there, and I thought I'd get a few things while I was here."

Her father accepted the answer with a pleased smile. "I'm glad you're here."

Her father placed his tools down at the door, as was his routine while the women readied the table. As they gathered together for the dinner, conversation led to the real reason of Deborah's visit.

Supper passed relatively quietly after the discussion at the table left everyone to their own thoughts. No one wanted to talk about anything that had happened in the past. Deborah's father was repeatedly tempted to bring up his friend Fredrick again in hopes that she would be persuaded to change her mind. But that story had been told over and over, and he could not see the use in telling it again.

Everyone knew there was nothing to be said about Deborah's loss of her husband Robert. And the argument of her coming home to stay had been well played out. Instead, they broke the silence from time to time with idle chitchat and empty conversation, catching up on the day-to-day routines and happenings in the town.

After dinner, Deborah silently decided to see for herself if she could find Ehrig. She took her shawl and walked to the other side of town. Making her way across town along the torch lit streets, Deborah came to the tavern. Pausing just slightly but not stopping as she neared the entrance, Deborah walked in and looked around. Clutching her shawl closely to her body, she moved to the bar.

"Has Ehrig been here?" she asked the barman.

"He hasn't been here all night. Shame, too. I was looking forward to the extra coins he tosses our maids," he said, wiping down the bar top. "My understanding is he went hunting. He had a friend with him. Didn't say when they would be back, though."

"This friend, was he a tall man with dark hair? He carries a bow."

"Yes, that's the man. He stayed with us last night. Said it is possible he would return but was not sure. We saved his room anyway, just in case."

Deborah thought, *It's possible then I am not too late.* She thanked the barman and left for her parents' home. On the way, she stopped a young teenage boy and whispered in his ear. The boy nodded, and Deborah smiled, handing him a copper.

*   *   *

The curtain in the window moved slightly, followed by the sounds of fumbling with the latch, and the door cracked open. The light from the room behind him illuminated the large frame of the butcher in his long pajama and nightcap, squinting nearsightedly into the night. His wife was behind him, peering around his shoulder.

"Who is there?" he asked through the crack in the door.

"It's Hawk, the huntsman. I am here with the boar we discussed this morning."

"At this hour? I did not expect you for another two days, if at all," he said, still squinting from having been roused from bed. He widened the crack of the door a bit and focused on Hawk, then turned his gaze to the large boar on his porch. "My goodness! That is a prize!"

Hawk could not fail to notice the wince as the man's wife punched his lower back in response to the comment.

Quickly recovering his composure, the butcher continued. "I believe we agreed upon seventeen silver pieces, but I expected delivery at my shop. If you believe you can just drop it on my doorstep, I can only give you sixteen and a half."

"Sir, we agreed upon twenty," Hawk replied quietly. "If you wish to haggle, we can allow the scales at your shop to be our negotiator. As you have already observed, this boar is larger than either of us was imagining this forenoon, and you will also find that it is young for its size." With each word Hawk's voice became slightly softer.

"Twenty? I cannot pay twenty…that is too much." The butcher's head tilted slightly to the right and back in the direction of his wife, a slight plea in his voice.

So this is what Ehrig meant about the wife, flashed through Hawk's mind. *Perhaps it is time that her reputation catches her,* he thought shamelessly.

Hawk looked stoically at the woman. Without taking his eyes off her, he replied to the man, "And I cannot afford to take less than twenty-five."

"Twenty-five!" The butcher's wife clearly could not believe her ears.

At this Hawk moved a half step to the side and faced her directly. "Twenty-five, madam." His voice was cold. "Not only is this animal large and tender in its youth, it is two days fresher than your husband expected." Turning his attention back the butcher, he said, "Have you sons? If so, fetch them to haul the boar to the shop."

The woman was not quite cowed. "Twenty-five, and we must perform our own delivery? I think not," she said, raising her voice to her husband.

Hawk continued to stare directly into her eyes. "Yes, madam. Your own delivery. A bargain for this beast at twenty-six pieces of silver."

"WHAT?" she howled.

Without a word, Hawk turned and stooped, grabbing the far end of the pole to which the pig was tied. He hauled it down the steps of the porch into the street and turned back to her, no small feat considering the full weight of the animal. "I believe I shall take it to your competitor. I am sure he will make available the twenty-six silver pieces and have it in the marketplace by tomorrow." Then Hawk thought better of the idea. Sitting down on the carcass he smiled. "Better yet, the pig and I are removed from your property. Here we shall stay for a month, if necessary. The price goes up from the twenty-seven you owe by two pieces of silver per day until either I am paid or only a skeleton remains in the street. I am sure the neighbors will love the smell as it rots. I will send for the intestines, which I left nearby, to enhance the flavor."

"You *cannot* do that!" she cried, pushing herself past her husband and onto the porch. "The…the…constable will not allow it…and I *will* call for him."

Hawk's face broke into a wide grin. "Do that. He is a good man, with a fair sense of justice…and old and fat enough to know the value that I have brought to you. Further, a few coppers in his palm should cover whatever fine for he will surely deem this matter too trivial for the magistrate." Hawk gave her an exaggerated wink that could not be missed in the dim light emanating from the open doorway.

As the shrew stood on the porch, mouth agape, Hawk furrowed his brow. *How did I know that? Those words were not bluster and bluff. I spoke true. But how did I know that?* He looked down at the boar, half expecting it to be glowing. It was not. He looked up again. In the darkness, none of them noticed the slightly green tinge fading from Hawk's exposed skin.

"Enough," the butcher said firmly. "We agreed upon twenty silver coins. I will, here in the darkness, concede that two days' freshness warrants some extra measure. As for the rest, let us take the animal to the shop where I may see exactly what I am buying. My sons are not available this evening. Will you assist me with transporting it over?"

"I can assist you," Hawk said.

The butcher took a firm hold of his wife's arm and pulled her into the house, closing the door behind them. Hawk could still hear the woman's voice from where he stood in the street. Significantly, he thought, Hawk heard no replies from the butcher. Five minutes later, the man exited the house with a cleaver through his belt and a torch in his hand.

Grasping the pole as to take the lead, the butcher grunted once under the strain of lifting the weight as Hawk raised his end. The men made their way to the icehouse of his shop. After lighting torches in their holders on the walls and tying the carcass with a rope strung through a shackle, they lifted the boar to a hanging hook where the butcher would do his work. The butcher carefully looked over his purchase, outside and in, using the torch he had carried from home for additional light during the thorough inspection.

"The animal is all that you claimed, my good man. I need not the scale to tell you now that he is worth thirty pieces of silver, but a deal is a deal, and we agreed upon twenty. You have demanded twenty-five for the extra value you brought and raised it to twenty-seven for having to listen to my woman's greed. I now offer you twenty-six, a compromise," he said, standing straight and looking at Hawk unapologetically. The man's demeanor had returned to that of the person Hawk had met earlier in the day.

Hawk looked at him for a moment, "Done." He smiled.

The butcher released a small sigh and extended his hand. Hawk took it without hesitation. *An honest merchant. Should we do further business, it will not be in the presence of his wife. He deserves better.*

The man turned, snuffed the lights on the walls, and moved toward the door of the icehouse saying, "My cashbox is in the front. You will have your payment shortly. By the Light, man, how did you get such a large beast back in such a timely fashion? Surely you had help."

"I did. We carried it for some distance but the burden was not so great," Hawk admitted.

"Not so great?" The butcher laughed. "Well, for his sake, I hope you paid your helper well. I'm glad it was not me who had to run through the forest with that thing on my shoulder."

Hawk smiled. In the main shop, the butcher opened the box and carefully counted out twenty-six coins. "Perhaps if you come this way again, we can make another arrangement."

"Perhaps," Hawk said, turning to leave. As he stepped out the door, Hawk stopped short. Turning back to the butcher, he said, "What was that expression you used? 'By the Light?' What does that mean?"

"Huh? Oh? It doesn't mean anything really. It is just a nonsense exclamation that gives you something to add to your words. It comes from the legends of the keep at the far end of the valley. Children's stories. Why?"

"Ah. Nothing. The phrase just struck me as peculiar. I am not from this area. Thank you. And yes, I think I would like to do further business with you should the opportunity arise. Good night."

Hawk exited the butcher's store and started his way to the inn where he would seek out that bath. He wanted to get some rest before the sun came up. Ehrig had been clear about not being late, and Hawk did not wish to miss his opportunity. Hawk did not know where he was to be led, but certainly it would be interesting. Plus, Ehrig promised answers, and Hawk was eager to have those. Arriving at the tavern, Hawk made his way into the bar.

Chapter Five

It had been a long day. Hawk was counting himself lucky that the hunt was so successful. *With the extra money I've just earned, I should be okay for some time,* Hawk thought. Pushing the door open, he entered the establishment and looked around but did not see Shilah serving in the main parlor. The tension of the hunt and then the cleaning and hauling of the pig back to town was evident in the stench Hawk brought back with him.

The barman recognized him straight off. "Hello, sir! Welcome back. I have your room waiting for you in anticipation of your return. The fire used to heat the water was allowed to burn out so it's not quite as hot as earlier, but I can fix that if you so desire." Remembering his last encounter with Hawk, he added hastily with a nervous smile, "No extra charge for rewarming it, of course."

Thinking about it for a moment Hawk said, "Yes, please, fire it up. I will be down shortly." Hauling the pig was heavy work even if the load was lightened somehow, especially from the butcher's door to his shop.

"Very good, sir. We took the fire down not long ago. The water should not be so cold as to take to long to heat up. I will send Shilah to fetch you when it's ready," the barman said.

"That would be perfect." And with that, Hawk took the key handed to him and headed to his room. Stopping on the stairs, it struck Hawk that he was not sure where the entrance Ehrig had stated he would be at in the morning was located. He turned to the barman and called out, "How far is the west gate from here? And how do I get there from here?"

"Not far at all, a small stretch from here following the street corner to the left from the town center," the barman responded.

Nodding, Hawk continued up the stairs to the fourth door. Opening it, Hawk entered and placed his things down, again looking at the inviting bed. *This may be my last chance to enjoy a comfortable night's rest for some time*, he thought as he pulled off his boots where he stood. Hawk loosened the belt holding the pouches. Slowly, the weight of all he was carrying began to shift from his body to the table and floor.

The sand in the hourglass was three-quarters gone when Shilah came to the door. She knocked lightly.

"Who's there?" Hawk inquired, in spite of recognizing the knock.

"Shilah."

Hawk did not put his boots back on this time. Hawk did not even attempt to reach for his blade as was his custom. Wearing only his pants and undershirt, he opened the door and let Shilah in. He walked back and sat on the bed as she entered the room. Shilah's eyes were filled with lust as she eyed Hawk. Reaching out her arms, she went to embrace him, but the smell of dead pig and sweat prevented her from achieving her goal.

"Oh," she said, taken aback from the stench, "your bath is ready now. The boy is just about finished filling the tub. The water is just as it was earlier." She looked at him directly. "I checked it myself."

"That's good news. I am going there straight away."

Shilah retreated a bit, more to distance herself from the smell than to give Hawk the room he needed to prepare for the bath.

As Shilah made her way out the door, Hawk raised up off the bed to follow her out. Taking nothing more than the clothes on his back and the key to the room, he locked the door behind him, headed out into the hallway and down the stairs. Hawk glanced over at Shilah as he made his way to the bathing room. She was back in front of the bar clearing mugs and placing fresh ones down. Shilah looked up to see Hawk entering the bathing room.

There was no delaying preparing for his bath this time. Hawk quickly disrobed and moved over the tub, sticking his fingers into the water to check the temperature. Slipping into the tub, Hawk's tired body quickly relaxed, but his mind was still extremely active trying to recall the moments when he would have sworn the events that occurred just did not seem right. Grabbing a sponge and bar of soap, Hawk began scrubbing himself. His movements were automatic and his stare was distant as he cleansed himself. *That pig was much heavier when we killed it than it was when Ehrig and I were carrying it from the woods,* he thought, *and in dealing with the butcher's wife, aside from seeing the constable drunker than most of the patrons the other night...*Hawk was again lost.

*   *   *

A knock on the door came. Deborah quickly rose to answer it, trying to prevent her parents from being awakened. As she was talking to the person through the door, her mother approached.

"Who is that, dear?" she asked.

"No one, Mother. A boy," Deborah explained.

"A boy! At this hour? Whatever does he want?"

"Nothing, Mother," she said then whispered, "Thank you, young man," through the door, closing it behind her. Moving across the room and removing her shawl from the peg in the wall, she said, "Mother, I shall return shortly."

"And where are you going at this hour, child?"

"To see a friend. I won't be long." Deborah opened the door and quickly closed it behind her. She made her way across the town and toward the tavern.

*   *   *

Hawk was drifting in and out of sleep. The water was perfect, and his mind finally relented to the fact he had no real clues to any of his questions. Thankful for the second bath in as many days, he truly was now in debt to Ehrig.

Shilah was busy clearing a table of mugs when she glanced over at the bathing room. Lifting the tray of glasses, she placed them on top the bar. "I'll be right back," she said to the bartender. The barman did not say a word, managing only a knowing and silent shake of the head and crooked smile in response. Shilah made her way to the bathing room where she knew Hawk would be busy taking a bath. Opening the door, Shilah watched as Hawk enjoyed the water with his eyes closed. She entered and carefully closed the door behind her, leaving it slightly cracked so her entry would not alert Hawk.

Quietly, Shilah stepped across the room and wrapped her arms around Hawk. "Hello again," she cooed. Without saying a word, she leaned over and gently pressed her lips to Hawk's. "Oh, that's much better…"

Feeling the light pressure of Shilah's full lips, Hawk's eyes opened to see familiarly colored hair from a tilted head resting on his face and neck. He reached up and took hold of her and returned the favor.

*   *   *

Entering the inn, Deborah looked around to see if she could find Hawk in the crowd. Not seeing him, she approached the bartender. "Excuse me. Do you know if the gentleman who was to return this evening made his way in?"

"Two men arrived today, ma'am. Of which do you speak?" the bartender said, hardly looking up from his task of wiping dry the freshly washed mugs.

"This man was tall with dark hair. His eyes are also dark. A strong jaw. He was to be returning from a hunting trip if I am not mistaken."

"Ah, that man is currently down the hall to the left. Only door there, you can't miss it."

"Thank you," Deborah said.

Only then did the bartender look up at the person who had spoken to him. *My goodness!*

Deborah wove her way through the crowd, making it to the other side of the room. Looking toward the left, she saw the door mentioned by the bartender. Nearing the entrance of the room, she stopped cold in her tracks. She had expected to see Hawk. She had not expected to see what came next. Through the opening, Deborah witnessed as a woman approached Hawk.

A pang hit Deborah in her chest. She watched as the girl kissed Hawk. Deborah thought for just a moment, trying to decide what to do next. She wanted to make her presence known, but in a burst of clear thinking, Deborah simply turned and left. On the walk home, the night air felt colder than before.

*   *   *

"Shilah!" her father called out as he entered the bar. "Where the hell is that girl?" he yelled at the bartender. The mugs were emptying on her side of the bar, and she was nowhere to be found. Shilah heard her father cry out her name. She froze and looked at Hawk, her face inches from his.

"Will you be back this way again?" Shilah asked in a hushed tone.

"I'm not sure. I'm leaving in the morning with a friend. I don't know where I'll be heading exactly," Hawk responded in a whisper.

A frown crossed her face, "I hope you do."

Then Shilah giggled as she kissed him again, rose up from the side of the tub, dried her hands quickly, and left the room. Hawk was smiling as she left. Her father saw Shilah as she entered the bar from the hallway leading to the bathing room.

"What the hell were you doing over there?" he asked.

"Just checking the water is all," Shilah responded.

"'Just checking the water is all,'" her father mocked. "Get to work! Those men want more drink! Checking the water my ass..." His voice trailed off to a mutter.

Shilah looked at her father with a nervous smile, shooting a glance toward the barman as she passed his side, grabbed the tray of full glasses off the bar, and headed into the room of men waiting for their refills.

Deborah caught herself rushing as she moved down the street away from The Rusted Lantern. She slowed to a more natural walk as she chastised herself. *What's wrong with you? You have no claim on him. Why did seeing him with that, that girl make you run out of there like a broken-hearted twelve year old?* She stopped momentarily when it struck her that "that girl" was Shilah. She had known Shilah almost since the younger woman had been born. They had played together often while growing up.

Deborah was about the age of six when they first met, yet when they did, their friendship was sealed quickly. Deborah had few close friends growing up. Though there were many children that would gather in the center square, Deborah usually kept to herself, often finding a corner to sit not far from her mother and watch the others. She was mostly a shy child who would prefer working in her father's shop to running with the other kids in the park.

Deborah's mother would try to find ways to get her child to engage with the other children as they played, but nothing seemed to work. She adored her child, doing the best she could to accommodate every whim that crossed Deborah's mind. Her mother was never far behind when Deborah fell or needed a hug or word of encouragement. The bond of mother and daughter was strong between them.

It was Shilah, walking along with another girl, who approached Deborah one day. Shilah was younger than her companion by several years. They were walking past holding hands when the younger girl broke free from the grasp of her friend and walked straight to Deborah sitting alone.

"Hello," the young girl said, smiling. Her long hair fell in her face on one side, tucked under the ear on the other. Deborah smiled back. The smile quickly faded as her friend caught up.

"I've seen you before," the older girl said. "You don't play," she said as a matter of fact.

The younger girl stood idly by in front of Deborah, still smiling. Deborah shrugged in response, not making much eye contact, choosing instead to stare at the ground. The older girl plopped down next to Deborah. "Can I sit with you?"

No reply.

"Good. I'll sit with you. I was getting tired anyway. I'm Abigail. I'm seven. That's Shilah. She's my neighbor. She's four. I'm watching her."

"Hello," the younger girl said again. She waved her little hand and smiled broadly. Deborah could not help but smile back at the pretty little girl.

"Well? What's your name?" Abigail asked.

Deborah nervously glanced over to Abigail. "Deb- Deborah."

Abigail sat there pondering for a moment. "I like Deb better," she replied. Deborah shot Abigail a glance then smiled.

From that point on the three girls became inseparable except for days when Deborah would accompany her father to work in his shop. She'd spend hours running around, sometimes cleaning up behind him, at other times causing the mess. Her father would always shower her with affection regardless of her actions. Deborah was quick to learn and before long had a great understanding of the various tools and their uses in the carpentry shop.

Along with working in the shop, Deborah would also go on hunting trips her father would sometimes take. She loved to walk through the woods—though she was not always the quietest companion.

One day her father planned to leave on a hunt to try and refresh the supply of meat. Deborah wanted to go with her father, but he insisted she stay home. Deborah pleaded to tag along.

A bit frustrated, her father made Deborah a deal. "If you can promise to be quiet and walk softly, when we get back I'll make you your own bow and teach you to use it. What do think about that?"

Deborah's eyes lit up. "Yes! I can do that!"

Her father smiled. "Go then, grab your things."

That day, Deborah was as quiet as the animals around her. Her footsteps were the softest they had ever been. Before darkness fell, her father was prepping a six-point buck to haul back home. True to his word, a few days later, he presented Deborah with a bow of her own, along with some instruction.

Abigail and Shilah would come by and watch as Deborah spent time practicing shooting the arrows she had been provided. It was not long after that her father allowed her to bring the bow with them on the hunt. Her work with a bow was exceptional even if not every hunt was successful.

And now here she was, upset at what she saw. It had been no ordinary bar wench she had walked in on. Had it been merely been one of the working girls, she would not have thought twice about it, but Shilah was her friend.

Arriving at her parents' home, Deborah tried to ease her discomfort by telling herself again that she had no claim on Hawk, though she was surprised at her reaction. Up to that point, she had not any reason to suspect that he was attracted to her. The thought helped a little—but not enough.

All right, young lady, Deborah thought firmly as she prepared for bed. *You did not come here to chase men. You have a journey of your own to get ready for, and you have missed Ehrig twice now. If he has not been frequenting The Rusted Lantern, Abby at The Griffin should know where to find him.* She laughed at the irony of her matter of fact attitude toward Abby and Ehrig's relationship. She had known Abby as long as Shilah and held no prejudice toward the girl's profession. *Would I have felt the same way if it had been Abby rather than Shilah? Oh, stop it!* If Ehrig were with Abby, he would be getting up late. She fell asleep going over the items she wanted to get at the market in the morning.

*   *   *

A heavy rap on the door and a husky voice awakened Hawk. He stretched as his mind slowly slipped from the clutches of unconsciousness. Lifting himself out of bed, he was dressing when there was another knock on the door. This time it was a barmaid bringing hot water for Hawk's morning wash. Emptying the jug into the basin, she left just as quickly as she came. Hawk peeked out the window. Sunrise. He had an hour to make his way to the west gate.

Hawk gathered his belongings. Checking the straps of the knife tied to his leg, Hawk slung the quiver over his shoulder, grabbed his bow, and departed the room. He walked down the stairs, turned over the key to the man standing behind the counter. Hawk peered one more time around the room, drew the conclusion that Shilah would not be here this early, and left.

Hawk had made his way through the center only minutes before Ehrig would pass the same point. Turning left as directed, he walked past a series of homes as he made his way to the meeting point. Deborah was also moving about in her parents' home, preparing her father's luncheon while her mother was setting breakfast. She glanced out the window to glimpse Hawk carrying his gear and the bow she had given him. *He is moving on,* she observed as he continued on his way. Still bothered by the image she had seen last night between Hawk and Shilah, she watched in silence as Hawk walked past. She would find Ehrig later and seek his assistance in her mission.

As Hawk approached the main gate leading to the west, he saw that Ehrig was not there. The gate was open and without a watchman, as had been the case when he had entered town from other directions. Thinking maybe he was late, he looked to the rising sun. *It couldn't have been an hour already.* Looking back in the direction from which he had come, Hawk did not see Ehrig approaching. He checked the road leading out of town, knowing that he would not see him in that direction for he had already looked. Hawk decided that he was early, but just to be sure, he moved down the path a short way, checking for recent tracks. Not finding any, he came back and stopped short of the gate. There was a large rock off to the side of the road that would make a good backrest where he could sit and maintain full view of the entrance to the town.

*   *   *

Ehrig prepared to leave The Griffin and make his way toward the west gate where he was certain he would see young Hawk. Settling his tab, giving Abby more than a friendly squeeze, and saying goodbye, he picked his belongings off the floor and made his way out the door and into the street. A cool breeze was blowing; Ehrig stopped to take a deep breath. *Storms. I love storms,* he thought as he ambled along. Ehrig noted that very few people were out on the streets, but many candles were burning in the homes along his path.

Ehrig headed to the meeting point. He made his way taking shortcuts between houses, across gardens and worn patches, not particularly taking notice of where he placed his foot or where the next one would land. Nearing the gate, he did not see Hawk anywhere.

"Hmph," he said, a bit disappointed but continued walking without hesitation. Passing through the gate and toward the woods, Ehrig kept his direction constant, neither turning with the road at its bend nor veering left or right, but straight away with purpose.

Hawk, deciding to relax a bit after keeping a vigilant watch, had just settled on the ground when Ehrig passed. If it were not for a pointy stone forcing him to readjust, he would have missed Ehrig altogether. Grabbing his gear and picking up the bow, he chased after Ehrig, whose pace had not slowed even after hearing Hawk's approach from behind.

"There you are! I was thinking maybe you had changed your mind and at this very moment were snuggling up to the lovely daughter of my friend at The Lantern," Ehrig said maintaining his pace.

"I was there just past the entrance only sitting off to the side. I didn't see you approach at first. How is your morning?" Hawk asked cordially.

"Fine, just fine. A storm is coming. I love storms," Ehrig said.

"I was trying to gauge when it will reach us when you passed me by," Hawk replied. "I am thinking around midday."

"Before that. Not much before, but before." Ehrig nodded to himself as he continued his pace without checking the sky as he responded.

* * *

The morning was quiet and after helping her mother straighten up from breakfast, Deborah gathered her bow and arrows and placed them by the door.

"So? You are intent on going to the Keep?" Deborah's father asked. Standing by the door preparing to leave, he picked up the basket of food she had prepared for him. "That quest cost Fredrick his life, and you are intent on following him to the grave? Those of the Hold leave us alone—if we leave them alone," he warned.

"Your friend Fredrick was seeking adventure and glory," she replied quietly. "This is different. I told you. I am drawn to do this. Yes, I want to know what happened to my husband, but there is more. I don't know how to explain it to you. I told you last night during supper, I have no fear of this, and I can't attribute it to courage. You know full well that I have gone into dangerous situations before, and I can say that I had to draw upon courage to do so. This is different...I don't know...it's just different."

Deborah's father listened as she revealed what was on her mind. While she spoke, one name came to his mind: Ehrig.

Though most in the town new the family, Ehrig was a friend who routinely passed by to visit. During his visits, Ehrig was always quick to tell his stories. "Let's see if we can't expand your imagination!" he'd say. Deborah was always enthralled by the stories Ehrig would tell. She loved to hear Ehrig's tales.

"Stop filling her head with these dreams!" her father would say, scolding Ehrig.

Ehrig would wink at Deborah and wince playfully as if caught in wrongdoing.

As she grew, Deborah's trust of Ehrig also grew. At times, she would bend Ehrig's ear, seeking advice for an issue that would matter only to a young girl, but was too embarrassing to discuss with her parents. He never seemed to mind spending time with her. Ehrig always watched over Deborah. Of all the girls who played in the center park, Deborah was easily his favorite. Now, here, Deborah's father cursed the ideas Ehrig had placed in her head.

"Hmmm. My daughter, the carpenter's daughter, an adventurer." The man shook his head. "You are a bright girl, Deborah, and you should be smart enough to allow me to talk you out of this. The legends speak of people being called to the Stronghold of the Deviants, but why you? Why my daughter?"

Deborah laughed softly. "You have always said I am a little strange, more at home in the woods than in the kitchen." She stood tall and smiled broadly. "Maybe I am a Deviant!" She winked at him. Her mother walked in from the kitchen, listening to the exchange.

"Tease all you want. You are still my little girl. Should I not be concerned about you?" He frowned. "And what if I forbade you?"

She stepped over to her father at the door and kissed him. "We discussed all of this last night. I will be all right. I shall stop by the shop before leaving town. Expect me before the sun is high." Giving Deborah a hug, he left.

Turning back to her mother and seeing the look in her eyes, Deborah said, "I shall do what I must." Her mother stared but did not reply.

Deborah went back to gathering her things for the trip. Her bow and the arrows Hawk had left her were set near the door. There was not much said as she moved about the house. Having prepared for the most part the night before, it was not long before Deborah was standing at the entry of the home. Knowing full well her mother was silently petrified of the idea of her daughter going out toward the Keep alone, Deborah gave her a long embrace.

"Don't worry, Mother. I'll be careful. I promise to return soon. After getting my supplies I will go by the shop then be on my way. Don't let Father see your sorrow, it is unwarranted." Her mother did not say a word, but the expression on her face spoke clearly. Deborah hugged her again and was out the door.

Heading toward The Griffin, she heard a woman complaining about her flowers being trampled. She arrived at the tavern and was greeted by the owner. "Hello! Deborah, how are you? It's been quite a bit of time since you have come by way of this side of town. Come, sit...stay awhile," the owner said.

"Hello, Mr. Gelmher. I was hoping to find Ehrig, actually. Have you seen him?" she asked.

"Ehrig! Ah yes, Ehrig. He was here last night. Came and visited Abby, you see. But he left well over an hour ago. He looked to be ready for travel."

"Gone? This early? Did he say where? Or when he would be back?" Deborah knew that Ehrig would come and go on a whim, but to miss him again…

"No, no he didn't. You know Ehrig," came the reply. "Maybe he said something to Abby."

"Abby. Yes, Abby. Don't tell me she's gone also."

"No, she is here. You know where her room is."

Trying not to run, Deborah wasted no time going up the stairs. Bam! Bam! She rapped on the door harder than necessary. The door opened.

"Wha—Deborah! By the Light, what are you doing here?"

Deborah pushed her way into the room. "Abby! Where is Ehrig? Has he left town? Where was he headed?"

"What? Slow down. Yes, it is nice to see you again, too, Deborah. You have been up on that mountain too long." Abby giggled at her old friend.

"Damn! I'm sorry, Abby. I have been looking for Ehrig for two days now and have missed him every time. It is good to see you, but if Ehrig has left, I'm afraid I may not have time to visit."

"Slow down," Abby repeated. "What is it so all-fired important for you to see the old rake?"

"I am going to the Stronghold. I *need* to talk to Ehrig."

"'Need?' You have heard his tall tales and lies about the Hold more than I. Why do you *need* to talk to him?" Abby giggled, and then frowned. "You should not be going there."

"Abby, *please!*" Deborah paced the room. "I know the stories, but what if they are not just all fairy tales? Ehrig knows the way. You know I can get there on my own. But if Ehrig knows something that would help me along the way, I must talk to him."

Abby sighed. "You know he never confides in anyone about his business. No, he did not say where he is headed or when he would return."

"Is there anything?—"

Abby looked at her hard for a long moment. In her line of work, it was not wise to be too talkative about what she saw and heard. She had known Deborah since they were girls, but that was all the more reason to be wary—not of Deborah, but of herself.

It was too easy to gossip with old friends. A flicker out of the corner of her eye distracted her, and she turned her head. There was nothing. Turning back to her friend she said, "The other night Ehrig took me to The Rusted Lantern with him. We met a young man there...we took drinks up to his room. He said he had been looking for Ehrig. He mentioned your name. Good looking, too. We only stayed a few minutes."

"Hawk!" Deborah could not control the exclamation.

"I don't think his name was mentioned. Is he why you are going to the Stronghold?" Abby smiled. "He is worth chasing," she said as an afterthought.

Deborah let out a small chuckle. "No. He passed by my place on his way here. I thought maybe Ehrig might be able to help him. So I told Hawk to look for him. He seemed nice enough. Did Ehrig say anything more about Hawk?"

"While we were at his room Ehrig told him to meet him here about noon, then we left. Ehrig was gone the rest of the day and did not get back until quite late. Stunk to high heaven when he did return. I don't know what they were doing all day. We had a good time cleaning him up though." More giggles.

Ehrig has taken more of an interest in Hawk than I imagined. If I were that sort of girl, I would wager they are traveling together. Oh hell…who am I kidding, I am that sort of girl. They are together. Now what am I to do?

"I am sure you did." Deborah winked at her friend. "When do you *not* have a good time?"

"I try. The gods know I try." Abby laughed. "I am afraid that is about all I know. Ehrig got up earlier than usual today. He packed for the road, but did not say anything more than that a storm is brewing. He loves bad weather. The man is nuts. Fun, rich, generous, but I tell you he is crazy."

"Thank you, Abby. I do appreciate your help. I wish I could stay, but if a storm is coming I must get on the road."

"When did you go crazy, too? You want to be on the road when the storm comes?"

"I think I must. The storm will not stop Ehrig, and it will make it harder to follow him, to track him. I do want to speak with him. I'll have to try and find him before the rain comes."

"Okay, if you say so. It truly was nice to see you again, Deb. If you really are going to the Hold, I will pray to the gods that I will see you again." Abby hugged Deborah, too much like a final farewell.

She walked over to her dresser and opened a jewelry box. Removing a pendant from within, she said, "Here, take this with you, Deb. Be safe." Abby handed her dear friend a necklace with a small jade stone carved in the shape of a cloud. It was her favorite.

Deborah looked at Abby affectionately. "I will do that. And you will see me again." Abby had not referred to Deborah as Deb since they were children. The look in Abby's eyes expressed more than her words. With that, Deborah left the room and the tavern. Back on the street, she could see the clouds moving from the west across the valley. *I have a little time, but I had best not dawdle.*

Hawk, she thought. *Ehrig is traveling with Hawk.* The visions of the previous night came back to her. She was not anxious to see Hawk right now. *If Ehrig left with Hawk, maybe he intended to be his guide. Maybe I will not have to encounter either of them. At least not right away.* It occurred to her that this might be wishful thinking, but for now it somehow comforted her a little. Though she was eager to speak to Ehrig, Deborah was still not ready to see Hawk after witnessing him with Shilah.

Deborah made short work of her business at the marketplace. In her haste she did not get quite everything she had planned, but as she left the business area toward the west gate, she considered the lighter load: It would allow her to travel faster. She did not want to catch the men right away, but she could not allow them to outpace her too quickly.

Deborah's father worked in silence. Normally a conversationalist during the work hours, this day he was without words. Moving back and forth along the piece of lumber, he measured and cut, trimmed and sanded. His motions were precise, direct, purposeful. His focus was so intense that not one of the apprentices thought to interrupt his concentration. He finished the project and placed it safely away but in view and turned his attention to the other work that he had neglected during the morning.

Deborah made her way to her father's shop to say good-bye. Upon entering the shop, she could sense that her father still had not come to terms with the notion of her heading to the Hold in the west.

As she worked her way toward him, he paused and looked at her. "You shouldn't be going anywhere except perhaps to your cabin," he said, resuming his work.

"Father, we discussed this. I must go. I must find my answers. If I don't go now, I will just go later," Deborah said.

"I don't like this. I don't like the idea of you heading out there alone." He looked around cautiously trying to keep his voice down.

Deborah stood firm. "I came to say goodbye for now, Father. I know you don't want me to, but I must be going." She hugged him and kissed his cheek. "I love you."

Deborah, her bow, quiver, and pouches in hand, turned and started toward the door. As she made her way across the floor, she stopped and turned, only to see her father hard at work again. Opening the door, Deborah moved across the threshold and was about to close it when she realized her father was standing beside her holding the staff he had labored so vigorously on that very morning. The piece of wood was beautiful, about six feet long, an inch and a half in diameter. Smooth as glass and as straight as a measuring stick. The look in his eyes had changed from anger to sadness as he handed it to Deborah. Deborah's eyes welled up as he guided her through the door and to the street in front of the shop. As she turned to leave, she heard him say, "I love you, sweetheart."

Chapter Six

Deborah knew that Hawk's destination was to the west, and if nothing else, Ehrig would also be heading west to meet the storm. At the west gate, Deborah stopped. She was not surprised that tracks on the dusty roadway were too jumbled to be useful. Hoping for a clue, she slowly moved away from town. A freshly crushed flower just off the path caught her eye. Someone, coming from the gate, had walked out to the large boulder a little farther off the road. With no other clue to go by, she decided to have a closer look at the area around the rock. There was evidence of someone pacing, like they were not sure which way to be looking, then sitting down. *Whoever came out here was waiting for someone.* Following the new leg of the V-shaped trail of footprints from and back to the road, she could see that they came alongside a second set of prints. *And had to trot to catch up.* The footprints slowed to a side-by-side pace. The road turned southerly a short distance from the gate, but the pair of tracks she had chosen to follow continued straight off the path toward the woods.

Standing by the side of the road, Deborah stopped and looked around for any other signs but saw none. *They are heading due west. Ordinary travelers or merchants would follow the road,* she reasoned and broke from the road to follow the footprints into the brush.

*   *   *

The pace was brisk at first but soon slowed down to a casual stroll. The deeper Ehrig and Hawk pushed their way through the increasingly dense forest, the darker it became, the treetops slowly removing the rays of light as if one by one. The conversation was brief and meaningless. Ehrig sensed that Hawk's mind was turning, and the time for some explanation was coming. Although Ehrig knew he had some answers to the questions running through Hawk's mind, he would not divulge everything to the other man. Some questions could not be explained; others required actually seeing to gain understanding. Ehrig made his way up a shallow streambed lined with trees as Hawk followed.

Hawk started to speak as Ehrig cut him off. "In my lair, there are some belongings I would like to show you. 'Toys' I like to think of them but actually 'tools' would be a more accurate term."

"Tools?" Hawk said.

"Yes, tools to keep you safe, defend yourself, and of course take the offense with," Ehrig replied. "You will need them where we are going."

"That is what I have wanted to ask you, Ehrig. Where are we going? You seemed to have known all along I was coming, where to find me, and now, where to lead me."

"The Arena! And it was not my doing, young lad. No, it was by way of the Light that I saw you."

"That term, I have heard several people speak it in town but I have never heard it before then. What does it mean? The Light?" Hawk asked. "The people in Falkenwrath seem to use it to refer to some part of the legends, but you never mentioned it in the stories back home. And why do you now call yourself Ehrig? Your name is Eth. Even after all these years, I have not forgotten you."

"Actually, my young friend, it is neither. For now continue calling me Ehrig. That is the name you have been using, and it will flow most easily from your mouth should we encounter others. For now, consider the name just a label to distinguish one man from another."

"But is not a man's name his bond? When a man hides his name, he hides himself. When you know not the man's name, you know not the man." Hawk stated this as a matter of faith. These were not questions; they were as true to him as gravity pulling an arrow from the sky.

"Fair enough," Ehrig replied. "But you do not know me. I came to your room as a stranger in the night, with a female unknown to you, and intoxicants. Yet you allowed me entry to your room and after no more conversation than my demand that you meet me at a location unknown to you, you in fact kept the appointment, then allowed me to invite myself to your hunt. Why?"

As Hawk thought about the question, he slowed his pace. "I don't quite know. Deborah told me to ask for you. Your name was not unknown to me. And I recognized your face."

Ehrig interrupted. "My name was not unknown to you? You heard the name Ehrig once only from Deborah. You said that as if you had heard tell of me in stories or gossip. This was not the case, was it?"

Hawk stopped. This conversation was not going the way he had planned. He was supposed to be getting answers, not more questions. "No, that was not the case."

His companion had slowed, but had not quite come to a halt. Rather, Ehrig turned to face Hawk, who stood among the trees trying to clear his mind to regain control of the conversation, and continued slowly walking backward. "Come. You will receive some of what you are looking for. All that you seek may not be yours to have, and none of it will be offered up to you as a mother's willing teat." Ehrig turned and again walked forward, but at the slow pace he had used when backpedaling. The retreating brought Hawk back to enough of his senses to start walking again, closing the short distance between them before the dark green cloak became one with the forest. With Hawk again at his side, Ehrig increased his pace.

They continued in silence for a few minutes before Ehrig repeated his last question. "Why do you not consider me a stranger? A name you only recently heard from another stranger, a face you had seen over a matter of days a decade before, when you were still a child? Yet here you are for the second time in as many days, alone in the forest with me. Why?"

"Well, as a starting point, you saved my life yesterday," Hawk began.

Ehrig interrupted him. "I did *not* save your life. At best, I did what a hunting partner is supposed to do: finish the kill. You know even better than I that taking down a boar with a single arrow is more luck than skill. That you came as close as you did is a tribute to your skill. With that shot, had I not been there, you would have survived, though perhaps a little worse for the wear. Try again."

"But the way you finished kill!" Hawk protested. "Your positioning was perfect. It could not have been any better had it been practiced for weeks with a hog that knew its part in the dance!"

Ehrig chuckled. "Well said, and maybe you are right. Attribute it to my skill. But you have still evaded my question."

Hawk fell silent again. *He said I would receive what I am looking for. What am I looking for? Receive?*

"Why have I taken up with a stranger? With you?" Ehrig nodded as Hawk continued. "The easy answer is that I do not really know. But now I don't think you will accept that from me." Ehrig nodded in agreement, eyebrow raised. "You are demanding that I tell you my mind, which I cannot do if I do not know it myself." Ehrig nodded a third time as his expression changed to a smile. Hawk could not tell if the smile was one of encouragement or satisfaction, but in some way the fact that he was smiling helped. Hawk felt reassured.

"I don't know if I can find an answer to your question." As he spoke, Hawk had slowed their pace considerably; Ehrig matched his stride without objection.

"Why with you?" Hawk thought about his answer. "Deborah must have felt you could help me. She gave me your name, and I didn't question or analyze her. She was helpful and kind to me. I admit to being taken by her beauty, which probably had something to do with my acceptance of her assistance. When I didn't find you right away, it was of no great concern, but..."

The woods were quiet save for their slow footsteps, which were themselves barely discernable from more than a few paces away.

Hawk searched for words, and Ehrig kept his peace as he observed that even with his companion's distracted state of mind, Hawk moved effortlessly, instinctively among the trees and the underbrush. He also noted that the wind had increased somewhat. *The storm is on schedule. I love storms. This one will be healthy for the valley.*

They had continued for several dozen paces before Hawk resumed. "...but you found me and when you did I was...bewildered. A face known to me in a place far removed from anywhere I had ever been, a face...I do not know how to say it otherwise...from my childhood."

"A face trusted in the innocence of childhood?" Ehrig offered.

"Yes. I suppose. Something like that."

"...with the intrigue of a new name?" came the amused reply.

"Most certainly. You barged into my room, and I found at least five mysteries confronting me all at once," Hawk said. "Just how did you know I was seeking you? I hadn't asked for you by name. Which brings me to your name. Why is your name different than before? And why did you seek me without knowing my business? No one here knows me. I have certainly changed over the years, but you seem to have escaped the hands of time," he said, holding up a finger as he counted off each new point. "And how in the name of the gods did that girl appear and disappear under your cloak like, like—"

Ehrig could not keep a straight face at the last question. He burst out laughing, hands to his knees, bent over with mirth. Hawk just stood and stared. "I am happy to so amuse you," Hawk said unhappily.

"Sit, my friend," Ehrig said, once regaining his composure. "It is time for a short rest. We will come back to your answer in a moment." Hawk dropped his pack to the ground and sat next it, then reclined onto his left elbow. Ehrig's eyes continued to twinkle as he noticed that Hawk had made a point of pinning a strap to the ground with his elbow as he changed position.

"You make it hard to answer you," Ehrig said seriously. "You ask so many questions at once and as I start to answer one, the beginnings of an answer prompt many more."

"It seems to me that you have more than I. You respond to my questions with questions of your own. I have not perceived any answers," Hawk retorted, bothered by Ehrig's humored reaction.

"The answers you seek are not the ones you expect. He who cannot teach, cannot claim to know. If you cannot tell me of your mind, I must assume that you do not know it yourself. Without clarity in your own mind, you will neither understand nor accept the answers that you seek. Now, once more: Why are you here in the middle of nowhere with a stranger?"

Teach? My mind? The words caught Hawk off guard. *I hunt. Is this what he is looking for? Is he asking how I will know that I found what I am hunting for?* Hawk kept to himself for a moment, attempting to gather his thoughts. Not quite sure what he was going to say, or how he would say them, the words came slowly.

"My father always said that I am a hunter by instinct. Things he had to learn, I knew without instruction. He said that he never taught me to hunt, he only taught me refinements that improved my skill. Now I am hunting answers rather than game. I guess I have to say your presence created many questions. Instinct told me my answers may lay around you as well, if not with you."

Hawk paused for a moment. The lack of reaction told Hawk maybe Ehrig was looking for something else. Hawk shifted again. Ehrig sat comfortably next to him, patiently waiting for Hawk to continue.

You convinced me there was something more to my dreams. You are the reason I decided to search for answers behind the dreams, Hawk thought. *How am I supposed to say that without revealing too much? The answers are before me somewhere; perhaps they are in the castle, maybe not, either way I have to find out what is behind my visions. If he wont provide answers, maybe he can provide direction. Regardless of whether it is good or bad...I need answers.* Hawk decided to try a different tack.

"It was not my mind that attached to you. It was more basic than that. A mottled fawn does not lie still in a field in the presence of danger because its mind knows that its protective coloring will make it difficult to see. It does this because it is its nature to do so. I already said that I do not really know why, rather, I can only say that finding you was the correct thing to do under the circumstances," Hawk said.

Ehrig said nothing as he gave Hawk the time he needed to gather his thoughts.

"The only way I know how to answer you is to say that my father can look at tracks in the forest and pick out those that are the most fresh, knowing whether they are new enough to be worth following. He can tell you why he has come to the decision, the clues that give him the information he needs. Even as a boy I could look at the same tracks and *see* the answer without knowing how it came to me. Even as your presence has continued to generate questions, my mind tells me that as the mysteries accumulate, they are all somehow related to my quest."

Ehrig shifted his position on the ground. "What you now seek is more elusive than the tracks leading to a deer. Instinct. From one man this could be a conveniently vague answer that begs the question, from another a talent devoid of intellect, and from yet another…" He let the thought trail off.

Suddenly changing the direction of the conversation, Ehrig asked, "Tell me about your nightmares. What do they have to do with all of this?"

Again Hawk was caught off guard, this time with Ehrig's question. *How does he know my thoughts?* Hawk had not forgotten their conversation so long ago, but remembered only talking about the stories his father would tell. *How does he know to ask about the nightmares?* Hawk recalled as he approached Eth, how he knew him then, sharpening dull blades on a stone behind their home. It was this talk so long ago that had planted the seed for Hawk to embark on this journey. Hawk took a moment as he tried to put the words together.

"At first the dreams weren't so bad. Everything was green. It was like I was covered in a blanket almost. It wasn't scary…just green. Then one night things changed. I started seeing images of places I couldn't recognize."

Ehrig sat, listening intently, not saying anything or giving any hint of thought. Simply listening.

"For a while there I was having them almost every night. It was strange because the visions were always broken, flashes really, never with any kind of pattern, random in occurrence. Often I would wake, and my father would come to me to calm me. Once I saw a field. I was in that field jumping from side to side. I don't know why I was jumping, but I saw myself getting farther and farther from the center as if I were taking flight with each leap. I was amazed at what was happening. Like my mind could control where I went or what I did. I recall waking from these dreams feeling at ease," Hawk said, pausing slightly to recall the feeling he had back then, the feeling of letting go and of being released from the limitations of gravity as if he was flying.

Hawk's face was euphoric then troubled. "But then, there were other nights when I woke to the sound of a large explosion. I could feel it literally reverberate through my body, shaking me! Jumping out of the bed, I would wake to find myself in the center of my room prepared to fight, the explosions were so real to me." Hawk thought about mentioning the cemetery that plagued his dreams, but decided against it. Even now after all these years that vision scared him most.

As Hawk recounted the events that led him to this journey, Ehrig had made himself comfortable against a tree.

"One night, after my fourteenth birthday, my father came to me after one of these dreams. 'Let me tell you a story,' he started. 'It's about a place very far away. A place called Deviant Stronghold said to be inhabited by men with great skill, a place where men would meet to compete in games of combat much like in the days of the gladiators.' As he described the events, I would revel in his stories, wanting to learn more and more as he described it all to me. He never told me how he knew of such a place. And at that time, I never thought to ask, either.

"For a while, every night before bed he would come to my side and tell me a little more about Deviant Hall. He often spoke of Sapient6 saying he was the center behind the legend of the Deviants. The crux. Although I must admit that even to this day, I really have no clue as to what or who Sapient6 is.

"I must also admit my father's stories helped. They took my mind off what was happening in my sleep. I didn't have another dream for some time after that. Then one day, I had another. I found myself again running, but this time I was facing someone...or *something*. The vision I had was convoluted. The strange thing about the dream was how the faster I attempted to move toward whatever it was in front of me, the further away I seemed to be trailing. Like I was not supposed to get there...no, that's not right...more like it didn't want me to get there," Hawk said. "I told my father about the dreams but he explained them away to the stories he had told.

"It wasn't until you came into town that I thought there had to be more to the stories than what my father had led on in the beginning. The tales you entertained the children with, me, were so similar to those that my father would tell me at night. There were differences to be sure, and you didn't repeat them word for word. But when you spoke, I could sense the similarities between your version and his. I could see the pattern in them. It was about that time I decided I was going to find out more about this Keep and the entity or being that dwelled within its walls. I felt the need to see it for myself," Hawk said.

"So? Do you think your acceptance of me now had anything to do with what you have just related? And I will not be convinced it was purely on account of your father's stories or some such nonsense," Ehrig said, still resting comfortably at the base of the tree.

Hawk looked at him, stared at him. Ehrig's face was bland, even passive, while Hawk tried to unveil the other man's thoughts as he studied him. A long minute passed before Hawk replied. "Yes and no. Yes, you are related to my dreams and, no, not because of the similarity between your tales and my father's. Back home you made a comment to me when I asked about the stories. You said something, like 'Legends and myths often are based upon fact.'

"Ever since I crested the mountaintop and started my way down into this valley, strange things have happened around me. Most of them subtle. Some brutally obvious. All of them in some way have pointed to you."

"Really? Go on," Ehrig urged.

"You ask why I took up with a virtual stranger. You." Hawk's mind and heart were merging. He could hardly hold the words back. "The stories intrigued me. You insinuated there is more truth to them than anyone believes. There are too many unusual things happening around you, too many things that are the stuff of legend. I want to find out what that truth is. And even more, I want to find out what the truth has to do with me. I want to know where I fit in concerning all of this. Why did I take up with you? Because if you don't have the answers to my questions, then maybe you can lead me to them!"

Ehrig considered Hawk's argument. After a moment of silence between the two, Ehrig decided to speak. "You asked about 'The Light.' Everything that has happened in your life has been the doing of The Light in one way or another." Ehrig paused as he weighed the outcome of revealing any information here, in the woods, at this time.

"Your dreams. I cannot say whether the Light brought them to you or whether you used them to draw the Light to you. In either case, it does not matter. Its presence in your village brought me there as well. The Light brought Deborah to you in the woods, although she is, as yet, unaware of this. And she pointed you to me."

"My pack!" Hawk interrupted. "There was a greenish glow above it when it disappeared! You did that."

"No. The fate of your pack will have to wait for answers from another. Some answers I have for you now. Others will have to wait. Still others are not mine to give...and still more...may take a lifetime."

"The pig? You said we were to have help. It was greenish after you said that. I thought it was a trick of light...and it was so much easier to carry."

Ehrig smiled. "Yes, it was, 'lighter,' if you will allow the turn of a phrase, but even that was not of my doing."

It took Hawk a moment to catch the wordplay, and then he chuckled. "I half expected to see a green pig at the butcher's house when I threatened to let it rot in the street. I'll have to tell you about that later."

"You won't have to. I was there."

"That was really unlike me. Were you responsible for my stubbornness with his wife?"

"Hehe. No. Had I wanted to be part of the play, I wouldn't have left. No, my purpose then was merely to observe. I watched from the butcher's rooftop. When you started talking about taking the pig to the other butcher, I was disappointed. I thought for a moment that maybe a mistake had been made. No, it was not the pig that glowed green then, it was *you*. When you said that you would send for the guts, I almost rolled off the roof." Ehrig laughed.

"Me? Green?" Hawk was dumbfounded.

"Yes, you. The way you drew the Light to yourself then was remarkable."

"I what? I did no such thing. I didn't even know there was such a thing. I'm still not sure I believe any of this."

"My friend, we could sit here in the rain for weeks just going over the things that have happened to you in the last three days. As it is, we have been bouncing from one thing to another without making much progress." As Ehrig said this, three large raindrops bounced off Hawk's right cheek. As they had talked, the wind had gotten stronger, bringing the storm clouds with it.

"Ah! The storm is right on schedule. It will last until mid-afternoon, then move on. Grab your things, and go sit under that tree. You do not want to get rained upon." Ehrig pointed to a young oak about fifteen paces from where Hawk sat. Ehrig picked up his own gear and moved in the direction he had pointed. Hawk gathered his things and followed.

As Hawk resettled, Ehrig remained standing. "I have some business to attend to. I shall be back no later than when the storm clears—well before dark. While I am gone, think of what you have seen and heard this morning. Rest. Sleep even, if you can."

As Hawk began to protest at being left behind, Ehrig stepped out from under the tree and started walking away. There was a loud crack above their heads, forcing Hawk to duck instinctively. The storm had reached their position and was directly overhead. Ehrig stopped and turned to face Hawk, lifting his arms outward toward the sky. Smiling, he yelled, "I love storms!"

As Ehrig finished the sentence, a dazzling blue-white light with a simultaneous explosion of sound flashed the sky directly in front of them, landing right where Ehrig stood and throwing Hawk to the ground. The thunder was deafening.

Momentarily blinded by the intensity of the lightning bolt, Hawk blinked several times before his eyes cleared. He expected to find Ehrig's charred body smoldering in front of him.

Instead, Ehrig stood, still smiling.

The ringing in his ears made Ehrig's words incomprehensible, but the movements of his lips were clear even with the spots still dancing in Hawk's vision. "I love storms." The shimmering green glow that encased him was equally unmistakable. Hawk stared, speechless. Ehrig stepped back to where the young man stood and put his hand on his shoulder—the glow remained where it had been.

"Say 'please.' It will probably keep you dry here under the tree." The ringing in Hawk's ears had subsided enough to understand these words.

Hawk opened his mouth. "Please?" It was hard to tell whether it was a question or just incredulous parroting of Ehrig's command.

Ehrig chuckled. "Close enough, I think," he said, stepping back toward the glistening green light. The glow slowly moved in Hawk's direction, growing as it did so. If he had tried to look, Hawk would have seen that the entire tree had become surrounded in green. The leaves stopped dripping the rain on him. Through the shimmer in front of him he watched Ehrig retreat. As the man disappeared into the trees, he also seemed to be rising into their branches as if carried by the wind. Still stunned by what he had seen, Hawk sat down. Unconsciously, he took a piece of jerky from his pack and began to gnaw on it.

* * *

The rain began to fall as Deborah followed the tracks into a shallow streambed. Dry during the winter, the warmth of early spring had allowed a rivulet to run in the lowest part, but the going was easy where the water had not yet reclaimed its path. Footprints in the patches of snow still remaining in shadowed areas made tracking a trivial task. The rain came earlier than expected as Deborah followed the tracks up the streambed. *What a nuisance*, she thought.

The further she traveled up the streambed, the more the rainwater from the mountainside began to claim its territory. The fresh prints in the snow were quickly dissipating in the tributary that was forming. Deborah began to search for tracks that may have steered away from the forming river but saw none. The prints that were visible kept along the same route as far as she could make out. She had no choice but to continue her hike through the streambed until she saw a sign of their departure from its path.

Deborah stayed as close as she could to the treeline, hoping to keep as dry as possible. Around a small bend, she came to a fork where the runoff of the mountains joined. The water had risen enough that no prints were apparent anymore. She walked up one side, then back and up the other side, trying to find a trace that would indicate which path Ehrig and Hawk had taken. She saw none. *Obviously they had continued along the dry streambed as before, but which fork?* Either fork led in the general direction she had deducted would be the logical path. Unconsciously rubbing on the stone of the pendant Abby had given her earlier, she followed the path to the left.

The chill of the rain of early spring was more annoying than welcome, but Deborah loved the smell of the freshly cleansed forest. The thunder in the distance, mostly back in the direction of the town, prompted her to stop every now and then to try to catch a glimpse of the lightning. Suddenly a massive blast of noise engulfed her. "That strike was close!" she exclaimed out loud. Looking to her right, she sought smoke as evidence of where it had hit. She slowly did a full turn, staring into the hills that surrounded her, but saw nothing. The rain kept falling and the trees swayed in the wind, but she did not see any signs to indicate anything was out of the ordinary. *Strange.* Accepting there was no danger, she moved on, knowing the rain and an early season fire from the lightning was not a real concern for worry.

*   *   *

Hawk had decided that a nap in the rain sounded like a good idea. Up on a small hill, the oak was providing the shelter Ehrig had promised. Adjusting the sack against the tree, he laid his head down to rest. The image of Ehrig still standing as the lighting bolt crashed to the ground where he stood was inexplicable to Hawk. His being unscathed just did not make sense. But Ehrig had given no opportunity for answers, and Hawk was too dumbfounded to ask had he had the chance. The rain was soothing and it did not take long to lull Hawk to sleep.

*   *   *

Deborah followed the left branch of the stream, hoping she made the correct choice, knowing that if she had not, the trail could be lost for good and she would not have any clues to track. The water in the stream was a little stronger now that the rain had some time to collect on its way down to the larger rivers in the lower valley. She walked along the side of the stream looking for signs of the two men, but saw none. Without knowing it, she passed Hawk asleep on the hill. Deborah was unwittingly creating a distance between Hawk and herself. The separation between them was already such that the glow surrounding the tree under which Hawk slept was not visible to her. The rain was constant but tolerable as she decided to continue pushing further into the forest, unaware she was separating herself from her goal.

The storm let up slightly, and the rain turned to a light drizzle. Deborah found herself lost—not in the sense that she could not find her way home, but rather any sign that Ehrig or Hawk may have left had completely vanished in the storm. As she continued walking through the forest, she looked to the sky, trying to keep on a westerly course. The valley was huge, and she knew it could be some time before she ran into another person. Deciding to rest, she sat along a fallen tree and had fruit and pieces of jerky she had picked up at the market. Deborah knew she would need to begin looking for shelter before dark.

*   *   *

Hawk was tired. He ran with every ounce of energy he could muster. Try as he might, he made no ground against the vision in front of him: It continued to remain the same distance regardless of every labored step. His breath was heavy and his lungs stung deeply every time he inhaled. The image moved gracefully, without any hint of effort, while Hawk, struggling, fought for each advance. The silhouette was closer this time although he still could not make out exactly what he was seeing.

Suddenly, he was jumping. Higher and higher he went. He felt the rush of taking flight as the ground below him fell away. The image was still present, maintaining its distance as before. Without warning a blast of air hit Hawk, causing him to tumble out of the sky. He was falling! Hawk had no control over the freefall. In his mind, he could see the distance of the earth closing on him fast. He tried with all his might to regain control but couldn't. The land below him seemed to reach out to grab him. Hawk screamed as he was about to make impact when he felt the blow to his arm and side.

"Wake up, boy!" Ehrig yelled, having just pounded Hawk's arm.

Hawk came out of his sleep shaking, uncertain of his location, unaware of the green light that was dissipating around him. He was drenched in sweat. And his arm ached for some reason.

Ehrig, kneeling on one knee, handed Hawk a skin. "Here, drink some water." Looking him over and seeing Hawk was all right, Ehrig stood, smiling. "That's the closest you have ever been, isn't it? Come, we must move on before darkness falls."

Shaken by how real the dream was, Hawk had no words. Hawk's breathing returned to a normal rhythm as his heart slowed its pace. Standing, he grabbed his things and followed Ehrig through the forest. Only remnants of clouds remained of the storm. The ground around the tree where he had slept was dry. Except for the sweat, so was Hawk. As he navigated his way around the muddy puddles, Hawk could tell the rain from the storm must have been heavy.

*   *   *

Deborah's frustration was evident. Every sign of Ehrig and Hawk had disappeared in the storm, erased by the flow of rainwater down the hills and swept into the streams. Using the staff her father gave her, she manipulated her way around rocks and fallen trees as she made her way up a hill, hoping to get a better idea of where she was and if possible, get her bearing on the stronghold that lay before her.

The storm had all but passed now, and the sky was clearing. Reaching the top, she looked about the skyline. Off in the distance she could see another storm brewing, circling directly to the west. Deborah scanned the view in front of her looking for something she may have missed or any sign of Ehrig or Hawk. Nothing. Deciding the time had come, she began looking for the shelter she would soon need.

Deciding the best course was to follow the lowering sun, Deborah crossed over another stream as she searched for a place to rest for the night. She came upon a slightly larger hill that seemed as if its face was taken off. A small but strong waterfall filled a small pond below it. Deborah stopped long enough to take a drink and rest. She climbed a pile of large logs to the top and made her way up the cliff over its ledge, pushing into the forest above.

*   *   *

The pace that Ehrig set after leaving the tree had precluded any continuation of their conversation. Hawk and Ehrig headed down the hill.

"Come, we are not far now," Ehrig said, looking up to the sky. "We should make it before sundown."

Chapter Seven

The two men continued their march through the forest. As Ehrig maneuvered his way through the trees and around brush and rock, Hawk followed step for step. The trek was not difficult but did seem to be taking a long time.

"Where are you taking me?" Hawk asked.

"To my place in the woods."

The sunlight was starting to dim as Ehrig and Hawk had come upon what looked like large logs that had fallen in a pile stacked against a hill. Ehrig stopped for a moment and observed the surroundings curiously, then circled the waterfall next to the logs. "Come," he said.

Hawk followed as Ehrig disappeared behind the tree trunks into a small opening. Ehrig lit a torch that was resting near the entrance and led Hawk through a narrow S-shaped tunnel into the mouth of a large cave. Inside, Ehrig stood next to the entry, holding the torch high. Hawk moved past him into the room and turned back toward Ehrig. The room went black. The torch had simply ceased to burn. "What happened?" he asked into the darkness.

"It is not needed here," came the reply, as a diffused green glow slowly began to brighten the room.

"What is that? More magic?" The tone of Hawk's voice was tinged with awe as the globe before him became brighter and brighter.

"No and yes," Ehrig replied. "This illumination is not exactly the work of the Green Light. It is a harness if you will. To you, it is probably the equivalent of magic, but in reality it is no more magical than striking flint on stone to light a fire. For your purposes, think of it as lightning in a bottle. This is just the beginning of the events that you will witness. You are destined for greater experiences and challenges that your mind has not yet been prepared for. But you will be," Ehrig said, placing the torch against the wall at the entry of the cavern.

Hawk could now see that the glow emanated from several sources around the juncture of the cave walls and ceiling as the light being emitted radiated into a crystal blue hue. As he squinted in the unusual light, Ehrig continued, "Give it time to let your eyes adjust.

"Soon you will witness quite a few new enigmas, mysteries better explained by example rather than words. But there will be a time and a place for all of that later," he said, waving his hand in dismissal, moving toward a passage entrance on the opposite side of the room.

"The lighting is just the first example. Everything new that you see here will astound you, but, like the lights, none are magical. Rather they are merely beyond your experience. The magic, as you call it, is in how they can operate in this place. The answer to that is the Green Glow, the Light...the purpose of your quest. It is the Light that I will answer about, not the toys. Now take off your pack and make yourself comfortable while I get us some food."

Hawk shrugged off his pack and placed it, along with his bow and quiver, against the cave wall at the end of a couch covered in bearskins. But he did not make himself comfortable. Ehrig was correct. There were many strange things in this room, and it was clear that there were hallways leading to other spaces.

Hawk scanned the area as his eyes adjusted in the light. A minimal inspection told him this cave was neither naturally formed, nor dug out by human hands. The walls were smooth and glasslike, as if the rock had been fused by intense heat. Although the room was not filled with furniture, it had the basic necessities to make it comfortable. Off to his left was a set of chairs surrounding a table. On the opposite end of the couch was a large cabinet about the height of a tall man and half again as wide. Divided into thirds, the center door was glass while the two on the ends were solid wood—all had locks. Through the glass Hawk could see several weapons: a bow and quiver, two swords, knives of various sizes and shapes, and a crossbow.

On another wall was a bookcase about the same size as the weapons cabinet. Even more amazing than the sheer number of books here in a cave in the middle of a forest was the fact that none of the printing on the bindings seemed to have been lettered by hand.

Hawk continued to explore his surroundings, touching the bindings of the books and admiring the trophies on the walls. There were many different species of animals that Hawk did not recognize.

As he stared about the space, Hawk noticed other passages. His curiosity began to get the better of him as he made his way closer to the entrance to one of the hallways.

Ehrig emerged from another path in the cave just as Hawk had started his way into a hallway that led to another room.

"That is for later," Ehrig said. "Come and eat something."

Hawk moved to the table where Ehrig had placed a plate piled with fruit, slices of pork, and a tankard of ale. The meat was fresh and hot, the tankard covered with frost. Hawk started to question but thought better of it as Ehrig turned and left the room again, returning a few moments later with a plate and tankard of his own.

*   *   *

Deborah continued walking through the forest. With the light fading, she still had not found a place to rest. Realizing time to find shelter was running out, she reached a clearing in the trees and decided this area would do. Using large leaves from a fern to form a bed, placing her bow, staff, and sacks near the edge, she was satisfied with the arrangement. Setting up a makeshift pit, she quickly found what pieces of logs and sticks she could to make a fire and settled in for the night. Deborah heard the occasional owl call out in the woods and the water of the stream passing by, the sounds of the night comforted her. Soon she was sleeping.

*   *   *

"Rest now. The day was long but tomorrow will be longer. There is much to discuss and new adventure before us!" Ehrig said enthusiastically as he grabbed the furs off the couch and threw them into two piles on the floor. "You will be comfortable there," Ehrig said pointing to one pile. "We will talk in the morning." Ehrig turned and disappeared through another passage in the cave.

The man is maddening, Hawk thought, even as he recognized the need for rest. Although he had slept while Ehrig was gone, the final trek to this place had been fast paced and long. He eased upon the pile of furs and made himself comfortable. It was not hard to do. The lighting of the room dimmed and went black, along with Hawk's consciousness, as he fell into what started out as a dreamless sleep.

*   *   *

As Deborah lay sleeping by the fire she had built, the glow approached through the trees. It had emerged from out of nowhere and watched as the reflection of the flames danced upon her face. Her breathing was slow and deep. The glow, floating above the ground, made no sound as it hovered near her position. Closer it came to the figure resting on the ground. Slowly, the green glow covered Deborah, swallowing her bit by bit. She felt nothing as she and everything she carried were immersed in the light. The light became brighter as it hovered above her. Then she was gone. Even the embers from the brightly burning fire were snuffed out, leaving no trace.

*   *   *

Ehrig rose from his slumber. As sleep cleared from his head, a smile came to his face. "Good," he whispered. He dressed and stepped into the hallway, making his way toward Hawk.

Ehrig stepped out of the tunnel and into the room where Hawk slept. Hawk awoke startled from another dream.

Sitting up from the furs, Hawk turned around to see Ehrig standing above him. The look on Ehrig's face said it all. Hawk could only sit there with his arms crossed over his knees. Movement in the second pile of furs caught his eye. Hawk stared at the pile. It moved again. Glancing around he noticed a second bow with a second quiver of arrows. *I know that bow*, he thought, recognizing his knots on the arrows. Hawk looked up at Ehrig and back to the furs.

Deborah woke. On her stomach, she lifted her head, disheveled hair falling in her face, and gazed about the cave. "What?…" she said slowly, pushing herself up, sitting on her ankles.

"Deborah?" Hawk said.

Hawk and Deborah sat on the cave floor simply staring at each other. After a few moments of awkward silence, Ehrig started to laugh. They both turned to stare at him. Deborah giggled then stopped, still confused. Hawk just stared.

Getting to her feet, Deborah walked over to Ehrig, who was starting to regain his composure. She hugged him and stepped back, "Ehrig! In the name of the Light, how the hell did I get here?" she said, glancing about the room. "And where is 'here'?"

Ehrig reached out and took her hand, leading her to the couch. "I was led to believe that you wished to speak with me."

"What is going on? Last night I was in the forest, and now I'm here with you and Hawk. Hawk!" She turned to see him still sitting on the rugs.

"It's good to see you again, Deborah," Hawk said after clearing his throat.

"I did not bring you here, Deborah. Hex brought you here," Ehrig said.

"Hex? You mean from the stories of Deviant Hall?" Deborah asked incredulously. She was twisting her hands.

"Yes, Deborah, that is the Hex I speak of. Hex is real," Ehrig replied. He leaned over and opened the center door of the cabinet with the weapons Hawk seen the day before.

"Who, or what, the hell is Hex?" Hawk had gotten to his feet and walked over to the table to pull out a chair, looking first at Ehrig, then to Deborah, and back to Ehrig.

"Though the legends have spread, the name has not. You are not from this valley. It stands to reason you will not have heard of Hex. But Hex is not our immediate concern."

Deborah visibly shivered when Ehrig pronounced that Hex was real; goosebumps covered her body each time the name was mentioned. "The stories say Hex is the Light," Deborah answered.

"Hex is *not* the Light...and the stories do not tell that he is," Ehrig interjected. "The legends say that Hex is *seen* as the Light. There's a difference. But retelling the legends is not our purpose here. Hawk, go sit on the couch. I will be back in a moment." Ehrig disappeared down the tunnel.

Deborah looked confused. "Where *are* we? Do you know how I got here?"

"No. I woke just before you did. It wasn't until you moved that I realized anyone other than Ehrig and I shared the space," Hawk replied. "Ehrig said this cave is where he lives. Look around you, the things in this room, I have no clue as to where half of these would come from."

Deborah gazed around the room from where she sat on the couch. Getting up, she walked over to the open weapons cabinet. She picked up the crossbow and tested its weight and balance. She started to raise it to her shoulder when Ehrig stepped back into the room.

"Do you like it?" he asked.

Startled, Deborah hurriedly lowered the crossbow, placing it back in the case then whirled to face Ehrig. Her face was that of a child caught with her hand in the sweets jar.

"It's beautiful," she stammered. She edged her way back to the couch.

Both of Ehrig's visitors sat patiently. Neither knew what to say or do. Ehrig understood. The time to begin explanation had arrived.

Chapter Eight

Ehrig knew there would be resistance to the reality of what he had to say. He also knew there were ways to educate the uneducated, to remove ignorance and doubt, replacing it with knowledge and acceptance. Ehrig had waited patiently in the wings. It had taken years before these two were ready to hear what he had to share. When he realized that Hawk had found his way to Falkenwrath, Ehrig knew the time had come. Deborah following behind Hawk was unexpected. But now that they were both together, Ehrig's next step made sense.

Ehrig smiled at Deborah's discomfort. With his free hand Ehrig grabbed a chair from the table and dragged it across the room to face them. He lay the thing he had brought back with him on the floor next to the chair. "You have both heard the legends of Deviant Stronghold from me and others; however, you have not both heard the same stories. The legends and myths are just that: stories told and retold, added to and subtracted from in each new telling. Some have been invented out of pure imagination, but the fabric of all is based in fact."

Ehrig drew a deep breath as to drive home his next point. "At this moment there is one thing, above all else, that both of you must understand: Your lives have not prepared you to comprehend the vastness of what you are about to experience. There are facts and ideas you will encounter that will not be learned nor accepted in this world for many years to come. In the beginning you will be required to accept what is revealed as it is given to you. Understanding will come in time."

Picking up the object he had placed on the floor and holding it vertically, the butt on his thigh, he asked, "Do you know what this is?" He did not offer it to either.

"No, but I would guess that it is a weapon of some sort based on the design of the part resting on your leg. It also appears to have a trigger, like a crossbow," Hawk answered.

"Very good. A weapon it is. But without me to show it to you, you would have to live a great many lives before you would ever see such a device. Later today I will show you what it is capable of. This demonstration will surely bring forth more questions—all valid—and for that you will have to trust that I am telling the truth," Ehrig said.

Ehrig continued speaking, first turning his attention to Hawk. "Hawk, you left your home to find out if Deviant Stronghold exists, but the true meaning of your quest is to find if there is a connection between the legends and your dreams. Deborah, you know the Stronghold does exist. You have seen it from across the valley."

"What does any of this have to do with me?" Deborah asked.

"You are searching for closure as to the fate of your husband, Robert—information not mine to impart. But I can say that Robert's destiny lay at the Stronghold, and you will not grasp what you find there until you understand his quest, which was not terribly dissimilar from Hawk's,"

Ehrig said, cautiously resting the weapon on the floor. "Neither of you had an inkling of what you were walking into when you most recently left your homes."

Deborah's mouth opened, but no words escaped. She looked in Hawk's direction and back at Ehrig. *How did you know what I was searching for?*

"You cannot begin to comprehend until you have grasped two concepts: nothing and Deviance," Ehrig continued. Raising his index finger, Ehrig drew a circle in the air in front of his face and told them to do the same. "Now what is *in* the place where you drew your circles?"

"Nothing," Deborah stated as a matter of fact.

"Air," Hawk said.

"Well, which is it?" Ehrig asked.

Hawk explained, "If there were no air in the circle you would suffocate if you were to put your nose in the place where you drew the circle."

Again Ehrig replied, "Very good. Just because you cannot see it does not mean that it does not exist. Yet even the absence of air in the circle would not mean that there was nothing there. When I say 'nothing,' I mean just that. In this case, if we were to remove the air from the circle, there would still be something, a place where we could put an object...air or anything else. The 'nothing' of which I speak not only does not have air in it, it also has no place to put air. Not even time."

"That is nonsense," Hawk interrupted. "I can envision a place that is empty, but a place that is not even a place? Nonsense."

"Deborah, you are shaking your head," Ehrig said.

She looked up at him. "In the beginning, Sapient6-"

"Excellent! The creation. No need to go further!" he said waving his hand in the air, cutting Deborah off. "Whether Hawk's creation story is the same as yours is immaterial. Both, of necessity, begin with the idea of nothing. For if there was something, then creation would have already occurred...except for one small problem..."

"Where did Sapient6 come from?" Hawk said.

"Better and better! Indeed, where did Sapient6 come from? For that matter, where did *you* come from?

"Do you remember being born? What evidence do you have that your parents are your parents, other than being told this?" asked Ehrig, not allowing time for answers.

"Sapient6 can only say that his first awareness was of the Green Light. BUT! The Green Light claims its first awareness was of Sapient6! Simultaneous creation? And by whom or what? Are they both the creators? Both say no. Neither remembers their birth any more than you do. The difference is that you have others to tell you of your beginning, they do not," Ehrig said, excitement rising in his voice.

"Now you are talking in circles," Deborah declared. "And what does this have to do with us?"

"Hold on," Hawk interjected. "Light that talks? Thinks? Remembers?"

"You have already seen some evidence of this, Hawk," Ehrig said matter of factly.

"Deborah, I will get to you shortly...now, the ultimate creation will probably be forever unknown. But what we do know is that if there is a point of creation, then by definition, prior to creation—whatever that means—is pure nothingness, not even a place or even a time for something to be created in." Ehrig's voice was building again as he continued speaking.

"The question then becomes: How can creation even occur? The only answer that I am aware of, like all such answers, begs the question, but...that answer is Deviance!" he said, eyes wide open. "Deviance is not a thing or a place or a god or even an idea. The best we can say is that it is a condition of difference. Our immediate reaction is that something must cause or create the condition. This may be, but we will probably never know exactly. The best we know is the original sin of difference was the Green Light or Sapient6 or both. The Light is properly called The Green Glow of Deviance. The thing we can say for certainty about it is that it propagates Deviance. It is the embodiment of that which is different."

"But are we all not different?" Deborah asked.

Shaking his head as if to stop Deborah in her tracks, Ehrig replied, "You are jumping to the end of the story. Please, hear me out—"

"Religion!" Hawk snorted, interrupting the exchange. "You are a priest trying to convert me to yet another religion. The gods are all well and good, but they have done nothing for me, and I prefer to return the favor. The stories I was told represented Deviants and Sapient6 as heroes, as warriors with remarkable abilities and skills, but now you are telling me they are the gods? Bah! Is this what I traveled all this way for? I'm going home." Hawk stood and moved to where his belongings lay propped against the wall.

"Hawk, please listen." There was a plea in Deborah's voice as he stepped past her.

He picked up his pack and turned toward her. "I would prefer to have the bow with me when traveling alone. But it is yours, and I shall leave it should you so desire."

Deborah said sadly, "No. Take the bow, it belongs to—" A horrendous crash of thunder interrupted her, echoing in the room.

The sound caught both Hawk and Deborah completely unprepared. Hawk dropped everything, jumping about four feet away from the source. Sitting, Deborah could only cringe as she covered her ears. Ehrig sat still in the chair.

The weapon he had brought into the room was in his hand, pointed toward the ceiling. Ehrig was glowing green, the floor around him littered with chunks of fiery red rock. In the ceiling above his head there was a gouge almost a foot deep and about two feet in diameter. Bits of molten rock dripped from the ceiling above him. When the rock landed on the glow encasing Ehrig, it slid down to the cave floor—like rain off an umbrella.

"Religion? You think I bring religion?" Ehrig said evenly, shaking his head. Standing, he said, "Both of you, follow me." The glow faded as Ehrig headed toward the hallway.

Hawk stared at Deborah as she stood nervously and careful to avoid stepping on the hot rock around where Ehrig had sat, slowly walked toward the hall. Hawk's gaze followed her for a few steps, and then he followed as well.

The tunnel that served as the hallway was long, fifty paces or more, illuminated by the same lighting that was in the main room they all had just departed. It was empty except for the cobwebs lining the corners of the rock. The trio passed numerous closed doors as they made their way to the end. The entry at the end of passageway was closed, but swung open as Ehrig approached—without him touching it. The light was bright as Hawk followed Ehrig through the entrance. Deborah stopped just outside and looked in.

The space was huge. It was a round, dome-shaped area that appeared as big around as the hallway had been long. Along the walls where they stood were cases and boxes, some of them wood, others metal. There were cabinets alongside the boxes and a small table and two chairs off to the side. In front of them were more boxes, but these were empty, some scattered about in pieces. There was other debris and markings of explosions in the ground covering the area in front of them.

Deborah, walking cautiously, stepped through the door and stopped again. Ehrig was about a half dozen steps inside the door with his back to Hawk. Deborah closed the distance behind Hawk, pressing her body against his.

Hawk wasn't expecting Deborah's touch and was surprised as he allowed himself the pleasure of her breast pressing into his arm as she looked around the room.

Chapter Nine

Looking about the space as if deciding how to proceed, Ehrig initially turned to Hawk since he was closest. But after a moment the big man decided on a different course of action.

"Deborah," Ehrig said, "straight in front of me, walk twenty-five paces, stop, and turn around." She looked at him, questions in her eyes. She was still trembling from the shock of the explosion in the other room. "Please, do as I ask."

Ehrig shifted the weapon to his left hand, pointing toward the ground. He put his right hand on her shoulder and nodded. She looked past him back at Hawk, and then began walking in the direction Ehrig requested. As she did so Hawk took two steps toward Ehrig.

"What are you doing?" Hawk asked.

"Hold there. Do not take another step nor say another word," Ehrig commanded, his tone serious and firm. Hawk stopped in his tracks.

Deborah walked the specified distance, paused for a moment, then turned around to face Ehrig and Hawk.

Without switching hands, in one smooth motion Ehrig swung the weapon up to hip level and pulled the trigger.

Again, the thunder roared and echoed in the room. Deborah's body exploded into hundreds of fist-sized chunks. Nothing in the mess on the floor where she had stood resembled anything human.

The first time the weapon had fired, Hawk had been facing Deborah, his back to Ehrig. This time he was facing the man, but the firing caught him no less by surprise. He instinctively jumped again, finding himself crouching, knife in hand. His mind told him to spring and plunge the knife into Ehrig's back, but his muscles did not obey. He could not move. Ehrig had lowered the weapon again and stood silent.

A long moment passed with neither man moving, Ehrig because he chose not to, Hawk because he could not. Ehrig's focus was on the spot where Deborah's remains were splattered on the ground. The fragments that had been Deborah were glowing lightly. This glow was golden. It was not bright, but it was definitely there. Hawk watched in shock as a few moments later the remains seemed to evaporate, and in seconds both they and the glow were gone. There was no evidence remaining of the murder.

"Religion," Ehrig huffed. "This is not religion. There is no religion here. Only death." Ehrig spun on his heel and walked toward Hawk. Looking down at the hunter, Ehrig said calmly, "Put your knife away and come with me. Do you think you can do what the lightning in the woods could not?" He walked to a cabinet near the door and put away the weapon, locking the door on the box, then starting slowly back down the hall.

Hawk found that he could stand, but he could not walk. The urge to kill Ehrig raged in his core, but he could not move. He had control of his arms; he could twist to see

Ehrig walking away from him. Hawk sheathed his knife and stumbled forward, walking again. This time when he grabbed his blade, it was of his own volition…and his feet were again glued to the floor. One more attempt, and it finally registered. If he wanted to follow Ehrig, the blade had to remain in its scabbard. Hawk reluctantly followed after his new enemy, managing nothing better than a fast walk.

Ehrig stepped into the main room seven or eight paces ahead of Hawk. "Deborah!" he called out, as if she were still within earshot.

As Hawk entered, a glow was evident on the couch where Deborah had sat earlier. It was golden, as had been seen in the cavern, but brighter than before. Hawk stopped and stared in awe as he watched the young woman materialize before his eyes over a period of several seconds. When the transformation was complete, there was not a mark on her. The confusion on her face was as evident as the golden glow that accompanied her back here.

Ehrig had taken a seat as he too watched Deborah complete her return. The rubble on the floor that had surrounded the chair was gone. Hawk looked up—so was the gouge in the ceiling. "Hawk, take a chair and be careful, do not touch Deborah," Ehrig said, continuing to watch Deborah, not looking in Hawk's direction as he spoke.

Too stunned by what he had seen and what he was witnessing to do anything else, Hawk dragged a chair from the table and pulled it to the opposite end of the couch where Deborah had materialized. He sat staring at her.

The bright glow that surrounded Deborah faded entirely. It took a moment for her to regain her senses. "What just happened?" she exclaimed, looking to Ehrig for answers.

She stood and walked over to Ehrig and repeated her question. "What just happened?"

Hawk's attention was on Deborah; his mind was reveling in what he had witnessed. He wanted answers.

Ehrig shifted in the chair slightly. "You tell us," he answered. "You know parts of what happened that Hawk does not. He knows parts that you do not. I will fill the details in between."

"What *was* that *thing*? I paced off the steps, as you asked. I turned around. I saw you spin it up in your hand. I thought I saw a flash, suddenly everything disappeared: both of you, the room…even me. My entire awareness was just…just…" Her eyes were directed at the ground as she groped for words. "Green." She stood there without saying more.

"The Green," Ehrig corrected. "Go on," he said.

"I don't know how to go on. There was nothing to see, no sound, I tried to move, but had no sensation of doing so. If I had moved there would have been no way to tell that I had."

"Please continue," Ehrig said, for she had stopped speaking again. While they waited for her to gather her words, Ehrig stood up and walked across the room to the table where he and Hawk had eaten the night before. Turning to face the pair, he leaned against it, perched on the edge.

"I heard my name. No…that's not right. I…became aware of my name as if I was being called out to…now, I'm just not sure," Deborah said as she moved back toward the couch and slowly took a seat.

"I tried to follow the sound, find where the voice was coming from. At the time it seemed so simple…like…being told to stand up or sit down. Now I don't even know what it was or how I could do it...or anything else...there was just The Green."

She looked at the two men. Neither spoke.

"Then the green was gone and bright, glowing, yellow flecks seemed to be rising before my eyes. This room and you two started to come into focus, and I was here!"

Hawk rose from his chair and started toward Deborah. "Hawk!" Ehrig barked. The hunter turned toward Ehrig and saw what looked like a small cloud of vapor floating in the air toward him. It was moving very quickly and gradually expanding in size, but still slowly enough for Hawk to see that Ehrig had a long, slender 'stick' in his hands, pointed directly at him. The glowing ring of vapor was almost a foot from Hawk's head when he dropped to the floor and rolled. As he moved, a slender stream discharged like a rod piercing the cloud from the stick Ehrig was holding.

The ring expanded into a globe of intense blue-purple energy with a loud *crack*! The sound was not as loud as that from the previous weapon, but it still caused Deborah to flinch. The intensity of the light from the exploding ball forced her eyes shut. Even though the sphere of energy expanded within less than two feet of her, she felt nothing.

Hawk was gone. The floor was covered in blood and chunks of flesh—the scene was almost identical to the one Hawk had seen in the larger room—including the eventual evaporation of the evidence. Deborah stared at the fading gore, open mouthed.

"This is what Hawk witnessed happening to you," Ehrig said, placing the weapon on the table behind him.

"Hawk," Deborah whispered the name, frozen in horror.

"As I said, there were parts of the tale that neither of you knew. Now you have both experienced the story," Ehrig said quietly.

"Hawk!" His voice cracked the name like a command.

In a moment, the shimmering golden glow appeared on the chair in which Hawk had been sitting. He materialized, as Deborah had just minutes before.

Ehrig walked to where Hawk sat and faced him, standing about three feet away. Bending at the waist, he looked directly into the still dazed eyes of the hunter. "Is there anything you would like to add to Deborah's account?" Hawk shook his head slowly.

Straightening, Ehrig moved to where Deborah sat and again bent at the waist. He kissed her on the forehead. "He will be all right. As are you."

Ehrig walked back to the table. Their eyes followed him. Neither spoke. He picked up the new weapon, opened his cloak, and slipped it inside. It disappeared, as Hawk remembered Abby having done that night in his room.

Moving back toward them, Ehrig smiled broadly. "Well, that was fun. Shall we do it again?"

Hawk opened his mouth and closed it again. Then with a confused look he stated, "I wanted to come back."

Ehrig continued to the couch and sat down on the end in front of Hawk. As he had with Deborah, he simply said, "Explain your meaning."

"I heard you call out, and when I turned I saw what looked like a ring of vapor coming at me. I tried to roll across the floor to avoid it. It was instinct more than anything...then everything was green. It was like Deborah said, the only reality was *the Green*. Nothing else existed. My first reaction was to check myself to see if I was hurt. But I was gone, like everything else. I had not felt anything. I was on the floor, and then I thought I heard my name. No, Deborah was right, I did not hear anything, but my awareness was reacting like I was still whole. I tried to look around to see where my name had come from…but looking had no meaning. The first time I thought I had heard my name, but the place or whatever it was, was so unreal. I had to be imagining that I had heard anything. The second time…was there a second time? I *knew* my name had been, had come to me."

Hawk's chin dropped to his chest. His hands clenched his knees. The words to describe what he had experienced came to him with the same difficulty that Deborah had exhibited in telling her tale. "I wanted to return here. When my name penetrated to me…I wanted to."

Hawk lifted his head and looked at Ehrig, then Deborah. "Wait a moment, what happened here? Was it…was it like…in there?" he said pointing to the hallway. Deborah turned her head away.

After a moment, Ehrig answered softly, "Almost."

Deborah looked back at him. Tears rolled down her cheeks. "It was like a big flower expanded around you…then you were gone."

Hawk averted his gaze from her as his eyes welled up as well. "I wanted to come back."

"Did you find that easy to do, Deborah?" Ehrig asked when Hawk stopped speaking. "Want to come back? Not everyone can."

Deborah looked up at him sharply. "Not everyone can come back?"

"Not everyone can *want* to come back."

"What?" Hawk wiped tears from his cheek. "Some do not want to come back?"

"I did not say that. I said not everyone can want to. Although, in some cases, you are correct. No, not everyone wants to. Most, however, simply cannot want to do so. They find the Light so foreign they cannot break themselves out of themselves. As you both experienced, there is no 'reality' there, the only existence is your awareness of self. With nothing but 'you,' there is no Deviance. Without that essence of existence, there can be none, and the Light of your own difference fades and disappears. Some have called this 'true' death. Without the will to return, you do not. This time I cheated a little by ensuring that you were able to recognize something outside of yourselves. While I neither brought you back nor had you brought back, I gave you a clue that there was still more to your existence than just yourself. You had to do the rest on your own. There was no point to the lesson otherwise."

"Are you saying Deborah was not really dead?" Hawk demanded. "I saw you kill her. I take it that she saw me die…no, I did not die…what did happen to us?"

"Oh, you were quite dead. From the look on Deborah's face I was not sure which horror she was reacting to most: the fact that I murdered you in cold blood or the thought she might have to clean up the mess," Ehrig replied, chuckling.

"Ehrriig! Please!" Deborah pleaded.

Ehrig winked at her. "You'll be pleased to know, young lady, that Hawk's reaction to seeing you in bite-sized pieces was pure hatred. He would have killed me on the spot had it been allowed."

"Ehrig, was that really necessary?" Deborah's eyes still held tears.

"It was not," he replied. "However, you two—" Ehrig stopped, thought better of revealing too much information so quickly.

"Hawk was not the first to dismiss this as religion. He will not be the last. You wanted to know what the creation of Deviance had to do with you, while Hawk dismissed it as irrelevant. You both have now experienced the essence of the creation story yourselves, alone with the Light. The Light was all around you, the one thing that was different from yourself. Your focus was internal. 'There is just me.' No thought of differentiation, just you, no Deviance, only you. Without deviance, you cease to exist. You die. The beasts of the fields and woods cannot cope with this and they die. The vast majority of people likewise find the situation so far out of their realm of experience and so disconcerting that they, too, have but one life and one death."

Hawk stood up from the chair he had been sitting in since he reappeared. There was a glazed look in his eyes that revealed he was deep in thought. Deborah watched as Hawk paced slowly back and forth in a small figure eight. Deborah glanced at Ehrig and realized she must have had the same look on her face.

Ehrig continued speaking. "At the point of creation, there was no Deviance. Then Deviance became itself, the deviation from Nothingness. Your own recreations today could not have occurred without the Light. The deviance was, for lack of a better term, all around you. You merely had to use it. But before you could use the Light, you had to recognize that the Light was available to you, that there was something other than 'you.'"

Ehrig patted his belly as if he had remembered there was something else bothering him. But instead of yielding to the growl in his stomach, Ehrig pressed on in his explanation.

"That is where my cheat helped you along, although it was really for my convenience rather than yours. Given enough time you might have come back on your own, but you also may have dimmed to nonexistence. Time has no meaning in the Light but it does here, and I did not want to wait for your return. If possible, I wanted you back here before lunch, so I gave you a hint. If it was not possible, well…"

Ehrig let the thought hang and changed the subject again. "Hawk started to leave. If you had not been here, I may have just let him go his own way to oblivion. But Hawk referring to me as a mere priest pushing religion in front of you pissed me off…and Hex would have been angry had I let him leave—and I didn't feel like hearing it."

"What? Hex? Why would he have been upset?" Hawk stammered.

"He figures you owe him."

"I *owe* him?"

Deborah made a sign as if warding off an unseen evil. "Ehrig! Be careful how you speak of Hex!" she exclaimed. Ehrig looked at her slightly confused. She formed the sign again with her hands. He smiled. He grinned. He laughed. Deborah looked at him dumbfounded.

Ehrig stood up, winked at her again, and said, "A dead girl telling me to be careful. You are a sweetheart. Thank you. Don't worry about how I speak of Hex. The worst he can do is kill me, after all." Pausing, his face turned serious and he said, "However, you…and he," Ehrig tilted his head in Hawk's direction, "probably should use respect in your words toward Hex."

"I do not owe him a debt," Hawk said solidly.

"You can take that up with him, if you like. His object lessons tend to be less subtle than mine."

Hawk could not believe what he was hearing. "Turning me into chunks of meat was 'subtle'?" he said, shrinking back into the chair at the table.

Ehrig shrugged. "It was the easiest way to introduce you, first hand, to the Light. Do you still think I am feeding you religion?"

Hawk shook his head slowly. He was not sure what he thought, but if nothing else he was not ready for another "object lesson."

"Good. Now as I suggested a bit ago, let us give it another go. That was fun."

Deborah scowled at him. "That was not fun. You talk like we were cats with nine lives."

Ehrig smiled again. "Be assured that you have many more than nine if you want them. But no, I did not intend to spend the day having us killing each other."

"Each other?" The phrase caught Hawk's attention instantly. "You will let us use those things?"

"It would be a good idea. You will have more success at the Hold if you have some familiarity with them. Once you have handled them, you may find it easier to accept some of the things you are told without requiring, shall we say, personalized demonstrations of everything new."

"Personalized. Yes. I suppose you could say that," Hawk replied. "As long as I...and she...stay in one piece, I guess I'm ready."

"I'm hungry," Deborah said.

Considering all that had taken place, the thought had not occurred to Hawk until Deborah mentioned it. Then his stomach would not let him think of anything else as the hunger pains grew. Ehrig was quick to accommodate the Deborah's request.

"Very well then, let's have something to eat." Ehrig moved toward a path in the cave opposite the entrance to the room they had exited earlier. "I have just the thing to satisfy your appetite," he said with a gleam in his eye. Hawk and Deborah looked at each other suspiciously.

Ehrig returned shortly with biscuits and what looked like a mixture of eggs and meat and placed them on the table. "Sit down, please," he said, gesturing toward a vacant chair for Deborah. Hawk rotated inward, facing the table.

The two were ready to join Ehrig in filling their stomachs. Hawk looked at his plate as Ehrig served him. "Ahhhhh, doesn't that look appetizing?" Ehrig exclaimed. As he placed a plate in front of Deborah, neither made a move to begin eating. Neither could decipher the substance Ehrig had served, and both sat staring at the meal in front of them.

"What? Eat up!" Ehrig said sitting down and helping himself to a healthy first bite, obviously enjoying himself.

Deborah spoke first. "Ehrig...what is this?"

"It's good!" was the reply.

"But what *is* it?"

"Mmpher 'n' Osslidgeegzz," came the reply. Ehrig chewed happily on a mouthful, a grin spread from ear to ear.

"Excuse me?" Hawk said. "What did you say? Did you say ostrich eggs?"

"Uh huh."

"What's that?" Hawk asked, not recognizing the animal.

"Big bird, huge," Ehrig spread his arms, never letting go a biscuit he was holding, "taller than you fully grown, can't fly but runs its ass off. It'll kick your ass, too, if it catches you stealing an egg. Hehehehe!" Ehrig laughed.

"And what?" Hawk continued.

"Gopher," Ehrig said plainly.

"*GOPHER?*" Deborah shouted.

Ehrig nearly choked as he swallowed. "Yes, gopher!"

"And why ostrich eggs?" asked Hawk.

"Because a robin's eggs are too damn small!" Ehrig pounded the table with glee, thoroughly enjoying the exchange.

"Ughhhh," Deborah said, shaking her head.

"Have you tried it? How can you say you don't like it if you have not tasted it?" Ehrig asked, sounding hurt. "If you are going to refrain from eating it, then you must also refrain from insulting me as well."

Hawk was the first. He took a biscuit in one hand and a fork in the other. Stirring the mixture, Hawk smelled the food and tentatively put a small portion in his mouth followed by a large bite of the biscuit. As he chewed it, his head rocked side to side as if judging the flavors in his mouth. Swallowing, he paused. "It's not bad."

Ehrig smiled proudly. "I know."

Hawk took a bigger second bite. Still nodding in agreement with Ehrig, he began eating his meal in earnest. Deborah was still having nothing to do with it. She rose from her seat and found her sack. Producing some jerky, she returned to the table and ate. Ehrig shook his head with a disappointed look. "When have I steered you wrong? Ever?"

Deborah thought about that question for a moment. She had grown up listening to Ehrig tell his stories of Deviant Hall. But back then they were only stories. There was nothing to indicate Ehrig was talking truths instead of fairy tales. She would get caught up in every detail about Hex and Sapient6, fascinated as Ehrig spun his webs. Never in her wildest dreams did she think any of what was happening now would ever take place.

For the first time since she had met her father's friend Ehrig, she wondered who this man really was. Still, for all that had occurred up to this point, Deborah could not think of one time when Ehrig led her astray. All the advice he gave as she grew, every warning or piece of assistance he provided—none of it ended with her regretting having listened to him. Ehrig was always there when she needed him. Deborah knew she could trust him, never thinking to question. Until now.

"No, Ehrig, you haven't. And I am not going to let you start now."

"Ah well, more for us!" came Ehrig's reply. "Eat up, Hawk!"

Deborah picked up a biscuit.

The growls in their bellies subsided. After finishing the meal, while clearing the table, Ehrig decided there might still be time for more demonstrations. He moved toward a cabinet. Unlocking a side door, he pulled out the weapon he had produced that morning and turned toward Hawk and Deborah. There Ehrig stood, staring into a pair of stony faced travelers. Without saying a word, Ehrig raised the weapon.

Chapter Ten

Hawk and Deborah did not say a word as Ehrig removed the weapon from the cabinet, but their glance at each other told them they were thinking the same thing. Both were startled as Ehrig made a sudden move. Turning toward them and holding it up, Ehrig started to speak, but the pair's reaction stopped him. Deborah had recoiled. Hawk had been less obvious, but he too had shrunk back. Ehrig smiled gently. "My first reaction to this was similar," he said quietly. "There is no need for fear, Deborah." Deborah looked anything but convinced.

"Come with me back to the quiet room, and I'll show you how and why it works. You already know more about it than you think."

"Quiet room?" Hawk asked.

"Where we were before breakfast. At the end of the hallway."

"You call that quiet?" Hawk countered.

"Well, it allows me to think when I practice, you see," Ehrig said. "Come."

Deborah hesitated before following the two men back through the tunnel. Ehrig and Hawk made their way into the quiet room. Ehrig began moving and opening some boxes, pulling containers away from the walls. Hawk stayed out of the way, to the left of the entrance. Deborah entered the room and stood quietly near Hawk with no intention of leaving his side.

Ehrig took a few minutes and said little as he worked, placing items on the table and carefully preparing his next demonstration. The delay was negligible. When he was done, what looked like string, a bottle, and a small bowl sat atop a rectangular table next to the weapon. Also on the bench was the stick Hawk last saw in the main chamber after being introduced to the Light.

Pointing, Hawk asked, "What kind of magic makes that stick work?"

"That is not a stick. It's a rifle—a special type of rifle. One that uses dissimilar gases that when combined, cause an incredible reaction. It's called a 'Flur,' and Deborah couldn't have described it any better. It looks like a large flower, but I wouldn't spend time trying to sniff the scent out of this bud! But let's not get ahead of ourselves.

"In time you will see many different types of weapons. That is just one of many…as is this!" Ehrig said, drawing attention to what lay before him on the table. "Allow me to demonstrate something to you. Stand still and watch." With that, Ehrig opened the bottle on the table and poured some finely powdered dust into a bowl. He took the string and pushed one end into the pile of dust. Almost as an afterthought, his attention turned to the ground. Finding a stone large enough, he placed it on top of the bowl, which he carried about fifteen paces away from the table; the string, about five paces long, trailed behind. Setting down the bowl, he moved back, straightening the string. "Hawk, your flint and steel, please."

Hawk walked over, staring at the bowl, and handed Ehrig his fire starting tools, then returned to Deborah's side. Striking the two, Ehrig made sparks fly, igniting the string. As it burned, spitting sparks, the string quickly shortened, and a large ball of fire erupted from the bowl, the force so strong it sent the stone flying to the ceiling of the room. Both Hawk and Deborah jumped back at the explosive flare of light and smoke.

"You see that?" Ehrig asked. "That is what happened inside the weapon I fired before, only that explosion took place inside a metal case filled with smaller pieces of metal called *shards* or *flak*. It is a very simple concept, you see. The force within the case is so great the case itself breaks apart and flies in every direction. So to control that explosion, the case is put inside a tube closed at one end and opened on the other," Ehrig said, picking up the weapon and continuing his explanation. "The force of the explosion forces those pieces of flak out of the tube at an incredible speed. The outcome, as you have witnessed, is devastating. The case used for the device is called a *grenade*. Simply put, it's a handheld cannon deployed with devastating effects."

Having seen the results first hand, Hawk still could not believe the power of the weapon Ehrig was holding. *The devastation that could be brought upon an animal would leave nothing to carry home*, he thought.

"Despite appearances," Ehrig replied, "what makes it work are the same things that make your bow, your knife, your flint, and steel—all work—but this is neither the time nor the place for this kind of instruction. You may be permitted to have this knowledge at a later time. It depends on you."

"Well, I do *not* like it at all! Why would anyone want to have such a weapon? What's its purpose? It seems like overkill," Deborah said.

"Yes, I suppose it would be under normal circumstances but," Ehrig paused, "the circumstances you will encounter are not normal. In fact, they are just the opposite." Ehrig went to a locked cabinet, opened it, and removed a second cannon from its shelves. Placing it on the table, he went back and removed two rather large boxes and brought them to the table as well. He then relocked the cabinet. Hawk and Deborah watched in silence.

"Right now it is time for you both to make a decision. Has your resolve to continue your quests been diminished by what you have seen and heard this day? Or are you ready to prepare for the next phase?"

"What do you mean 'next phase'?" Deborah asked.

"Acceptance," Ehrig said simply.

"Acceptance?" she echoed. "Of what?"

"That there is more to the world than your experience has led you to believe. Acceptance of new experiences, concepts, and realities—Deviation—deviation from truth as you know it."

"Practically everything we have done today has been like that. It is hard to deny what we have experienced. But you say it is not magic," Hawk interjected.

"It is supernatural. Black magic," Deborah whispered.

"Deborah," Ehrig responded, "haven't you already agreed that for as long as you have known me you have you never known me to lie? That I have never tricked you?"

"Since I was a little girl," she said, "and up until today I would say no to both, but now how do I know everything I thought I knew was not all trickery?"

"A fair question. The honest answer is that you do not. The equally honest response is that it was not trickery. If there was any deceit on my part, it was due only to omission. I did not offer what was not asked. After what you have seen today, can you say that if I had given this information freely, would I have been believed—by you, or anyone else?"

"No. I guess not," she conceded.

"For now, if it helps for you to think of The Green Light as magical, do so. The power that it…controls, for lack of a better word, is little understood. I do not call it magic, but for now that may be the best way for you to think of it. Black magic it is not, however. At worst it is neutral. It is neither good nor evil. It just is.

"This," Ehrig said, pointing to the cannon, "on the other hand, has no magic. I believe you can best be served by spending the rest of the day trying to come to grips with the reality of this weapon. It is a weapon of war, just as a bow, a knife, or a sword. But like these, it functions predictably and without fundamental variation. Used properly it is a useful tool. Used improperly, it is dangerous both to you and everyone around you."

"What do you have in mind?" Hawk asked. His voice held more than a little suspicion. "You said no more visits to the Light."

"No, no more visits." Ehrig chuckled. "All I want you to do is handle the weapon and convince yourselves that it is just as real as your bows or a sword…even if it is noisier. That you can shoot and miss, that you can shoot and wound, that you can obtain a clean kill, that you need no special powers to use it."

Hawk approached Ehrig. He stared at the cannons resting on the table. Deborah watched, not moving closer to inspect the weapons as Hawk had. Picking up one, Hawk turned toward Ehrig with a bit of unease yet much curiosity.

In a quick motion Ehrig twisted the gun from Hawk's grasp. "Please do not point that at me. Or anyone else you do not intend to kill," he said quietly. Sliding a lever at the top of the weapon back, Ehrig showed Hawk that it was, in fact, not loaded and how to determine if it was. Deborah came a few steps closer, attempting to see.

"Unlike a bow, you cannot just look at this to tell whether it is armed or not. Therefore, you always treat it as if it were— even if you personally disarmed it yourself only moments before," Ehrig admonished. Leaving the breach open, Ehrig set the weapon back down and opened one of the boxes containing grenades for the cannon he had earlier placed on the table.

Ehrig explained how to load and unload the weapon. As he demonstrated, Ehrig continuously gave instructions that emphasized the safe handling of both the gun and its ammunition. Ehrig was careful to point out key parts and names of the various pieces that comprised of the weapon. Although he was thorough, Ehrig knew he was moving quite rapidly through the explanations and hoped his pupils were catching on. Finally, Ehrig placed the cannon and a magazine of ammunition back onto the table. "Now, tell me: How do you know whether this weapon is armed or not?"

Hawk fell for the trap. Picking up the cannon, Hawk extended his hand and looked down the weapon's tube at the sight, and then turned it over and checked the magazine slot to see it was empty. Not fully pulling open the breach and letting it shut close, he placed the weapon back on the table stating, "It's not armed."

"No!" Deborah said. "You didn't pull back the slide completely. It could still be armed. Check it again."

Ehrig smiled broadly as he nodded. "Good, Deborah. Not paying attention with a knife will get you cut. Not being careful with this can get you, and anyone nearby, killed."

Hawk again picked up the weapon, careful to keep it pointed away from Ehrig and Deborah, and reopened the slide. Pulling it back completely ejected a round from the chamber. With a quick hand Ehrig caught the unspent cartridge as it flew from the weapon and held it up to Hawk. "It is always armed," he restated more forcefully. "Always.

"Go ahead, take the magazine and load it, Hawk, and go out so you are about twenty paces from that box over there...and try not to point it at us on the way." Ehrig winked as he said "try." "It fires much like a crossbow. Be sure to stand sideways to the target and hold it very firmly against your body before firing. Brace yourself with your hind leg and fire at the box. There's a bit of a jolt for sure, but nothing you cannot handle."

Hawk pointed the weapon at the box. It amazed him at how easy and balanced the cannon felt in his hand. With a nervous grin, he squeezed the trigger. *Blam!* The cannon fired, rocking Hawk back a bit. The top of the box in the center of the quiet room disintegrated into splinters and fragments. Hawk's eyes were wide open now. He was grinning from ear to ear as he looked at the cannon with pure amazement. "I can't believe this. I would never have believed this had I not seen or fired it for myself! This is truly amazing! Try it, Deborah!"

Deborah was intimidated by the challenge. She was having a much harder time accepting what was going on around her. Ehrig walked up beside her. "You don't have to, Deborah. For sure the one thing that I cannot do for you is force you to accept anything going on here."

Hawk steadied himself for another shot. Deborah braced herself for the shock of the round going off in front of her. *Blam!* A few splinters flew from the top of the remaining portion of the box, but it would have to be said that he missed. Hawk frowned as he lowered the weapon.

"Both shots were high," Ehrig said. "You are flinching as you pull the trigger. Try again. The noise will not hurt you."

Once again Hawk prepared himself and fired. This time the entire box exploded into thousands of fragments. Hawk beamed.

The hours had passed and the repeated explosions from Hawk firing the cannon had taken their toll. "It's almost like the pounding of metal at Father's work," Deborah said, looking at Ehrig. She smiled slightly and made her way out of the quiet room.

Ehrig watched her leave and turned to Hawk. "Maybe we should stop for a bit. We've been at this for quite a while. I am sure all this excitement has caused you to become tired. I will prepare another meal. You and Deborah sit for a while."

Hawk returned the weapon to the table and turned to leave the room. "Hawk!" Ehrig said sharply. "Do you leave your bow strung? Your knife unsheathed?"

Sheepishly, the young man turned back to the table and unloaded the gun. He set it back on the table with the breach open. Ehrig picked it up and inspected it. Closing the breach, he nodded to Hawk. Again Hawk moved toward the door.

Ehrig, close behind him, shut the door and followed Hawk through the tunnel back to the main living room. Deborah was sitting on the couch. As Ehrig left the room, Hawk sat beside her. "What's the matter?" Hawk asked.

"I am still trying to figure out what all this has to do with me. None of this makes sense."

Hawk did not know what to tell her. He was still trying to understand it all himself.

Ehrig returned with a tray of meats and bread. Deborah eyed the tray suspiciously; the look on her face said it all. Ehrig laughed. "Don't worry, this time the fare should be more to your liking," he said. "We have venison, slices of beef…oh, and quail."

Deborah had not eaten very much after having decided to avoid the unusual meal that Ehrig had served up earlier, but the idea of having fresh quail was more than she could take. She reached out quickly and snatched one of the small birds from the tray, only to drop it even quicker. "Mmmph!" She stuck her fingers in her mouth, clearly in pain.

"Oh, did I neglect to say it was hot?" Ehrig asked.

"Don't you dare laugh," Deborah said sternly, looking at Hawk. She reached out for the bird more carefully this time and placed it on her plate.

Hawk snickered but kept his mouth shut and his hands out of the way until Deborah was finished serving herself. She stabbed the quail she had dropped, brought it to her mouth, and blew on it. "I love quail." Taking a small bite, she continued, "Mmmmm. I never get to have it. They are so cute I just can't bring myself to hunt them." She took another, bigger bite, quickly stripping the meat from the bones of the small bird.

Hawk considered taking the second bird, but after having witnessed Deborah strip the first clean thought better of it. Even Ehrig left the last quail alone. Both watched as she devoured the fowl. Deborah finished her first bird and reached for a second. Slowing down, she began picking the quail clean.

"You eat with purpose now. Seems you are prone to moments of Deviance yourself. No wonder Hex wishes to see you," Ehrig.

Deborah stopped paying attention to the quail. She looked at Ehrig. "What do you mean he 'wishes to see me'?"

"Deviance in a woman is somewhat unusual. Yours especially so. The deviance you exude is subtle and feminine. Most women express their deviance as some sort of competition with men. 'I'm as smart as any man. I can do a man's job—'"

Deborah interrupted him. "Men and women are different," she stated bluntly. "I like being a woman, and I like being me. After Robert died, my parents, Abby, everybody expected me to come back home, mourn for a 'suitable' time, and get married again." She paused, staring at the table, obviously deep in thought.

"When I would not, they accused me of wallowing in my grief, which was expected at first, but then…then it was…I was trying to prove I did not need a man, that I hated men, that I resented Robert for 'leaving' me—everyone thought they knew my mind better than I did. I could not make them understand that it was not 'men' that I did not want, it was the expectations of *me* I did not want." She began slowly picking at the bird again. "Eventually, I was left alone. People began to see that I was fine and would continue to be fine. They saw I didn't hate men but didn't need a man to replace what I had lost." Deborah's tone was one of personal satisfaction.

Ehrig chose a slice of venison from the tray. "Hawk, are you going to just watch the lady gorge herself? There soon will not be anything left." Ehrig winked in Deborah's direction and stuffed the entire portion into his mouth. Hawk grabbed a piece of beef and wadded it into his own mouth. Deborah smiled at the remark.

As the men chewed, Deborah stood up from the table. Wiping her blade on her sleeve she sheathed it and turned toward the hallway to quiet room, taking with her the remaining piece of quail. She nibbled on the bird in her hand as she walked.

Hawk looked at Ehrig and furrowed his brow in a question. Ehrig just waved his fingers in a "let her go" gesture. They sat eating without further conversation when a loud explosion echoing down the hall suddenly disrupted the quiet. It was rapidly followed by two more.

Hawk's look at Ehrig matched what he was feeling inside. Both rose from the table and left the room. Another round blasted as Ehrig and Hawk entered the quiet room. The box Hawk had fired at before was in splinters, scattered about the ground along with several other freshly destroyed targets. The smile on Ehrig's face could not be measured.

"I have to admit there is something to this weapon," Deborah said. "I found that pushing this button makes it shoot differently. Check this out, Hawk." She turned back toward the boxes. *Thump.* She fired the weapon and an unexploded round flew through the air and landed close to another empty box. *Boom!* The round exploded upon impact, causing damage but not destroying the target.

Hawk was amazed at what he was seeing. Deborah seemed to be more at ease with the weapon than he. It looked natural in her hands.

Ehrig watched mumbling, "Deviance...it's a beautiful thing."

*   *   *

Though the time was spent inside the caves, outside night was falling. The day had been long. Deborah and Hawk had spent most of those hours firing rounds and were growing very tired. After ensuring the chamber was clear, Deborah returned the cannon to its place in the cabinet. Hawk followed suit soon after. They stepped through the door and into the passage that led to where their introduction to the Light took place that morning. Ehrig could see that the events of the day had taken their toll, since neither said a word as they made their way back through the entrance of the first room.

"Sleep now, rest. Tomorrow at dawn we'll leave for the Keep. You have much to learn and experience, and that will be the best place to continue. For now, I shall retire as well. Goodnight," Ehrig said, leaving Hawk and Deborah alone.

Deborah moved to the pile of furs from which she had awoken earlier that day. Hawk did the same. Both were exhausted. As they lay there in their beds, both were struggling to sort out all they had experienced. Neither spoke.

Hawk, for his part, was coming to grips with the revelations of all that occurred. Although he could see with his own eyes that all Ehrig had stated seemed true, he found his mind still arguing with the plausibility of it all. *Okay, so it's not magic. Fine. I still need to see for myself what is behind all this.* After a long moment, Hawk broke the silence. Speaking softly while staring at the ceiling, he asked, "How do you know Ehrig?"

Deborah lay there, pondering the question. All day long she had been thinking the same thing. Asking herself how she could think that she knew Ehrig for as long as she had yet know nothing about him in reality. Everything she had felt positive about was turned upside down by the events of today—and how much more was there about him that she did not know? There was no denying the things he spoke of today were real. She had experienced them, felt them, was shaken by them.

"He often visited the town I grew up in. Since he was my father's friend, I was used to him being around. Ehrig would always leave and return, just to leave again. We children used to play games, and at times he would join in. Other times, he would sit and watch. Then there were other times when he would tell us stories about the Green Glow. All the children were captivated by his stories."

"He told me stories once as well," Hawk said. Deborah lifted her head, curious. "That is partially why I am here. I would have these dreams that would fill my mind with visions I couldn't readily explain. Sometimes they were like nightmares flashing through my mind while I slept. My father had to start finding ways to soothe me back to sleep. One of those ways was to tell me stories about brave men fighting in battles and heroic deeds. He would speak of strange weapons and Deviant Stronghold, of Sapient6." Rolling over he continued. "Then one day Ehrig came to town. He would tell these stories that were very similar to those my father would tell, although not as detailed. But I could see a link between them. I could tell Ehrig's tales were of the same place. Only he didn't call himself Ehrig. He used the name Eth."

"Eth? Or do you mean Ith?" Deborah asked.

"I recall Eth being the name he used, but that was so long ago."

Deborah rested her head back on the furs. "When Ehrig would tell his stories, he would create a circle around a character that he called 'his favorite,' Ithaqua, or Ith as he would sometimes say. My goodness, the stories he would tell! 'Ithaqua would fly like walking on air and come down with a mighty roar' he would say." Deborah mimicked Ehrig's actions, waving her arms about. "We loved his stories."

Hawk and Deborah fell silent again, both lost in thought.

"I never had those types of dreams. I do remember dreaming, or at least thinking I was dreaming, but they were never violent. No, for me dreaming was very different growing up. My dreams always took me places. Sometimes I would see things from my past, familiar and safe. Sometimes I would visit places I had never been. But I never felt threatened. No matter where I was, I always felt comforted," Deborah said calmly.

Hawk sensed a difference in the way she spoke. It seemed Deborah had come to a conclusion about her place here at Ehrig's home in the mountain. The tone of her voice was no longer troubled.

"Well, we'd best get some sleep. Ehrig said we leave in the morning." Laying back again, Hawk tried to rest but could not. The tone in Deborah's voice bothered him.

Without looking, he asked, "Are you curious to see what is there? Do you wish to continue this?"

"Yes," was all she said.

After a long silence Hawk rolled over and closed his eyes. Hawk slept, but not well. Chaotic dreams of romance, lust, and rejection darted through his unconscious mind. None were complete; none gave the fantasy engendered by the casual brush of Deborah's breast against his arm when she had adjusted the weapon's position on his shoulder that morning. She had given no indication that it had occurred, in spite of the acute feeling on Hawk's part that a bolt of electricity had passed between them. Now his dreams of her were without resolution. They darted, started over, never complete.

Boom!

The explosive sound echoed down the hall from the quiet room and expanded into Hawk's mind. He shot to his feet, looking around frantically. "Deborah!" Hawk called out in a loud whisper. There was no answer. In the dark he moved in the direction of her bed and knelt. He quickly found her furs and determined she was not in them. Still crouching, he slowly turned in the room: a light glowed down the hallway toward the quiet room. Pausing for a moment and listening, Hawk heard no other sound beyond his own heart still pounding from the shock of being awakened by the thunderous noise. Slowly he rose to his feet and moved toward, then down, the hallway.

The green light emanating through the open doorway of the quiet room silhouetted Ehrig's frame. "Ehrig! What the hell happened?"

"See for yourself." Ehrig stepped into the room, moved immediately to the side, and allowed Hawk to pass.

Hawk moved past Ehrig and stopped cold. On the floor, in front of the cabinet where they had earlier returned the weapon lay the cannon, scarred and twisted. He turned back to Ehrig.

"Deb-or-ah?" he asked, speaking in syllables, the realization of what he was seeing sinking in.

"Yes, Deborah. The last traces were disappearing as I approached the door," Ehrig said quietly. "I have been forbidden to inquire or interfere. Beyond this I know no more than you."

"The last thing she said to me was that she wanted to continue...to find out where this was going," Hawk told Ehrig.

*   *   *

It was the same as the first time, the all-encompassing green.

Deborah's awareness was still giddy, as if the energy that had coursed through her body was still affecting her mind. The fear generated by the instinct of self-preservation was being replaced by a new fear, fear that her idea was not going to work.

*   *   *

"DEBORAH!" Hawk's voice cracked crying out her name. He waited. He looked around. Nothing. "Deborah!" he called again. Still nothing. He turned and ran down the tunnel back to the main chamber. It remained dark. "Deborah?" he whispered. The sparkle of gold he so desperately wanted to see did not appear. He heard footsteps approaching from behind. He wheeled. It was Ehrig. Hawk sank to the floor and put his face in his hands. The sound of the steps stopped; Hawk looked up into Ehrig's eyes. Ehrig's eyes said all that could be said.

"I cannot help her."

*   *   *

"HEX!"

*   *   *

Hawk felt an instant weight come upon him. "You, I can help," Ehrig said, concentrating on Hawk. Hawk's eyes grew heavy as the air around him started to glow green. Hawk raised a hand's length above the floor, his sitting position unchanged, his face lost in a trance. The furs in which he had been sleeping slid across floor and underneath him. Hawk was gently lowered onto them. He did not resist as he felt himself being pushed into a reclining position. As his head touched the fur, Hawk fell into a deep, dreamless sleep.

"Or maybe it is me that I am helping," Ehrig murmured as he turned back toward the hall. Pausing, he spoke to where Hawk rested on the furs. "You will not know the difference once you see her again."

*   *   *

HEX! Deborah again tried to shout the name. She had neither mouth nor vocal cords here, but shouting was the only way she knew to attempt to contact the mythical figure.

She waited...or she thought she was waiting. She remembered that Ehrig had said that time had no meaning here.

Time has no meaning? My thoughts seem to go on as usual. No! Do not say "I" or "me." Focus on Hex...someone...something other than yourself. Ehrig said "external" is the key...something other than yourself. This will work only by deviating from yourself. HEX!

Maybe this was a mistake. I am, no wait! DEBORAH is not alive. Can Hex find her here without dying, too?

Chapter Eleven

The next day at sunrise, Ehrig made his way into the living room to find Hawk already awake. His gear was packed and ready by the entrance of the cave. It was still rather difficult for Hawk to think of this place as a cave after seeing its interior. The furs in which he had slept had been shifted to the couch; Deborah's were still on the floor untouched, but Hawk paid them no attention.

Handing Hawk a small sack, Ehrig pulled out a biscuit from a sack of his own. "Come, we should be off now."

Hawk picked up his gear and followed Ehrig out of the mouth of the cave. Exiting the cave, they swerved around the small waterfall and passed the tumbled logs, turned up the slope, and climbed the rocks where Deborah had traveled two days before. Ehrig stopped at the top of the cliff. Hawk paused next to him. Turning toward the mouth of his home, Ehrig closed his eyes and opened them again slowly. "Done...let's go." The mouth of the cave was covered once more. There was no longer any way of guessing there was an entrance to the side of the hill.

"So what is our destination today, Ehrig?" Hawk asked.

"You shall travel to a small village just over those two

hills, about a half day's walk. Upon arrival, make your way across and wait at the far entrance opposite where you entered," Ehrig said.

"What do you mean 'you'? Aren't you coming with me?"

"No, not for this part of the journey. I must leave you for the moment and will join you later."

Hawk thought to question further but decided against it and simply followed as Ehrig turned and headed into the forest. As they walked through the trees Hawk reflected on the dream he had had the night before. Deborah, who had helped him on the mountainside when he had lost his pack, had appeared at the cave and kept him company the past two days. When he woke that morning, Hawk looked over to see there was no second pile of furs beside him; Deborah was not there. It had been just a dream. He sighed. If only she had really been there.

About a half hour's walk from the cave, they came upon a clearing. It was twice as long as it was wide. The width was roughly eighty paces from tree line to tree line, the grass was short and fresh. Ehrig walked out into the brush and led Hawk past the center of the meadow, but stopped not far from the forest's edge where the cast of the trees' morning shadow darkened the ground. Ehrig pointed through the trees in the direction Hawk needed to travel.

"If you keep the morning sun on your right, you will be fine. By the time it sits above you, you should be at a village called Bromelshire, a hamlet surrounded by small farming fields. There is no need for concern. I shall rejoin you soon,"

With that, Ehrig turned and walked away, keeping the sun at his back as he continued along the long portion of the meadow, not giving Hawk any more explanation. Hawk watched unsure of what to think. Seeing that Ehrig had no intention of returning, Hawk rotated into the direction he was given and started on his way. A heavy gust of wind hit him at his back as he reentered the forest, pushing him forward, throwing him off balance. Hawk paused for a moment and gazed at the sky, searched for the sun to gain his bearing, and continued into the forest.

The first hill was easy enough to climb. Though the trees were thick, the slope formed only a gradual incline. Hawk was sure to keep to Ehrig's directions as he trudged up the hill. The morning rays of sunshine felt good on Hawk's face as he crossed the occasional bright patch of sunlight illuminating the forest floor. Reaching the top, Hawk could see the second hill and quickly realized his easy walk would not last.

Hawk came to the bottom of the first hill and studied the ascent of the second. He was right in thinking it was not going to be a small feat. The hill was about one hundred fifty feet high. The first twenty-five feet or so went up almost vertically before slanting slightly into the hillside. Clumps of rock and boulders covered the face of the hill, patches of trees sparsely filling the space between. He surmised the trunks were thick enough to support him if necessary, but the wide space between them was something that concerned Hawk. One wrong move and he'd have to catch one of those trees. Would he be able to reach it in time? Hawk hoped he did not have to find out.

Hawk took a moment to plot his best course. Standing at the base, the slope appeared steep. Hawk readjusted his packs, ensuring his bow would not interfere with traversing the ascent, and started his climb up.

With a small running start, Hawk jumped up and grabbed hold of a jagged edge of rock, slowly pulling himself up and over the first boulder. Using the branches from a tree that leaned over his position, Hawk pulled himself closer to the next rock. Rock by rock, Hawk made his way up the hill. Occasionally, as Hawk climbed, he found loose rock that caused him to slip, but for the most part his footing held. Up he went, slowly progressing over the boulders protruding from the hillside, leapfrogging from rock to tree patch to boulder.

Not far from the shelf, Hawk paused to rest for a moment and gauge the remaining distance to clear the ridge. From where he was standing on the ledge of a rock, a couple of trees had taken root slightly below him, but they were out of reach. Beyond the trees, Hawk could make out two huge boulders. The closest boulder was smaller than the second but stuck out a bit more from the face of the hill than the larger one above it. Hawk searched for another way up but could not find one. If he was going to have any chance of reaching the trees, Hawk would have to scale his way closer to them.

Hawk readjusted his gear, fixed his bow, and then rubbed his hands against the hill, smearing dirt in his palms to dry the sweat. Stepping out, clinging to the side of the hill, he found was just enough lip on the stones to grab onto as he crawled, spiderlike, toward the trees.

The trees leaned awkwardly off the face of the hill like a limp fork. Though the bases of the trees were below him, the treetop closest to Hawk was thin and reached out above and over where he was perched on the cliff. Hawk scaled out as far as he could go before he found the ridges in the rock and stone had also thinned. There was nowhere left to hold on. Hawk's grip was weakening. It didn't take him long to realize he would have to jump.

Looking over his shoulder, Hawk tried to judge the distance to the closest tree. Taking in a deep breath, adrenaline pumping, Hawk rotated his head and upper torso and pushed off as hard as he could from the face of the hill, launching himself toward the trees. His arms and legs extended, Hawk attempted to land on the trunk but continued to fall through the air. He had missed his mark.

Hawk had only missed by inches, but with forward motion he landed instead on his side against the trunk of the tree closest to him, wrapping one arm around it and grasping it with the other. His weight coupled with the momentum of the fall forced the tree to bend. Hawk held on tightly as he continued to descend, hoping the trunk would not break. It held. Slowly, the resistance of the tree balanced out, supporting him over the side of the cliff.

Hawk hung on, letting the swaying come to a halt. Thanking his stars and realizing he had not been hurt in the landing, Hawk pulled up into the tree. He had to give himself a moment for his heart to stop pounding. Sitting there, he saw his first break of the climb. When he looked over at the smaller boulder, Hawk realized that the stone was much closer than he initially believed. It was just a step off the trunk and slightly below where the trees were rooted. Just above that was the larger stone, which looked as if there were steps chiseled naturally into the side.

The stones set deeply into the side of the hill, Hawk began to breath easy. He lowered himself onto the smaller boulder, readjusted his gear, and climbed the larger of the two plateaus of stone, reaching the crown of the cliff.

At the top, Hawk took a moment to look down the side

of the cliff. Drinking some water from his flask and taking time to relax, Hawk found his instinct telling him he was not alone. Without really focusing on any object in particular, he concentrated on his sense of sound. He noticed the birds stopped chirping and for a moment, the forest was silent. There! Hawk's ears perked up as a crack resonated in the woods. Hawk stood slowly, dropped his pack and what he could from his belt, and pulled his bow from his torso. Crouching, he started slowly, moving silently up the remaining part of the hill to find cover through the trees on his left.

*   *   *

Crack!

What was that? Deborah tried to focus her awareness. It had been like when she had thought she had "heard" her name the last time she was in the Light. This time the "sound" was much more distinct, louder, closer.

Hex?

The all pervading green shimmered in her awareness, seeming denser, thicker, even greener—if that were possible.

*   *   *

Crack!

Hawk was very patient. *Whatever it is, it is too noisy to be deer,* he thought. So he waited. Finding a tree where the bushes met the base, he crouched and waited for whatever it was that was approaching him to make its way to the clearing.

*   *   *

A bow pointed downward, an arrow in the rest mount, the man slowly made his way up the hill. He thought he had seen movement in the bushes in front of him. Standing slightly behind a tree, the man stood to make his shot. Drawing on the bowstring, he began to take a bead on the spot where he thought he saw the movement.

He hadn't expected to stumble on anyone this far into the forest. Having made the trip many times before, this was the first time the opportunity to fill his sack a little more presented itself before reaching Falkenwrath and unloading its contents. Deep in the forest, the man figured it would be a while before anyone missed this hunter, and by that time, he would have already traded the goods and disappeared.

A breeze rustled through the trees. The man slightly lowered his bow, scanning for the movement he had thought he had seen.

Hawk watched as the stranger slowly approached where he was crouched. The bow was lowered but still half drawn. *He seems to lack experience,* Hawk thought as he tried to assess what his own next move should be.

Crack! The other man broke another small branch on the forest floor as he continued to move forward. At the sound, a jay screeched and took flight. He reacted instantly by raising the bow in the general direction of the bird's former perch. The arrow released from the half drawn position and fluttered into the branches of a tree before dropping to the ground.

Hawk suppressed a chuckle at the pathetic display when he realized how dangerous this man might be if startled. The man had nocked another arrow, ignoring the first, which had fallen from the tree, focusing still on the bush Hawk was using as cover. Now he had the bowstring fully drawn.

Watching intently, Hawk unsheathed his knife. *This fool intends to shoot whatever he thinks he saw in this direction...me!* Even more deliberately he lay his bow on the ground. Adjusting his grip on the knife, Hawk watched for clues as to what, and when, the man would do next. Hawk knew that he would have no time to process the moment; thinking would make him too late.

Hawk was wrong.

The stranger stopped shuffling forward. He adjusted the bow's position and drew the string back a bit further. The arrowhead trembled in front of him, the adrenaline rush from the start the bird had given him had not yet subsided, and he was having trouble holding a steady aim.

Hawk decided to reveal himself. Slowly standing, he let out a call. The stranger looked over the tip of his arrow then drew the bowstring taunt. His eyes met Hawk's. Then he tightened to aim.

Hawk, realizing he was in trouble, still holding his knife, instinctively reared back. The knife flew from his fingers. The wood of the bow was not wide, but Hawk knew if his own aim was true, he could hit the bow and avoid bloodshed...especially his own. At a minimum, the knife would cause enough distraction to force the man to shift, buying time for Hawk to set his own bow.

Hawk was wrong again.

The adrenaline jitters heightened his awareness just enough for a glint of sun off the knife's edge to startle the man, causing him to flinch. The knife missed the bow. Hawk's blade sank deep into the man's neck. The shock of the wound caused him to release his grip on the fully drawn bow, which snapped back into his face. As the man fell to the ground his hands grasped ineffectually at the handle protruding from his neck. Bright red blood pulsed from around the blade. The man lay on his back gasping, his eyes moving frantically, choking on his own blood.

Hawk rose from his hiding place and raced over to the wounded man. "Damn it, man!"

The man's hands were still grasping the knife handle and had loosened it somewhat, now blood pulsed like a fountain from the wound. Hawk considered him for a moment, reached down, pushed the hands aside, and withdrew the blade. "You are a dead man. Another minute is not going to make any difference." His quiet, matter of fact words went unheard.

*   *   *

Slowly Deborah became more aware of her surroundings as she mentally stepped away from herself. Her awareness perceived a form coalescing. An image was being painted in her mind, but to her it was real. At first it was a shapeless ball, but gradually it resolved into a human form: a man, nude, curled into a fetal position. His face was not "visible," but she "heard" what sounded like a gurgling in his throat.

Hex?

HEX! Deborah screamed.

The gurgle continued. It sounded more and more like a death rattle.

When the form had assumed its final shape, it had been a very dark green. As Deborah tried to figure out how to interact with him, the color very slowly started to fade.

HEX!

Hex? What's happening? she thought, confused.

"He is dying, as well he should." From the depths of Deborah's mind came a voice, deep and dark. The voice was blunt and plainspoken. "But that is not Hex."

Deborah's mind was frantic. From where did this voice come? *With whom am I speaking? Is this Hex?* The image before her continued its slow dissipation in the glow.

Then help him.

"All die. Why should he not? He is of no importance."

I don't know. But we...you! You cannot just let him die. Why should he die?

"Do not concern yourself with this man. His path has been determined. Your concern should dwell within." The tone of the voice was unsympathetic. "Why did you insist on coming here?" the voice asked.

Deborah fell silent. She knew in the beginning why she decided to take her own life back in the cave, but seeing the man in front of her caused her to question her motives.

The voice's tone turned to anger. "Have you nothing to say to me? You come to my abode uninvited only to argue with me over this wretch? You know nothing about him or how or why he is here."

I came looking for...for Hex, Deborah answered, afraid of where she was, not knowing to whom she was speaking.

"You took your life into your hands to come here seeking Hex, but instead you find and take pity on this worthless trash! For what purpose? You had no regard for your own life. Explain then why I should have regard for his."

I come with purpose…my purpose, Deborah responded with resolve.

"Your purpose is not here. Nor is it in the form of a dead man. Return. You have other business. Complete that which you have begun, and you will find your answers. Hex shall not squander your deviance," said the voice.

My deviance?

"Return now to your journey. Hex still waits for you at the Keep."

And what of this man? You will allow him to die?

"I have no use for him, and neither do you. Return now," the voice commanded.

You cannot just leave him here to die! Deborah pleaded again.

Disgusted, the voice replied, "You may save him if you must. I will allow that."

How?

"You have already begun doing so. Finish your task."

These last words seemed to come from a far distance. She could barely hear what had been said.

Only the continuing gurgling sound from the curled up form broke the silence. She could see that soon the shade of color differentiating him from the all-pervading green would no longer be distinguishable.

*But how? I just want…*Then she abruptly chose to focus her mind on the task.

*   *   *

Hawk withdrew the knife and quickly stepped aside. Even so, droplets of the blood fountain pumping from the open wound in the dying man's throat spattered him. Moments later the spray subsided to a trickle. Shortly thereafter the chest moved no more.

"Damn it, man!" Hawk said again, grabbing the dead man's shirt. "Who are you? Why were you hunting me? I didn't wish to kill you, but you gave me no option!" Looking around, Hawk moved away from the corpse and bent down.

"Do you deserve the trouble of burying you?" Hawk said angrily, looking over at the body of the stranger. Straightening with a handful of mulch from the forest floor, Hawk wiped his blade clean and returned it to its sheath.

After retrieving his bow and replacing his arrow in its quiver, he went back to where he had left his pack when he had first heard the sounds of the man in the forest. He took a long drink from his water skin. "I need a drink. Why couldn't this be a wineskin?" he asked himself out loud. *How far did Ehrig say that town is? Half a day? I have used up most of that time already.*

Gathering his gear, Hawk prepared to move on. He walked back to the man he had killed and stared at the body for a long moment. "I have no desire to dig a grave with my bare hands, but I do not feel right about leaving you to the wolves and the bugs." He reexamined the corpse, not as a dead man but as a hunter's kill. The man was short and slender. The spray of blood from his throat had spewed mainly to the side and had not especially bloodied his clothing. Hawk grabbed him by a wrist and pulled him into a sitting position. "You shouldn't be all that heavy." Hawk bent and stripped the man's gear, leaving only his clothing in place. Then, bracing himself with the practiced movements of an experienced hunter, he hoisted the corpse over his shoulder. "Hmph" escaped him as the weight settled upon his shoulder. "You had better have family in Bromelshire," Hawk said as he began moving again. He hoped the village was at the foot of the hill and the slope on the downside was not as steep on the descent as it had been coming up.

His luck held. This side of the hill was gently sloped, the underbrush relatively sparse. As he walked, Hawk found his burden manageable; he had carried many heavier loads. Soon the woods broke open, and he found himself on terraced farmland extending up from a small village at the bottom. A short detour taking him to a path carved at the boundary between the fields and the woods made his travel even easier.

Hawk had traversed down about a half dozen levels of the fields when a boy with a hoe looked up and saw him approaching. "Bryce! A stranger!" he called to who Hawk could only assume was his brother. "Hail, traveler," he called up the hill. Hawk stopped and watched as the boys dropped their hoes and started running toward him. It was not until they were almost upon him that they realized it was a man Hawk had draped over his shoulder. The boys stopped cold.

"What is wrong with your friend?" they asked as Hawk approached.

"I'm afraid this man is dead, but he is not my friend. You should get the shire reeve."

"Our town is too small for a reeve. We have only a constable," the older boy replied. "Bryce, run and get Sem." The younger boy turned and sprinted toward town.

The older boy turned and watched his brother racing away. "He is going to outrun himself and fall if he is not careful," he said with a chuckle, continuing to watch for the amusing spectacle he had just predicted. Hawk shrugged his shoulders in an attempt to redistribute the weight a bit, then knelt and bent forward. The body slid onto the ground.

At the sound, the boy turned back to Hawk as he straightened again. "I'm Jason. What happened to him?" he asked.

Before he could answer, Hawk felt a soft nudge at his waist, just below his pack. It startled him slightly, but before he could react the whisper of a familiar voice immediately followed. "Let me explain this." His brow furrowed and turned to see where it had come from. As he did so, Deborah stepped from behind him.

"I'm Deborah. This is Hawk…and he is not dead." *I hope.*

"Ma'am! I didn't see you!" Jason exclaimed.

"I, uh…stepped into the woods," Deborah smiled.

"Oh. Sorry, ma'am," Jason said, blushing. He looked down at the man on the ground in an attempt to divert his face from the comely girl's. Noticing something odd about the man on the ground, Jason's face contorted curiously.

"I think he is breathing," he said. Jason moved in closer and knelt to study the body's head. He put his ear to the man's nose. "Yes. I do think he is breathing!"

Deborah smiled as she returned the older boy's gaze without shame, turned to Hawk and said, "I told you that all he needed was to get bounced on your shoulder as you carried him." Then she turned her attention to Jason. "We found him unconscious in the woods not too far back. I cleared some nuts that were caught in his throat." She smiled with the superiority of being right as she continued, "Hawk said we were too late, that he was already dead. *I* knew better."

"It looks like you were right, ma'am. He surely is breathing." The boy stood up, and Deborah stepped over to put her hand on his shoulder. "Go catch your friend. See if they can bring a cart so Hawk does not have to carry him any further."

"He's my brother, Bryce. Yes, ma'am. We will be right back." Jason took off down the hill, running even more recklessly than the younger boy had. They watched as Jason reached the end of the terrace where they stood and, as he jumped down the slope to the next terrace below, went head over heels. He rolled to his feet and brushed himself off. "I'm all right," he called back up to them, waving. Jason took off again, not quite as fast this time.

The man began coughing, reaching for his throat. He sat up and looked around in an attempt to gain his bearings. "How the hell did I get here? Where the hell am I? And who the hell are you?" His voice rasped out the questions.

"Are you okay? How do you feel?" Deborah asked.

Hawk stood and watched in disbelief.

"I don't know how I am. I am not even sure if I know *where* I am!" he said, looking around. "It was the strangest thing!" He extended his arm and held it up, waiting for Hawk to assist him. Hawk paused briefly, then reached down. The man grasped his wrist, and Hawk pulled him to his feet. The stranger slowly regained his composure, circling around the two. "Where are my things?"

Hawk had an ugly feeling about this man. Listening to the voice of someone he had killed such a short time ago made him feel more than uncomfortable. "Back up on the hill a bit, not far from here." Hawk pointed in the direction of the man's pack.

"How did you get here?" the man asked as he began to recall the recent events. The expression on his face as he looked at Hawk said it all. He lifted his hand to his throat but felt nothing except for the ragged scruff of beard growing on his neck. Confusion set in. "What the hell happened?"

The first of the young boys was returning with the constable just as he was ordered to do by his brother. Bryce was walking alongside and pointing in the direction of the three. As they neared, Bryce asked, "Where is Jason?"

Just as Hawk was about to answer, the constable spoke out. "Hello there! This boy came running saying there may have been some bit of trouble out here. Young Bryce here says someone has been killed?"

"That's the man I saw." Bryce pointed. Then he gestured at Hawk. "*He* said *he* was dead."

"No, sir, no one has lost his life here today. Everyone is fine. And you sir, who might you be?" Hawk composed his face into calmness.

"I'm Sem, constable here. Who are you? And why is the boy telling me of a dead man?"

"I'm Hawk from Rothersbucke. This is my sister Deborah. The man is a stranger to us. We found him in the forest. I thought he was dead. We seem to have been mistaken."

Deborah stepped up and continued. "We heard some strange noises coming through the trees. When we went to investigate, we found him. He was not breathing." She went on, relating the story as she had told it to Jason.

"You are a very lucky man," the constable said to the stranger. "And what were *you* doing in the forest?" He directed the question to Hawk.

"We were on our way to Bromelshire. We are to meet a friend there. Is this that village?"

"Yes, this is Bromelshire," Bryce interrupted helpfully. "Who are you coming to see?"

"A good question," Sem said. "No one has mentioned anything about expecting visitors, especially strangers."

"We separated from a friend earlier, and he told us to meet him here, although he didn't quite say where. He goes by the name of Ehrig."

"I don't know that name," replied Sem.

Jason had gone looking for Bryce and when he could not find him, ran to his father Henrik to let him know of the happenings taking place on the rim of the farm. Walking back to the edge of the field, Jason led his father as he retold the story.

Henrik and Jason could see the group standing up ahead. No one was lying upon the ground. No one appeared hurt.

As they approached, Henrik began to speak. "What goes on out here? Jason has been telling me an incredible story. And from the looks of things, it seems everyone here is fine."

"There may be a misunderstanding," Sem replied. "No one here has been harmed."

Hawk looked at Sem and glanced over at the once dead man.

"That is good news. I'm Henrik. It is a pleasure to meet you," he said, nodding his head.

"I'm Hawk. And this is my sister Deborah."

He was dusting the dirt off his clothes, still attempting to make sense of what just occurred as the exchanges were taking place. "I'm Felix," the resurrected man said, then turned and slowly began walking up the hill, back toward the trees.

"Where are you off to?" Sem demanded.

Felix stopped and turned to face them. "To retrieve my belongings."

"Well, how about you all join me now at my home where you can clean up and have something to eat? I am sure you could use a good meal," said Henrik. "Felix, you can retrieve your things later. I am sure they will still be where you left them. Most of the day is gone now, and I don't see you having time for anything other than setting up camp. Perhaps you folks would like to stay the night at my home. It isn't much but it's better than sleeping out in the cold."

Without waiting for an answer, Henrik instructed his boys, "You two get home and clean up. It's been a long day for everyone." Both the boys nodded and ran ahead, leaving everyone behind.

Felix looked at Henrik and half smiled, still trying to tie his memories together with what was happening around him now.

Deborah grinned broadly at the offer.

Hawk was ready for a good meal and the thought of traversing the hill again to rearm this man did not sit well with him. Henrik turned and started back toward the hamlet. Hawk followed, as did the rest.

Nearing the shacks that lined the edge of the small village, Sem said his goodbyes and headed home himself. Arriving at the doorway of a modest dwelling, Henrik opened the door and let in everyone. Jason and Bryce were finishing clearing the table when the door opened. Henrik, taking their belongings and placing them in a corner, pointed in the direction where Deborah could cleanse herself. She eagerly made her way into a tiny room to find a washbowl and towel. Meanwhile, Hawk and Felix took seats at the small table.

The residence was small. It had two bedrooms other than the room Deborah currently occupied. The living area was filled, even though the furnishings were simple. It was easy to see how cramped the home was, but Henrik and his sons made good use of the space available.

There was a fire burning under a stew well on its way to being served. The smell permeated the room, and everyone's stomach gurgled in unison. The sun in fact had begun making its way behind the hills and night was starting to fall. Taking note of that, Felix decided he was going to forego the meal for the moment and head out to retrieve his bow and gear. By the time Deborah finished cleaning herself, Felix had gone.

"Thank you very much. I needed that so badly," Deborah said as she entered the room. "It's a lovely home. Where is your wife?"

"She passed away at childbirth with Bryce. It's been many years now, but I still miss her," Henrik replied, silencing the room. Deborah looked over at the young boy but didn't say a word. Bryce stood quietly, lowered his head, and glanced at her through his bangs. After an awkward moment Henrik spoke again, "How about something to eat? There should be enough stew. I usually make enough for the boys and myself for two days." With that, Henrik began to set the table. Deborah rose to help.

Deborah noticed that Felix as no longer in the room. "Did Felix leave after all?"

"He decided not to wait until tomorrow to go find his things," Hawk quipped.

Deborah could tell something was bothering Hawk. She wanted to talk to him, but now was not the time.

After the meal, the boys were sent off to bed while

Hawk, Deborah, and Henrik stayed up to talk. "So where are you traveling to?" Henrik asked.

"We are heading to Deviant Stronghold," responded Hawk.

Henrik's intention to continue their casual conversation was suddenly brought to a stop. "What in the world do you want with that place? Don't you know about what goes on there?"

By the looks on their faces, it was evident to Henrik the answer was no. He moved around the table and took the seat closer to Deborah. "I...we, here in the village, we know about that place, and from what I can tell, nothing good comes from there."

Hawk's attention was riveted on Henrik's words.

"It seems that most people who go to that place have odd stories to tell. I have never actually gone there myself but from what I hear—"

"What kind of stories?" interrupted Hawk.

"Well, it is my understanding the walls are tall and the gates are shut, preventing most outsiders from entering, but excessively loud noises can be heard coming from within the castle walls and at times people screaming, I'm told. I hear the sounds can be horrific at times."

Continuing, Henrik spoke with conviction. His stories were much like those told by Hawk's father when he was a boy. Deborah did not know much about the stronghold other than what she was told as a little girl; what she did know did not match what she was being told now. The concern on her face was growing. Hawk could sense her uneasiness.

Henrik did not seem to catch on as he continued to fill in the two with the details he had gathered from other travelers. "...and even a few of the men here in town have tried to enter that fortress," Henrik continued, "though none were successful. There is a way you can go that will keep you safe, but you will need assistance. I have been told of a well. The word is that if you visit this place and drop a coin in the water, you will be granted a safe passage to the gates, but I know of no one that has actually found it. Getting within the walls is much harder still. For that, I cannot assist you. Though it is rumored they have, I have not heard of any way to cause the gates to open."

"Tell me what you know of this well," Hawk said. Henrik had his full attention.

"It is said to be about a day's travel from here, on a path that splits the position of the noonday sun and the sunset. The forest will become very dense the further you travel. But first, before you leave, you must prepare yourself. You cannot drink of the water from the well, but your body must be clean. You will need an extra skin of water for the both of you. With that you will cleanse yourself prior to dropping the coin. It is said, 'one coin only.' I don't know whether the value matters or if one coin is all that is necessary, or if more are required for more than one person. There is a stream beside the well, but you mustn't drink of it. It is said the tainted souls of those that fail on their journey are flowing in that river. Follow these directions, and if the legend holds true, you will face no danger upon your approach to the keep."

Henrik stopped speaking and rubbing his chin lifted himself from the table. Walking over to the wall, he grabbed a skin of his own and offered it to Hawk. "Use this."

Both Hawk and Deborah were unsure as to what to think, Hawk especially. Ehrig never mentioned anything about a well or the need for safe passage, but Henrik seemed confident in what he was talking about, and there was no point in taking chances. In the morning, they would head out and seek the well buried in the dense forest.

Hawk turned to Deborah. "And what about this man Felix?"

"You don't know him?" asked Henrik, puzzled by the sudden twist in the conversation.

"No, we don't. We found him in the forest," Hawk responded.

"I don't know, Hawk. I can't really explain right now, but I think I have seen him before," Deborah said, alluding to the event involving Felix that occurred while she was in the Light.

"Well, something about him doesn't sit right with me. I'm sorry but I just don't like him."

"I guess we can't really judge him at the moment, can we, Hawk?"

"No, I suppose not."

A knock stopped the conversation cold. Henrik opened the door, allowing Felix to enter. As Felix found a place to lay his belongings, Hawk and Deborah decided it was time to turn in. Henrik moved a small cabinet to make room for them then turned his attention to Felix. They found a place to rest while Felix was served what remained of the stew.

Feeling more comfortable now that he had his gear, Felix listened and ate his meal while Henrik told him of the legend of the well.

I've never seen a well, Felix thought as Henrik revealed what he knew about the stronghold. He had heard of Deviant Stronghold although he never entertained the thought of actually going there—not alone anyway. Felix considered all this for a bit while Henrik continued explaining all he knew about Deviant Stronghold and the well. Felix had traveled all this way to offload his cache of stolen goods, but following Hawk and Deborah had piqued his interest. *Maybe I can tag along…see what Deviant Stronghold is all about for myself.*

*   *   *

Hawk woke in the morning before the others after a hard night of restless turning. He could not understand how Felix was dead then alive and sleeping on the same floor across the small room. *And there isn't a trace of a mark on his throat!* Hawk thought. The sun was just beginning to lighten the night sky and dawn was close. Careful not to wake the others, he stepped outside for a moment alone. All night he had struggled with the events of the day before. Deborah did not seem to notice the oddities concerning Felix. Hawk was bothered by that fact, too.

Deborah woke to find Hawk missing. She looked around the room and noticed his boots were gone. Quietly, she put on her boots and stepped outside to see if she could find him. Hawk was leaning on a wagon, his back facing the home.

As his thoughts plagued his mind, Deborah walked up slowly from behind. "You are up early," she said softly.

"I couldn't sleep," Hawk said, turning to face her, keeping his voice low.

"Your sister?" Deborah smiled.

"I had to say something. What else would explain you in the woods with two men?" Hawk said, ignoring the jest. "It just doesn't make sense."

"What doesn't make sense?"

"He died, Deborah! I watched him die in my arms!" Hawk's voice was low but tense.

"Who died, Hawk?" Deborah asked. Her brow was furrowed, trying to understand what had Hawk so agitated.

"Felix died! You were there! You saw it, too! What do you mean 'who died'?"

"No, Hawk, I wasn't there," Deborah replied quietly.

The look of confusion was evident on Hawk's face. "What do you mean? What are you telling me?"

"Tell me what you remember, Hawk."

"We were making our way here to Bromelshire when we stopped. That is when I heard something approaching. While you rested, I stopped behind some bushes to watch and saw Felix sneaking up on me. I watched as he raised his bow. He saw me! He knew what he was pointing at!" Hawk said in a forced low tone. "I stood until he drew back on the string. By then I could only try to protect myself. I tried to deflect his shot by throwing my knife at the bow. He flinched when he saw it, and the blade struck him in the neck," Hawk said, looking at Deborah, truly disturbed at what had happened. "He fell back grabbing his neck and gurgling blood. There was nothing I could do. I knew he was a dead man even before I retrieved my blade. I watched him die. And then you came out and said he was choking. I don't understand—"

"What do you remember about me? About us coming here?" Deborah said, cutting Hawk off.

"We departed the cave with Ehrig. He left us at the field after giving us direction for Bromelshire."

"I never left the cave with you, Hawk," Deborah said hesitantly.

"What?"

"I never left the cave with you and Ehrig. I went back."

"Back? Back where?"

"Before you woke that morning, I shot myself with the cannon. I went back into the Light."

"You *what? Why?*"

Hawk's expression was that of disbelief, curiosity, shock all—rolled into one. "But you were with me the entire time," Hawk said when he was interrupted by a thought. *Is that what Ehrig meant back at the cave?* Ehrig's words echoed in the back of his mind, "You, I can help." *So she was there in the cave! Deborah experienced everything with me! It wasn't a dream!* "When did—"

"After we talked," Deborah said, anticipating the question. "You fell asleep, but I couldn't. I went back into the Light looking for Hex. I thought maybe I could find out what happened to Robert. I thought maybe..." Deborah's voiced trailed off.

"But that's when I saw him, Hawk! He was in the Light as well. I could tell he was dying. And then the voice told me to bring him back if I wanted—"

"Who exactly did you see? What voice? What are you talking about?" Hawk said, frustrated.

"After I went back...it was like the first time—nothing but green. I heard noises like a gurgling sound, and then I saw a figure. It was like me except that this light was fading...like Ehrig described. Also in the Light was a voice. It spoke to me. It told me that my purpose wasn't there and to keep moving to the keep. He didn't care that the person beside me was dying. He was cold toward that person. I couldn't be."

"Hex? He spoke to you?"

"No, I don't think it was Hex. The voice said Hex was waiting for me at the keep."

"Then who was it? Did he say?" Hawk asked.

"No. He did tell me that I could bring the man back if I wanted. He said that I had already started doing it. Then he, the Light, everything was gone. The next thing I remember, I was behind you, and Felix was on the ground. Neither you nor the boy seemed to have noticed me, so I just stayed quiet and listened while I tried to decide what to do next."

"So you brought him back...Felix, I mean?"

"I don't know, but I think so...yes," Deborah said quietly.

Hawk took a minute to absorb everything he had heard. He was still confused as to why Deborah decided to take the trip back into the Light, but everything else was starting to make sense.

Dawn had broken and the sun was beginning to make the surroundings visible. "I think we should start going," he said, shaking his head. Something about Felix truly bothered Hawk. For the moment, Felix was here and with nothing other than instinct to guide him, Hawk made a conscious and quiet decision: He would keep a close eye on Felix.

The two headed quietly back into the house only to find the boys were already stirring and Henrik was waking. Felix was still sound asleep.

Chapter Twelve

Hawk and Deborah were gathering their things when Felix woke. He saw the two preparing their belongings for departure.

"Where are you heading?"

Hawk turned toward Felix. "We're moving on."

"Where to?"

Hawk did not answer. "Beyond the valley," Deborah responded, glancing over at Hawk.

"Perhaps I could join you? Travel there with you?" Felix asked. Hawk continued to avoid Felix's questions. Deborah was well aware of Hawk's misgivings about Felix, so she did not say a thing. "Good. Then I'll join you," Felix declared.

Deborah's mind flashed on Hawk's misgivings, but her curiosity about this man she had brought back from the Light dismissed them. "Some company on the road would be welcomed." She smiled.

Damn it, Deborah! Hawk cursed silently, but did not say anything aloud.

The trio prepared for their trip into the forest. Filling the skins with fresh water and sacking some food given them by Henrik, they bid their farewell and thanked their host for his hospitality. Bryce and Jason stood quietly by as they watched them leave.

The sun was coming up, exposing the path through the small huts lining the hamlet. Besides the constable, Henrik and the boys were the only people who knew about the unexpected company. As far as the travelers could tell, no one saw them leave as they headed into the forest.

Life in the forest was beginning to wake. Hawk silently pushed his way through the trees, occasionally cutting through the brush or bushes instead of finding a way around them. Deborah and Felix followed behind not saying a word.

The trip up the hill was exhausting, and the climb was beginning to take its toll. It seemed the closer they got to the Keep, the harder the trails were becoming. Hawk paused long enough to take a bearing on the directions given to him by Henrik. Felix decided to take a pull from his water skin.

"I would conserve that if I were you," Hawk said.

"There are brooks and streams everywhere. I can always refill later."

"Not where we are going."

"Where are we going? Rather, where are you going?" Felix asked.

"Currently, we are headed to the well in the forest," Hawk replied.

"And then on to Deviant Stronghold?"

Hawk and Deborah looked at each other. "Yes, that's right. In fact we are heading there after we stop at the well," Deborah said.

"Great! I will fill my skins there. I am from a town far north of here. Shackleford, have you heard of it?"

"No," Deborah said.

"Neither have I. And that well is not for drinking. Didn't you listen to Henrik?" Hawk began moving again, not waiting for an answer. Deborah followed him up the hill.

As they picked their way through the heavy woods, Hawk became more and more irritated. Henrik's warning about the forest being thick and the way difficult was proving more than true. Between the canopy and the broken cloud cover, the sun's position was hard to gauge and difficult to readjust their bearings as the trees and heavy ground cover forced them to zigzag their course. Felix compounded the problem by wandering off on "helpful" shortcuts and gravitating to paths of least resistance. More than once they found they had walked a full circle after Felix had convinced them to follow.

Finally Hawk had enough. "If I have to go after you one more time, I'll tie you a tree and leave you for the bugs and rats!"

"I have a rope," Deborah added.

"I am only trying to help," Felix protested.

"Hmph!" Hawk snorted as he turned and moved on. Deborah was only a step behind him. Felix stood there watching as they moved back into the dense forest, wondering if Hawk meant the threat. Not wanting to find out, he trotted to catch up just as he was about to lose sight of them.

Felix stayed with the two now, but this did not help Hawk's mood much. With the demonstrations of his path finding skills curtailed, Felix launched into tales of the exploits of the object of their journey. To Hawk, his stories were mere retelling of gods and heroes long past, with the names changed to those of well known Deviants, and had little resemblance to those told by his father and Ehrig. Hawk found the constant talk distracting, but held his peace when Deborah commented that the tales helped pass the time.

*   *   *

Echoes of metals colliding suddenly converged from all directions. No one could discern from where the sound was coming. All three paused and stared off into the forest trying to detect the source, but the denseness of the woods prevented it. Unable to discover the genesis of the noise, they continued traveling the path cut by Hawk, each paying close attention to the woods around them. The forest indeed became much denser as Henrik had forewarned.

A small stream trickling through the woods guided Hawk. He was moving slowly when from out of nowhere, between the clashes of metals, they heard a voice:

"You will never find it!"

They all stopped and looked at each other, but no one could figure out where the voice came from.

"Hehehehe. Shut up, will you?" the voice demanded.

Hawk froze. He recognized that voice! He put his finger to his lips for silence and motioned for Deborah and Felix to stand still, then slowly began moving again.

"Look at him! Hehehe! Shut up! Shut up! Why can't you ever just shut up?" the voice shouted.

The voice seemed to be coming from above them and away from the stream. Hawk followed his instincts as he motioned for Deborah and Felix to remain where they stood. Moving gradually and silently up the hill, he saw a man slightly bent over. Hawk could see the man was dressed just as raggedly as the person he met on his way to Falkenwrath.

"You will not find what you are looking for," the voice echoed from the hill. The man's back was facing Hawk, yet he spoke as if he were looking right at him.

"And how do you know what I seek?" Hawk called out.

"All that come this way fail to find what they are looking for," the man said simply, having stopped his task. "Hehehehe, it doesn't exist! Hehehehe. Would you SHUT UP?"

Hawk moved to the left as he climbed closer to the man who was still bent over, face obscured. As he neared, Hawk noticed the man was holding a hammer in his right hand and a small copper plate in the other. The sleeves of his shirt were just high enough to expose the scars on his arms. "Timothy?"

"Up Yours, boy! Up Yours!" he screamed. "SHHHHHhhhhh! I see you found your way to the place where others have come to fail. Is that your intention as well?" the man said, still not looking up at Hawk.

"I don't know what you mean," Hawk replied.

"Do you not seek to throw yourself and your loved ones into the stream of lost souls?" the voice beneath him asked, stifling his laughter.

"What are you talking about? I have no intention of throwing anyone into a stream. I was given directions to this place."

"Directions? And now I suppose you'll want guidance again? Bah!" he said, waving a dismissive hand in the air, his face still hidden. "Let him look! Let him look! Hehehehehe."

"Timothy?"

The old man rotated toward the young traveler. His face confirmed the voice as he rose up into a tirade. "Get him out of here!"

Hawk rotated, and seeing Felix, growled, "Felix! You left Deborah alone?"

Timothy yelled, continuing his rant. "Six says I cannot kill him, but death will be the least of his problems. Get him out of here!"

Deborah, hidden from view, stepped between Felix and the screaming man in front of her. "He didn't leave me behind." She added with a nervous smile, "Aren't you going to introduce me to your friend, Hawk?"

Timothy's outburst ceased the instant Deborah's voice touched his ears. A hand lifted to his ear and with a quick drawn breath he said, "You planned to throw this beautiful creature in the stream of lost souls? Six protects this man, but said nothing of you. And it would serve you right!" he said looking at Hawk in disgust. The deeply etched wrinkles on Timothy's angry face flattened to a smooth surface. Timothy's eyes softened as he gazed upon Deborah. He stepped up and taking Deborah's hand, gently kissed it, introducing himself, "*You*, my dear, may call me UY."

She smiled. "It is lovely to meet you, UY. I'm Deborah."

UY? Hawk thought. *I thought his name was Timothy.*

Timothy's attention turned toward the sky. "Yes, I know!" he said as he stormed off into the woods. "I know!" Without looking back, motioning his arm for the group to follow, he yelled, "See what you have done? Bah! Now he'll never shut up!"

Deborah smiled as Timothy departed. She thought this outburst was cute. She liked him instantly. The three began to follow before they lost him. Most of the day was spent, and it would soon be time to search for shelter.

The shadows in the trees began to swallow the forest as Timothy continued to walk through the woods in no particular direction, randomly turning between the trees and stones that blocked his path. To Hawk it seemed they were wandering without direction or purpose.

Felix had the same feeling. "Exactly where are we going?" he whispered to Hawk.

Hawk shook his head. "I don't know. Just follow."

Timothy continued walking in silence. Deborah trailed close behind as Hawk brought up the rear of the group. It was obvious to everyone but Timothy that the time to search for a safe place to rest had all but passed. It was getting harder and harder to focus on him as he darted from here to there, moving left then right, dodging between the trees.

The occasional ray of moonlight broke through the clouds quickly building above the treetops, illuminating the figure in front of them as Timothy led his followers farther into the forest. The fact that they were still walking after nightfall was wearing thin on Felix. His frustration got the better of him when he asked, "Excuse me, when are we going to stop and rest?"

Timothy's frustration was also evident from the pestering. "YOU can rest any time you like. It matters not to me."

"Best follow, Felix, and leave the matter alone." Deborah then added quietly, "but I, too, could use a break."

Timothy stopped and responded to the whisper he should not have heard. "Would you like a moment to yourself?"

"Yes, UY, I would."

"Good enough. We will rest here for a moment before carrying on." Timothy sat where he stopped.

"And what of the rest of us?" Felix demanded.

"Find your own damn tree!" Timothy fired back.

"Don't we have a say in when we stop?" Felix voiced.

"You are lucky to be here speaking at all!" he yelled at the top of his lungs.

Taking advantage of the pause, Hawk moved behind the closest tree he could find while watching the exchange. Above them the rainclouds opened, releasing their load. The base of the forest began to get wet. Hawk hoped they would not be traveling much further.

Deborah returned from behind a distant tree, found a place on the ground, and sat down to rest.

Although Hawk had not managed to enrage Timothy as had Felix, he was tired as well. Hawk sat next to Deborah after relieving himself. Felix sat opposite Hawk, furthest away from Timothy, not long afterward.

Taking their skins, each had a drink. Deborah felt as if she would fall asleep where she sat.

"Come, my dear. We must continue moving if we are to beat this storm."

"It's already raining, UY," responded Deborah.

He looked up and smiled. "Not quite yet, hehehe, this is only the beginning!" With that, he turned and pushed by Felix as he pressed into the forest.

The four walked through the night. The storm indeed gained strength, but that made no difference to Timothy as his pattern of weaving back and forth continued.

"There!" Timothy suddenly called out, startling everyone.

Hawk could barely make out what looked like a carving on the hillside. There was a canopy of trees above it but not much else by way of shelter. "We will be safe here?"

"And warm and dry," Timothy replied. "Just in time, too. Hehehe!"

No sooner had the four reached the clearing when the sky opened up and a heavy rain poured down. Thunder exploded above their heads immediately after lightning illuminated the trees all around them.

Everyone found a place on the ground to sit and rest except for Timothy. Felix and Deborah succumbed to their exhaustion almost immediately. Hawk sat silently and watched as Timothy walked over to a large stone and from behind it pulled out a cloak.

Hawk recognized that cloak! It was the same one Ehrig had worn the first night at The Rusted Lantern. Hawk's mind was reeling. *Who is this man? What is he doing with that cloak?* It was then that Hawk realized the rain was not wetting the ground around them. It was just like the tree where he rested on the way to Ehrig's cave.

Twisting to the side and looking over his shoulder with a knowing grin, Timothy said, "Best go to sleep, Hawk."

*   *   *

Morning came. The rain had stopped, but it was evident that the storm had been a major one. All around the shelter the ground was muddied and soaked, but the area on which they slept remained bone dry.

Deborah was the first to stir. She looked over to where Hawk lay sleeping. Felix was also still resting. Next to her sat UY, still asleep with his back against the hill. He didn't look at all comfortable. The assessing of her companions ceased suddenly when her gaze fell upon the bow and quiver filled with arrows atop a pack on the opposite side of where UY rested. Deborah recognized the bow immediately. She lifted herself from her spot and stepped carefully around him to the gear. Quietly picking it up and stringing it, she examined the bow. *Yes, this is mine*, she puzzled, *but how did it get here?*

"You really don't need those." UY's gruff whisper startled her. "But we thought you would be more comfortable having them with you." His eyes darted toward Felix and back to her. "Then again, you never know."

"We?" she whispered back. "What do you mean 'we'? These were at Ehrig's when I…Oh!…Are you a—"

"Shhhh." He silenced her with a finger to his lips. "In the present company some things are better left unsaid." With that he jumped to his feet and shrieked, "Up Yours! It is time to go! Have them catch up, if they can." He wrapped the dark green cloak around himself and moved into the forest with the rising sun directly on his back.

Timothy's strident voice instantly brought Hawk to his feet, knife in hand. He got his bearings just in time to see the cloak disappear into the trees.

Felix sat up and rubbed his eyes. "What the hell was that?"

"UY just left," Deborah replied, picking up her pack and quiver. "We should make haste, or we'll lose him."

Hawk sheathed his knife and quickly donned his own gear.

Felix said, "But I'm hungry."

Hawk took Deborah's elbow and turned back toward Felix. "By all means, cook breakfast. Bring us some, too. Don't let it get cold." Hawk guided Deborah toward the spot where he had last seen Timothy.

It was not difficult to follow Timothy's tracks over the wet forest floor. His path was now considerably more linear than the random wandering Hawk had perceived as they traveled the previous night. It was not long before they closed the distance. As they did so, Deborah trotted up to him and took his hand, "UY..." she cooed, looking up at him.

"By the Green Light, I hate traveling with women!" he growled. "Every bush and tree in the forest looks like a good place to pee!" He softened when Deborah smiled at him. "Okay, okay...find one to your liking."

Hawk quickly moved off. The rapid departure from camp had, in fact, given no time for morning niceties. Seeing that Deborah had not yet returned when he rejoined Timothy, Hawk shrugged off his pack and quickly retrieved some jerky and biscuits. When they had hustled after Timothy upon leaving their rest site, Hawk had noticed Deborah was carrying a bow, but in their haste to catch up, had not said anything to her about it.

Felix caught up as Hawk closed his sack. Hawk noticed Felix staring as he went to take a bite. Realizing that he was the only one digging into a pocket, and furrowing his brow slightly, Hawk offered the biscuit to Felix. Felix held up his hand to wave off the offer, pulling a chunk of dried meat from the pouch on his belt. Hawk then turned slightly toward Timothy and repeated the offer with a cock of his head. Timothy shrugged nonchalantly. Hawk tossed it to him anyway.

Deftly catching it, Timothy bit into it and smiled. "Not bad...now let's keep moving. I am tired of being out here."

Timothy pushed off into the underbrush. The group again found themselves scrambling to catch up to him with Deborah close behind and Felix again bringing up the rear—this time without straggling.

Now that the pace was a little less frenetic, Hawk also recognized the arrows he had made in the quiver on her back. Catching up to Deborah he asked, "How did you get those back?"

"UY returned them to me before we left the shelter."

"Timothy?" It became clear to Hawk that Timothy, or UY as he had taken to calling himself, was more than just a crazy old man. *He must be...Is he...a...just like Ehrig?* The thought was as much a statement as a question. *I knew there was something about the old man!*

Timothy continued through the bushes and shrubs among the trees, clearing a path for the others to follow. As they descended a small hill, a well came to view down below near a creek's edge. "Ah yes, let's see what we have today...hehehehe."

"Is that the well we were looking for?" Deborah asked Hawk.

"I don't think so. Timothy said there was no well."

Timothy continued toward the well. As they drew near, the incongruity of Henrik's story suddenly struck Hawk. *Why would anyone dig a well next to a stream?*

"Why indeed?" Timothy queried, seemingly in response to the unvocalized question. He took hold of a rope over the well's edge and began pulling on it. Slowly, and with no word of his intentions, he raised the bucket tied to the opposite end over the rock that formed its wall. Pouring out the water he looked inside. "Hehehehe...Look! Look! It's been a good day, indeed!"

The others watched as the old man reached in and removed a number of coins from the bottom of the bucket. "Some are more generous than others," he said with glee. He opened the pouch on his belt and clinked the coins into it, one at a time. "Hehehehehe...I just love that sound! Yes, it has," he said, answering himself. "I wonder how the others are doing?"

"Others? What others?" asked Hawk.

"That is none of your concern! Don't you worry about that, young man," Timothy scolded Hawk. "What you need is to continue pushing through this part of the woods until you find yourself between two hills, both with very large boulders on either side."

Hawk's confusion was evident.

Frustrated Timothy added, "Don't worry, the stream will lead you to it. From there, you must continue upstream where you will find it connects with the beginning of two other, smaller streams...Yes, the fork...hehe, the fork. Quiet! Now, at that point you must make your decision." Timothy paused for effect, looking around at the three travelers and waving a pointed finger in the air. "Some travel by day, others travel by night...and each will know which way is right!" Giving them no opportunity to question him further, Timothy turned abruptly and departed, disappearing as if he had been swallowed by the shadows.

"Wait!" Felix called and took a step to follow the old man.

"Don't bother," Hawk said before Felix had taken a second step. Felix turned and looked at Hawk. "It's clear that his path and ours no longer converge. We go this way now." Hawk started upstream in search of the hills with the large boulders protruding from their sides.

Chapter Thirteen

Once again the group found itself alone in the woods with nothing more than what they carried on their backs...and directions from an old man caught up in arguments between himself and occasionally those who surrounded him. Still, Hawk was glad they found the old man, Timothy, UY, whatever his name; again he had been there to point the direction for Hawk when he needed it.

The slope was slight and where there was a sandy bank the trek was smooth; in some places they had to walk in the shallow water next to the bank to avoid dense brush. Following the stream at times was considerably easier than pushing through the heavy woods. Yet in other places the brush or a steep bank would force them to detour away from the stream before finding their way back to it again. The hour was still early when Timothy had left them. They followed the waterway all morning and past midday. There was little conversation between them as they pressed on. They did not stop for a meal, but snacked as they traveled, and the breaks they did take were infrequent and short.

The winding stream coursed its way up through hills as it lead them farther and farther away from the tiny populated areas that surrounded the mountains and deeper into the remote woods. The canopy was once again becoming thicker, and Hawk was starting to notice a trend: Each time the sunlight began to filter off, he was faced with another challenge. The glow that caused him to lose his pack and belongings, the incredibly dense brush that followed, even the pig and carrying it back to Falkenwrath—each occurrence was preceded by the loss of light from above. As the others followed, Hawk did the best he could to not let on to them what he was sensing. Hawk took a moment to search his surroundings, looking for a change in color...looking for that distinct tinge of green. He could not see anything different, but something deep inside told him to be wary, they were about to deal with another obstacle.

The dense, dark foliage permitted occasional rays of sunlight to reflect off the stone and rocks along the streambed and sometimes within the shadows of the forest. Hawk decided to follow the patches of light for as long as he could. Doing this caused his path to become erratic. Deborah glanced over at Felix; both took notice of the change in pattern but followed just the same.

They came upon a gorge cut deeply between a pair of steep hills. Trees and brush from both sides of the stream crossed over and blocked the path formed by years of erosion from the water. As they approached the natural barrier, Felix was quick to point out the obvious, "Looks like we're going to have to go up and around."

"I don't like the idea of having to backtrack again or go around a hill. I say we cut right through," Hawk replied, looking into the foliage for an easier way to continue, searching for any signs of color change. Hawk's focus shifted and was no longer on his two companions. *There's got to be something around here, some kind of sign.*

"What about you?" Felix asked Deborah, who up until now had not said anything as Hawk moved around from side to side, grabbing at branches and pulling at brush, trying to find the best place to start, looking for something.

"Hawk is right. I don't think we should stray too far from the path UY set us upon. I think we should push through this and see what is on the other side," Deborah said, looking around at the surroundings. "And judging by the looks of this climb, I'm not sure where we'll end up before we can get back on the trail or even if we'll find the other side of these trees in the first place."

*There's got to be some kind of...*Hawk was not paying attention to the exchange, but almost on cue he pulled the blade from its sheath, raised his arm, and taking a heavy swing at the natural barrier, began hacking a path through the brush, striking at the area that looked *different.* At the impact of Hawk's blade against the foliage, the discussion between Deborah and Felix ceased, both startled from the sudden crack of splitting wood.

Progress was slow and the sun had long since crested above and began its persistent descent. Each had taken their turn clearing the path as they made their way through the twisted branches and heavy undergrowth. If not for the rush of the water below their feet, it would have been easy to lose direction while they pressed forward. It was Deborah wielding the blade when they finally broke through.

The trees became sparse. The underbrush that was so thick and woven was pushed back toward the banks of the stream. Now all that stood before them was the rock filled stream winding up the mountain. Hawk was tired. They all were. The denseness of the trees and brush was taxing to break through and their strength was depleted. No one said a word as they found a comfortable spot on the bank to the right side of the stream. Deborah handed the blade back to Hawk then rested on a large rock, her bow beside her. Hawk took the large knife and slid it into the sheath and then did the same. Felix found a spot on the soft dirt of the bank and laid his packs down beside him using one for a headrest. For the moment, no one thought of moving.

"That wasn't easy," Hawk said after a few moments of silence, his voice laden with exhaustion.

"No, it wasn't. I hope we don't have to go through anything like that again anytime soon," Felix responded. His eyes were closed as he lay just away from the water's edge.

"What do you think UY meant?" Deborah asked no one in particular, looking at the water passing in the stream, changing the subject.

"About what?" Hawk replied.

"You know…about traveling by day or night," she said, staring into the passing stream, lost in thought.

"I don't know. He didn't seem to make much sense the way he kept rambling on and on. Half the time, I didn't know who he was talking to: us or himself!" Felix said, chuckling.

"He's different, that's for sure," Hawk chimed in, but Deborah's question was not lost on him as was evident in his thoughtful expression. "Well, I'm sure we're going to find out sooner or later, but maybe we should get going. If I stay here any longer, I'm not going to want to move."

Grunts greeted him in response. No one wanted to leave the temporary rest stop, but they agreed they needed to keep moving. The group gathered up their belongings and started up the mountain walking along the bank. It was not long before the slope began to level off as they neared the top of the climb. Not far in the distance, the stream cut through the foot of two hills, a boulder was jutting from each like a stone appendage that had been whittled down to a large nub.

"That must be the marking UY was talking about," Deborah said as they pressed forward.

Hawk felt a strange sensation come over him as he neared the opening. He felt small under the huge stones as he passed below them. The feeling seemed mutual as Deborah and Felix followed closely behind. Passing just beyond the outcropping brought the small party into a broad meadow, better described as a narrow valley on the left side of the river, opposite where they now stood. On the right continued the thin crop of trees and brush. Naturally guided by the path of least resistance, they crossed the watercourse once more, this time moving toward the grassy field. The path was much easier on this side. The grasses were a welcome respite from the dense brush and trees through which they had toiled for most of the day. The grass was above knee high, lazily swaying as a breeze caressed its blades causing ripples.

Gazing forward, a distance that did not seem far, they could see where the river split near the base of a mountain, which struck Deborah as being as out of place as the stones in the hills. The mass of earth that lay before them was enormous. The two smaller active branches coming off each side of the mountain fed the stream they had been following, though the water markings of each of these were significantly wider than what was presently coursing through the channel.

It was reaching late afternoon as Deborah looked at the sky. No one noticed her furrowed brow as she spied the valley grass. As the three traversed the meadow, Deborah slowly permitted herself to separate from the others, walking closer to the receded treeline while allowing Hawk and Felix to continue on the straighter path through the field.

So slow was her course that they had not noticed the separation. It was only a matter of time, she figured, judging from the time of day and the way the group was moving slowly through the field. With no one talking or making any noise and the wind strong enough to cover any sounds of footsteps, the conditions were right. She hoped. *Don't speed up. Don't slow down...Just keep walking, just keep walking,* she willed.

Without any indication to the others, Deborah quietly pulled out an arrow from the quiver on her back and nocked her bow. As the group moved forward, Deborah scanned the grasstops. *Come on, I know you're in here.* No sooner did the thought cross her mind when out of the grass several pheasant took to flight. Both Hawk and Felix had not expected the sudden burst of motion from right in front of them. Deborah let her arrow fly and quickly nocked another. A wounded pheasant fell to the ground, flapping its wings frantically, an arrow protruding from its body.

"Oh! That was incredible!" Felix shouted. As he ran forward to seek the downed bird, a second flight of birds took off. Hawk turned to see Deborah loose a second arrow, and another bird fell from the sky.

Felix found the first pheasant still flailing on the ground. Picking it up, Felix wrung the bird's neck. Holding it up, he smiled. "We're eating well tonight!"

Meanwhile, Hawk found the second pheasant and quickly dispatched it.

Deborah walked up to Felix and retrieved the first arrow.

"That was a damn good shot!" Hawk called out laughing, taunting Deborah while she wiped the blood from the tip with grass. "I am thoroughly impressed."

"Uh huh...and you're not getting any!"

Hawk feigned hurt. Carrying the pheasant and returning the second arrow to Deborah, Hawk looked at her. His eyes said it all. Deborah smiled proudly and then blushed. They continued through the meadow with a lighter gait now that supper had been determined.

The distance was further than it looked due to the size of the mountain. As they approached the fork, it could be seen that the branch from the western side of the mountain stretched lazily along the meadow. The woods in that direction thinned as the path flattened, allowing for an easier view. The sun was bright on this side. The land was more level than what they had been traversing, and the thought of traveling an easier path immediately appealed to Felix, Deborah as well. The branch on the eastern side was a much different picture. This side of the mountain was as dark as night, and the trees were thick and dense, much like what they had recently cut through. The heavy, dark forest flowed off the mountain and to the north as far as they could see. This waterway came from the mountain more northerly than east.

Finally reaching the fork of the river and with the sun now sloping lower in the sky, they stopped for much needed rest and food. Each sat and pulled from their sacks as they found a place to rest in a clearing at the base of the mountain.

"Felix, help me gather some wood, and we'll start a fire for the night," Hawk said as he abandoned his resting spot. Felix rose up and headed off downstream into the lighter forest to the south. Hawk headed in the opposite direction.

The right side of the mountain cast a shadow that was immensely dark. As Hawk expanded his search for wood, he found himself further from the campsite and deeper in the forest. When he bent down to pick up a small log, he caught a shimmer in the darkness from the corner of his eye. *That's strange.* Recalling the loss of his pack, he decided not to approach the shimmer so quickly this time. Slowly, he made his way closer to where he thought he had seen the light. Nothing. Looking around and not seeing any more wood worth carrying, Hawk headed back to camp. He didn't make any mention of the light in the woods.

Off to the side of the camp near the edge of the stream lay a carpet of feathers. Beside them were the innards that had been discarded during the process of preparing the unlucky birds for the flame. By the time Hawk returned, Felix was sitting back in his chosen spot, and Deborah had cleaned the pheasants. Hawk tossed what little wood he found in the stack that Felix had gathered. Pulling one log from the pile and his now worn blade from its sheath, Hawk hacked thin slivers of wood off into a small pile. Starting the fire was easy enough since the wood was good and dry. Before long, the birds were dangling over the fire on a makeshift spit. The warmth of the fire and the smell of the meat cooking were overwhelming to them all. As they sat waiting for dinner to finish cooking, their conversation turned to what to do next.

"I'm not sure which way we should go next," Hawk said.

"It would be much easier to travel on the left side of the mountain, I think. The path seems much easier...and flat," Felix replied.

"I know I am tired of all that brush," Deborah chimed in. "Why don't we wait until morning. Let's see how the other side of the mountain looks then. Besides, I am tired and would prefer to rest."

"I could stand to rest myself," replied Hawk. "All right, we'll see what there is to see in the morning."

Night fell with their bellies full and the fire still burning, providing a warm barrier against the brisk breeze that continued to blow. Everyone managed to find a suitable place to lay. It was not long before Felix was asleep. Deborah was not far behind him as close as she was to the fire. The sky was clear, but there was no moon, and the stars were deep and bright, illuminating the night sky. Hawk lay there staring skyward. Although he was tired, sleep wasn't coming easy this night.

Occasionally, he gazed over at Deborah in the firelight as she slept. Her hair partially covered her face as the light of the fire danced upon it. *She truly is beautiful.* Here, now, in this light, she reminded him of a place that existed only in his heart. He could not help but wonder how things might have been, if only...

Tamara had been just as beautiful in her own right. Although her hair was lighter than Deborah's, she was of equal stature. Maybe Tamara was a little taller but not by much. She and Hawk had known each other since early childhood and were inseparable, even back then. It was of no surprise to anyone when they announced their intentions. The wedding had been humble but meaningful and as the days after their union quickly passed, Hawk found he was the happiest he had ever been. But the long life that Hawk had hoped to spend with his beautiful young bride was never to be. Only one month had passed when he found her. His beautiful young bride lay at the bottom of a low cliff alongside a basket of flowers she had been filling. Tamara had slipped on a loose stone and tumbled over the side. Hawk was devastated.

Time passed and there were others, but he never gave his heart to anyone the way he had to Tamara. Now, here he was, looking at Deborah with emotions he had not felt since he lost his true love.

With a heavy heart, he started to roll over to get some rest when just beyond Deborah, slightly up the mountain, in the heavily wooded forest he saw the shimmer again. Rising up on his elbow from his spot, he watched, studied. There! He saw it again. Hawk slowly stood and moved over to where his pack was stowed and quietly gathered his gear. As he slung the bow over his shoulder, Hawk turned back toward where he had seen the flicker of light, but it was gone. Quietly stepping past Deborah to the edge of the trees, he paused long enough to acquire the direction where he last saw the light, and pushed into the woods. He tracked the shimmer of light through the forest, repeatedly losing sight of it as he encountered difficulties in the night. Finally, after taking a particularly nasty blow to the forehead from a low branch, he lost the light altogether.

By this time he was thoroughly disoriented. Lost. He had no idea how far he was from the camp or even which direction to go to return to it. Worse, in his snaking after the glow, he had not encountered the stream that came off the mountainside to their campsite. Hawk managed to find a flat piece of ground and decided to spend the remainder of the night there.

* * *

Dawn's morning light brought Deborah out of sleep. She woke to see Felix bent over putting on his own gear. Looking around she asked, "Where is Hawk?"

"I don't know. When I woke, he was gone," Felix said emotionlessly as he continued dressing his gear. He pitched his head toward the eastern side of the fork. "I found some tracks that lead up the mountain along the east fork of the stream. He's welcome to it. I am going along the western side. I have had enough brush and thicket."

Puzzled, Deborah got up and looked for herself. As she verified Felix's observations, UY's words flooded into her mind. *"Some travel by day, others travel by night…and each will know which way is right!"*

It seems that he has chosen…or found…his path, she thought. She looked over to where Felix was preparing to leave. *Apparently so has Felix.* Disappointed both that Hawk had not told them that he was leaving and that his path obviously did not include her, she returned to the fork and stooped at the stream. Splashing the cold water onto her face, she rinsed away the grime and the remnants of sleep. Standing, she turned toward Felix, who was now packed and ready to travel.

"Hurry. Let's get started. Hawk has a head start on us, but he chose the difficult route. I am sure the Stronghold is close and if we don't delay, we can beat him there," he said, flashing a broad grin.

Deborah scowled slightly. *Felix is right in that Hawk chose the more difficult path—a path I don't relish…especially alone with little chance of catching up to him.* Looking toward the mountain, then back at Felix, she gathered her belongings. Staring off into the trees she turned to Felix and uttered a resolved, "Let's go."

*　　*　　*

If the sun had risen, it was not readily apparent to Hawk. The canopy of trees was so thick that the shadow below the surface dominated any semblance of day that might exist. Taking the time to attempt gathering his bearings, Hawk moved again but soon realized he was lost. He set out, pushing his way through the woods, listening for the sounds of the river that he knew passed through this side of the mountain. If he could find it, he could make his way back down the side of the mountain and find the others.

Disoriented from his trek in the night, he moved carefully through the shadows of the dense forest. Following the slope of the hillside, Hawk located the rushing water he had been hearing. He found himself at the saddle of two new hills that merged with the one he had been moving down. The stream was channeled between the hills and pronged down both sides of where he stood. Hawk stooped at the crux of the wye of the river and took a drink. Studying his surroundings, both branches of the stream running downhill, he decided on the branch to the left and continued making his way down the hill.

*　　*　　*

Felix was right. The traveling was easier. They followed the bank of the river as it lazily swayed back and forth along the mountain base. The meadow was blanketed with tall grasses and occasional groups of trees. For Deborah, if not for the clouds that were again building in the sky and the fact that Hawk had left in the middle of the night, the day would have been perfect.

As they walked, it seemed that Felix had become even chattier since Hawk had disappeared, continually speaking about this and that without any real beginning or end to his conversation. Deborah for the most part was cordial, if not fully attentive, as they continued their progress through the field. As the clouds became darker and the threat of yet another rainstorm loomed, Felix and Deborah edged closer toward the mountain and slowly followed the river.

Then the sky opened up and the rain came down heavily, catching the pair in the open. Moving as quickly as possible, they found themselves huddled up under a tree. The strength of the river they were following was quickly building as the rush of the current became obviously stronger, filling the widest margins of the waterway cut out by previous storms.

"We better cross while we still have a chance," Felix said. Deborah nodded in agreement.

He left the shelter of the tree and waded into the water, Deborah directly behind. The water level was already almost up to their knees. Just as he passed midstream, the current of the rising water pulled Felix's legs from under him. The water carried him about four feet downstream before he slammed hard into a boulder. Grasping it, he got control of himself and regained his footing.

Deborah had time only to gasp as she saw him fall then realized he would not be swept away. She altered her course slightly so she would be able to use the boulder for support as she crossed.

Reaching the other side Felix dropped his gear, stripped off his shirt and tried to wring it out, but in the rain it was a wasted effort. Deborah saw that a large bruise was already forming on his side, but he had not been cut. Felix did not bother to put his shirt back on, but simply grabbed his equipment and followed Deborah into the trees, thick at the base of the mountain. The woods gave them only a little protection from the rain. The pair continued for hours in the heavy downpour as they circled the base of the mountain. They stopped only once when Felix decided the wet shirt was better than the rain on his bare skin. By this time, Deborah was wishing she had followed Hawk into the woods. At least in the heavy forest, they would have been out of the rain.

Drenched, Deborah and Felix began making their way off the valley floor and back into the forested ground, following the river where it came down the mountain. Deborah was feeling the strain of traveling alone with Felix. His constant chatter about his travels and deeds was beginning to grate on her nerves. Inwardly, she was still upset with Hawk for leaving in the night without so much as shaking her to see if she would follow.

"I had spent some time near your mountains, you know. Those by Falkenwrath."

"Falkenwrath?"

"Yes, a lovely town. I stay at The Rusted Lantern," Felix stated. "Do you go there?"

"The Rusted Lantern, yes, I am very familiar with that

inn. I have never seen you there before. When did you say you were in those mountains?"

"Oh, it's been a while now. I don't quite recall just how long. It's a lovely town."

As Felix continued chatting to himself, Deborah faded back into her memory, attempting in vain to recall having ever seen Felix at the inn or anywhere else in town for that matter. That thought bothered, her but she did not understand why.

Deborah and Felix pushed further into the woods. As time passed, the climb had become steeper and rocky. The river was becoming harder to follow directly so they pushed up and away from the riverbank and instead walked along the hillside where the ground was easier to traverse. Circling the mountain, keeping aware where the river was, they continued their march with Deborah in the lead.

The climb was steep in most areas but passable. Both were happy just to be out of the rain as they continued the trek up the mountain. The woods were thicker, and the daylight was slowly disappearing the further they pushed through the forest.

*　　*　　*

The dense forest finally began to give way. Ahead Hawk could see more sunlight as he neared the edge of the woods. Slowly, as the ground began to clear, a path emerged. *That's odd.* Hawk followed the path as it circled slightly away from the river and into the forest. The trees lined the path neatly, as if placed intentionally where they stood. The sights and sounds of the forest filled his senses. The area he had entered was tranquil and peaceful. From the path emerged a small road in the middle of nowhere. Hawk walked along the side furthest from the river as he was led around a bend.

There in the distance, just barely in view, was a structure! Hawk's heart reacted to the sudden burst of adrenaline as calmly as he could while the beating in his chest grew. *Could that be it?* Hawk thought excitedly.

The trees draped lazily like a row of umbrellas as the road descended slowly toward the fortress. The stream Hawk had been following also drifted toward the foundation of the structure, filling the moat surrounding it. Hawk watched in awe as he made his way toward it. The cacophonic song of the birds and sounds of the breeze blowing through the trees created a serene calm. Hawk found the drawbridge lifted as he approached the crossing. Looking about his surroundings and further down the road that led away from the bridge, he could not see another crossing point. *Is this Deviant Hall?*

* * *

The mountainside Deborah and Felix were crossing kept pushing them further and further away from the stream they were supposed to be following. It wasn't long before they were moving more vertically than horizontally along the mountain. As they climbed, the trees began to thin out slightly and the view was becoming clearer among the treetops. Stopping for a moment to gather her bearings Deborah gazed at the beautiful landscape. Clouds against the skyline threatened rain yet again, but those seemed to be on the opposite side of where they were now. Felix, right behind her, was also happy to be stopping for a bit.

"Where do you think he is?" Deborah asked Felix.

"I'm not sure. He could be anywhere out there," Felix responded, gazing out over the canopy below. "Let's see, we came in from that direction and circled that mountain. That means he moved into those woods there."

Staring out into the general direction of where they both believed Hawk could be, Felix and Deborah saw the large structure at the same time. Partially covered by a different mountain and a blanket of trees stood what could only be Deviant Hall.

"Do you see that?" Felix asked.

"Yes, I do. What do you think it is?"

"It must be the Stronghold! That has to be it!" Felix could not hide his excitement. "We are some ways away yet, but I think if we can find a crossing over that stream below, we should be able to be there late today or early tomorrow."

"Hawk must have seen it already. I wonder if he is there."

Deborah started back down the mountain in search of a way to get across the stream blocking their path. Felix stood overlooking the castle for a few seconds longer wondering the same thing before following Deborah down the mountain.

Felix took that brief moment to himself. Stumbling into Hawk days before had been an accident. The plan to take his life and rob him would have worked had Hawk not seen him first. Felix remembered Hawk standing over him as the knife in his neck provided the only pressure available, keeping him from bleeding out. *I could have sworn he spoke to me. But what was the other thing? Where was I?* Felix had no idea it was Deborah who pulled him from the clutches of death. If it were not for her, he would have passed like the multitudes before him who had no clue of the existence of the Green Light. He put his hand to his throat, his brow furrowed.

Chapter Fourteen

The moat was much too wide to try to jump over. Looking into the water, Hawk could see a greenish tint reflected back at him. The stream he followed did not look like this. This was different. The water did not seem *normal.* Instead, the water below seemed to be teeming with…*something…maggots, maybe?* Either way, the thought of falling into whatever it was below did not sit well with him.

Hawk studied the fortress in front of him. From where Hawk stood, it seemed he was at a corner of the castle. The walls were tall and made of stone. They were overrun with vines of ivy and thickets of blackberry brush as far up as he could see. Between the walls was the link Hawk needed if he were going to get across the moat. The wooden planks of the drawbridge jutted over the height of the walls holding it up like an old man who had lost all his teeth except for a last precious one. And from the looks of that one, the old man still hadn't thought to take care of it.

Hawk stood for a moment not sure of what to do next. Glancing down, he saw a rock large enough to lob. He chuckled at the thought of throwing the stone across the water and at the large rotten tooth. *This ought to get some-one's attention.* Hawk bent over, picked up the rock, and wound up to hurl it over the moat when just then the bridge began to move, stopping him cold, exposing as it descended two very large doors attached to the walls just behind where the decayed bridge was hinged.

The loud cracking and snapping had Hawk almost convinced the bridge would destroy itself before it reached the bottom. As the bridge came to rest on the ground before him, Hawk studied the structure, unsure if it was safe to pass over. The logs of the planks were broken and splintered. The existing wood of the bridge looked as if termites and grubs had been feasting on its innards for decades. The iron braces that held the planks together were well rusted and in some places missing altogether.

Hawk was not convinced the bridge could support the weight of a fly much less withstand the burden of a full-grown man. *Well, there's only one way to find out.*

Hawk picked his boards carefully before he gingerly began his way across the bridge. He stepped on the first board, testing the integrity of the wood. It held. Hawk took a second step, and then another, slowly shifting from board to board, making a point not to look over the side at the maggoty water below. The crossing began to bow as he reached the center point of the bridge. The creaks and groans below his feet did nothing to ease his nerves.

As Hawk moved away from center, the wood below his feet seemed sturdier. Hawk's mind eased slightly. *I just might make it.* He leaped forward, skirting across the remaining length of the bridge in three wide strides. The sweat on his brow as he reached the other side masked his feeling of relief. Finding his feet on solid ground again,

Hawk turned toward the bridge, still not believing he made it across when suddenly behind him, doors once hidden from view began opening in unison.

Startled, Hawk watched in awe as the large doors, double his height, slowly opened to the fullest. Beyond the entry, he could see within a courtyard lined with statues and structures, tall trees neatly surrounded by trimmed shrubs and bushes. It was nothing like the natural harshness of the woods to the right and left of where he was standing. Hawk was taken aback by the serenity of the garden. For a keep of legend such as this, he was expecting to see more of darkness and turmoil, not the peacefulness and tranquility that was before him.

A path of stone led to a landing just before another set of doors just beyond the courtyard on the opposite side of where Hawk stood. *That must be the entrance to the castle.* Hawk followed the path, careful not to stray left or right. He paused to gaze upon the statues. *Odd.* The cold stare of captured intensity filled their eyes, sending a chill down Hawk's spine. It was an intensity he had never seen before. To his left stood a small line of huts pressed against the fortress wall. Uneasiness filled his belly the closer he came to the castle doors.

A series of steps surrounded the landing, each carefully placed before the next, leading to the large, heavy, wooden doors of the castle. Hawk paused briefly before making his way up the steps. A rumble behind the massive structure startled Hawk as he reached out to make his presence known. As had happened before, the doors began to open slowly.

From within the shadows of the doorway, Hawk could see a foyer dimly lit by sconces lining the walls. "Hello?" he called out poking his head through the open doors to no response. "Hello!"

Slowly stepping forward, Hawk entered the castle. His heart pounding in his chest, he was attuned to every sound as his feet scraped across the floor. The doors slammed closed as he crossed beyond the threshold. Hawk jumped at the sound of the bang behind him. There was no turning back.

Studying his surroundings, he noticed a corridor that extended toward the left from the foyer he had entered. There, the lighting greatly improved as larger flames lined the walls exposing a long and widening hall. Hawk moved forward into the hall. Paintings of men lined the walls. He studied the portraits, noticing the different dress and weaponry each held as Hawk made his way down the passage. Some were old, some young. As Hawk continued moving down the hall, he came across one painting that looked vaguely familiar. He stopped to study it further when from directly behind him came a voice.

"I was much younger then."

Startled, Hawk jumped, instinctively reaching for his blade. Ehrig laughed heartily.

"Ehrig! That is you? What are you doing here?"

"Waiting."

"Waiting?"

"For you. Waiting for you to arrive. I see UY managed to guide you well."

"UY? Do you mean Timothy?"

"Ah yes, Timothy," Ehrig chuckled, glancing at the hand on the blade by Hawk's side. "You have excellent instincts, Hawk. That will serve you well here. Come, you have much to learn."

Ehrig turned and briskly lead Hawk down the corridor in the direction from which he came, across the foyer and back toward the entrance Hawk had used to enter the hall. "Where are we going?" Hawk asked as they started out. This question, too, went unanswered.

*   *   *

A series of stones formed a jagged path across the rushing water. Felix noted Deborah was tiring. So was he. "Let's rest for a bit."

"That's a good idea," Deborah responded. It did not take her long to drop her things.

"I have wanted to see this place for some time now, ever since I caught wind that it may actually exist. Talk back at The Rusted Lantern is how I heard the tale. I enjoyed spending time out in the hills. You will be surprised the things you can see there if you just know where to look. I…"

Felix was rambling again. Try as she may, Deborah simply could not recall ever seeing Felix at the inn. The feeling bothered her.

"So why are you here? What brings you to search for this place?" Felix asked as he found a place to lay his pack.

Deborah revealed nothing. Stretching her back and twisting her neck to break free the knots, she landed herself on the ground next to her pack and bow. "Where did you say you were from?" she said, shifting the conversation back to Felix.

"Shackleford…it's a bit of a distance away from here for sure," answered Felix.

"Shackleford?" Deborah thought back to her father. Though he did not often travel, she could not recall him ever speaking of Shackleford when he returned from an occasional trip. "I've never heard of it."

"As I stated, it is a bit of a distance away. Why do you ask?"

"Curiosity getting the better of me, I guess. How long before we get there do you think?" Deborah responded, deciding to let the matter go.

"Oh, we are close...I can feel it. We are definitely close," Felix said. A few minutes passed before he spoke again. Looking around, he said, "But we won't get there sitting here. Are you ready?"

"Not really, but I agree, we should continue."

As Felix lifted his pack onto his back, his arms raised, slightly exposing scars on his left side. She had not noticed them before now. Even when Felix had his shirt off over the river, they had not been visible. Deborah regarded them as she bent over and grabbed for her pack. Although she could not see the wounds, the shapes were oddly familiar: two lines evenly parallel to each other peaking slightly above his pants waist. She gazed at them while they were exposed, making sure not to stare. Felix headed out, not realizing Deborah's discovery.

She watched as Felix departed. Shifting her pack on her back and slipping her arm and head through the bow, resting it across her back, Deborah started out behind him.

Deborah suddenly thought of Hawk. She had not realized it until then and even though they had not been separated for very long, she missed him.

*   *   *

Ehrig exited to the landing overlooking the garden and started toward the stairs Hawk had used to approach the castle doors. Hawk walked only a few paces behind him. As he stepped through the threshold of the door, Hawk felt a hard push from behind. Caught by surprise, he stumbled and almost fell. As he tripped on the landing, the doors behind him slammed shut.

Still in the awkward posture of catching his balance, he found himself frozen in place, unable to move, as he had been back at Ehrig's cave when he had attempted to attack Ehrig after Deborah's murder. "What the h—" began to escape his lips when suddenly the bow and quiver disappeared and his clothing, including his leather boots, burst into flames.

The heat seared his flesh. Immobilized, he could neither writhe nor cry out as the flames engulfed him. He could not even close his eyes against the flames consuming his garments.

Ehrig stood watching. He made no move to help. His expression was one of bemused sympathy, but no more.

Through the flames that flickered up in front of his face, Hawk could do nothing but watch Ehrig watching him burn. He tried to scream; he wanted to cry; he could do neither. It was an eternity as the cloth and leather disintegrated under the flames. All that was spared was Hawk's blade and the sheath that held it.

Finally the flames withered and died out. Hawk was still unable to move. Ehrig walked up to him. "I wish you had waited out here for me. You do not enter Hex's house with the filth of the world upon you." He removed the blade from Hawk's side, turned and preceded him down the steps that led into the garden. "You will not need the other things while you're here."

The door opened behind Hawk and closed again. In his peripheral vision he could see two figures, a brute of a man and a girl. The two were a hideous pair. The brute was large and crude in his features, his hair coarse and unkempt. His strength was visually evident in the mass of his body. The servant girl was petite and pale. Hair of straw covered her awkwardly long face and draped over a thin frame.

A tide of water splashed over Hawk's back, up his neck, over his head, and down his face. The water helped cool the burning, but the sandpaper that followed, scraping over his back, counteracted the effect. Hawk was still unable to wriggle away from it or cry out. The scrubbing was thorough, involving his head, neck, back, buttocks, and both legs.

The brute moved in front of him, a huge bucket in his hands. Standing before the helpless hunter, their eyes met as he emptied its entire contents, emotionlessly sloshing Hawk's face.

Stepping away he allowed the girl to take his place. She was holding a long handled brush. She promptly applied it to Hawk's face scrubbing briskly as she did. Then she began working from the front of his neck, across his chest and arms, before scrubbing down his torso, along his groin, and down each leg, finishing at his feet. Pausing only once when she had gotten to his waist, she stepped aside and allowed the brute to drench him with another bucket then finished her task. Neither attendant spoke as they worked. Now that he could see the instrument with which she was torturing him, Hawk realized that the bristles of the brush actually appeared quite soft and pliable. Somehow this made the pain of the brushing he was receiving somewhat more tolerable.

Her chore completed, she again stepped away and Hawk received a final dowsing rinse from the water bearer. The girl then used a large, soft cloth to pat him dry. Taking her time, she was much gentler than she had been with the brush and Hawk was able to actually feel some embarrassment through his pain, as her hands were thorough in drying him.

Once more she moved away to be replaced by the brute. This time he gently covered Hawk with a light robe, then grasped Hawk's shoulders. As he did so, control returned to Hawk's muscles. Without the brute's steadying hands, Hawk would have fallen from his frozen stumbling position.

Ensuring that Hawk had his balance and his feet, the brute released him and moved back a pace to the girl's side. She curtsied. "My lord." Her companion nodded, and the two disappeared through the door with their equipment.

Hawk closed the robe that the brute had draped over his freshly rubbed body. He felt awkward as Ehrig approached him.

Ehrig looked him over. "You will not blister," he said simply. "Come with me." Ehrig stepped off the stone step walkway onto the grass and headed toward a gap between two of the small buildings in the courtyard.

The grass was cool and soft on Hawk's feet, and it was easier for him to walk there than the stones had been. He kept silent as he tried to keep up with Ehrig, who led him into the dark gap. It proved to be a dead end about ten paces in. Ehrig stopped, half turned, and leaned with his back against the wall. In front of Ehrig, Hawk could see three rings of pale blue light swirling in front of him. They floated just above the ground and were about knee high. "Step into them," Ehrig said.

"What?" Hawk suspiciously eyed the lights and then looked back at Ehrig.

"We must move along if we are going to keep on schedule. Come...follow me. You didn't come all this way to stand around in this alcove." Ehrig looked up and then stepped into the rings.

Before Hawk could say a word, Ehrig was gone. Hawk glanced up and around obviously not understanding what was happening, but he did not want to stay here alone. Cautiously he moved closer to the swirling rings. He could feel the energy coming off the rings as he allowed himself to be engulfed by them. Green.

Oh shit. Hawk realized he was now standing on a wooden floor in a room with three young women staring at him and giggling. The girls were smiling and their stares told the story. Hawk looked down and up again before he closed his gaping robe.

The girls had a different idea all together. They jumped toward him and began tugging at the cloth draped over his body. None said a word, but all continued to laugh and play about Hawk's body, their fingertips occasionally dancing lightly upon his exposed skin through the robe.

The women were gorgeous, each with attributes that would make any man yearn for their attention. Hawk was no different. Each wore a long dress with sheer fabric. The light passing through the cloth as they gracefully danced about him revealed their perfect bodies. His want for them showed. Doing the best he could to hide it only made matters worse.

One, a brunette, took Hawk's face with both hands and teased with a kiss, then leapt away. As she did, the others, a shoulder-length blonde haired one and a redhead, whose long soft red curls gracefully swayed with every move she made, pulled his robe away, exposing his semi-erect penis and pink-scrubbed skin. Hawk instantly covered himself as best he could.

Suddenly the play and giggling stopped. Hawk was rushed backward toward a lone chair in the room by the blonde and made to sit. Still naked, he folded his hands over his lap. The blonde disappeared through a curtained doorway as the other two made their way to tables loaded with wool, needles, and various tailor's tools sitting next to spinning wheels. Within moments the blonde reappeared carrying large bolts of heavy fabrics, one of almost pure white cloth, and started unrolling them on a large empty table. The dark haired girl and redhead began manipulating the wool, constructing a special thread. The blonde began cutting from the cloths, freehand, as the machines whirred softly behind her. Within a matter of minutes she handed each of the other girls various pieces of cut cloth, and they began binding them together.

As they sewed, the blonde again went behind the curtain. This time she returned with a roll of soft leather. Working just as quickly with a blade as she had with the shears, she cut the leather into the desired shapes. The redhead handed her work to the brunette and took the leather pieces to yet another table with larger versions of the tools. The blonde sliced another narrow strip of hide and engraved an intricate design upon its surface.

Hawk sat watching. The speed, dexterity, and coordination of their efforts left Hawk quiet with respect.

They finished their tasks simultaneously and converged at Hawk's chair. Lifting his feet, the girls slipped a new set of pants onto Hawk's legs. A fresh shirt was pressed over his head, covering his shoulders. Hawk completed the task of inserting his arms through the sleeves. The brunette, carrying a completed monk's tunic with a cowl, stepped behind him. The others each grasped a hand and pulled him to his feet. Raising his arms over his head, Hawk felt the tunic slipped on him and an inscribed leather belt wrapped around his waist. They again sat him in the chair.

The girls moved continuously, placing new socks and boots upon his feet and combing his hair. Then, with their tasks complete, the girls began to move away, looking back, smiling and waving at him as they left. As the brunette and blonde disappeared through the same invisible door from which Hawk had appeared, the redhead raced back and stole a long kiss. Giggling as she pulled away, inches away from him, she batted her eyes and smiled, then raced to catch the others. Just before she disappeared, she turned to him and curtsied. "My lord." Other than giggling, this was the only sound Hawk had heard from any of them.

"You must have fancied her most," Ehrig said from out of nowhere.

Hawk jumped to his feet startled. "Where did you come from?"

"The same place you did. The gardens. How does it fit? Are the boots comfortable? Come take a look."

Ehrig led Hawk to a full-length mirror hanging on a wall. "These are the most comfortable shoes I've ever worn," he said as he inspected himself. "The fit is perfect. How did they do that? They took no measurements."

"Of course they did," Ehrig replied. "It looked to me like you enjoyed it, too."

Hawk acknowledged the statement with a wry smile.

"If you had waited outside, they would have bathed you, too."

Hawk's smile reversed. "You could have warned me." He scowled.

"Come along. We have an appointment to keep," Ehrig said, ignoring the comment.

"With Hex?" Hawk queried.

"No. I don't think you want another encounter with him quite so soon. Do you?" Ehrig grinned broadly, turned and exited through a door that took them to a narrow street lined with shops.

*   *   *

The clouds were getting angry once more. Deb and Felix were nearing Deviant Stronghold. As Hawk had seen before them, the thick woods began to slowly thin and a small path came into view.

"We must be close!" Felix said with excitement. Deb followed closely behind, her emotions building as well.

The path broadened as they followed it. It was level, smooth, and a welcome relief from traversing the landscape. Their pace increased when they caught bright glints of reflected sunlight through the thinning trees. It was not long before it was apparent that the flashes were coming off a bright white wall—a castle wall.

Felix broke into a trot. Deborah maintained her brisk

pace but did not try to catch up. As the path wound through the trees of the forest, Felix could discern various sections of the wall, but was unable to get a clear view of what he was approaching. Nonetheless, his anticipation of arriving at his destination grew and with it, his pace. He was almost running when he broke the edge of the trees and found himself in front of the most amazing looking structure he had ever seen. Felix stopped.

The castle was huge. The walls were dazzling white. Its many spires seemed to rise endlessly into the sky. Felix stared. When he looked up at it, it appeared as though he could reach out and touch the monstrous structure, but Felix realized that it would take most of an hour to walk the distance.

Every castle or fortress that he had ever seen had been constructed of rough-hewn stone, gray and drab and coarse. This was gleamingly smooth. The walls were like the blade of the finest sword. He could not see a single mortared joint. It was like every part had been carved and polished from a single stone.

As he stood taking in the scene before him, Deborah emerged from the woods. "It is beautiful!" she whispered from behind him. "Look how it shimmers. The Light that is green surely dwells within this place." Without stopping she followed the path into the fields.

Felix stood there. *Light that is green?* Felix felt more than vaguely uneasy at the reference. He followed after her in less of a hurry than before. Slowly he closed the distance between them.

As they approached the castle, Felix's excitement grew again. He soon passed Deborah on the trail and hurried toward the entrance. Guards tended the entrance, but Felix ignored their presence as he attempted to access the inner dwellings of the keep. Their spears crossed smartly, causing Felix to stop suddenly.

"What business do you have here?" questioned one guard.

"I wish to see the Deviants. I am to make my bid!" Felix demanded.

"Tradesmen do not submit their propositions to Deviants." The guard laughed. Pushing the shaft of his spear against Felix's chest, he continued, "Go to the end of line and wait your turn. You will then be directed to the proper place." Felix looked around but saw no line.

"Do it!" the guard sneered.

Felix grasped the spear shaft and pushed it back. "I'm no tradesman. I am here to join—"

Before he could finish the sentence a hangman's noose at the end of a rope ensnared Felix under the chin and smoothly lifted him about a foot off the ground. Instinctively he released the spear and grabbed at the rope with both hands to relieve the pressure on his throat.

Deborah stopped short. She had not seen the rope appear, but Felix's feet leaving the ground got her attention. She stared. A rope about three feet long stretched above him with no visible means of support; it was simply suspended in midair with Felix dangling below it, legs kicking. As he hung from the air, Felix's tunic rose, exposing his midriff. There on his side was the scar that caught Deborah's attention before. This time it was fully exposed. Deborah stared at the mark on Felix's body in shock. She knew that cut! She had seen that mark before! Her surprise was transitory as Felix's choking brought her back to the moment. She rushed up to the guards. "Help him!" she pleaded. "What did he do?"

"It appears that he has offended one of the lords of the Keep." The guard smiled and then sighed. "I was hoping this would be a quiet watch. You are both under arrest."

*   *   *

"Then who?" asked Hawk. "And who *is* Hex, anyway? You have told me some about Sapient6, but it is Hex's name that kept dogging us on our journey. You have said practically nothing of him other than his name."

"There are two in all of existence that you do not want to meet. Hex is second on that list. The fulfillment of your quest requires Hex to be your goal. I am tasked to see that you are prepared to meet your goal."

"Prepared? I am ready to see him now!" Hawk said.

Ehrig smiled. "No one is ever 'ready' to see him. Now, about your appointment, let's see, how to get there..." he said, contemplating the journey, tapping his chin. "Walking will take half a day, and you cannot afford the time."

Ehrig stared at Hawk intently, then around at the people walking about the shops. As he contemplated, a smirk broadened into a wide grin. "A person of your namesake should really enjoy the pads." With a decisive pat on Hawk's back, Ehrig exclaimed, "Let's do that! Let's ride the wind!"

Hawk hustled behind Ehrig to keep up. As they approached an intersection of the cobbled streets, Hawk noticed a square in the middle of the junction that sparkled in the sunlight. There was little traffic in the street, but all were obviously careful to go around it. As the two men drew closer, Hawk could see that the sparkle came from inside the square itself and not from the glistening sunlight.

"It is easiest if you do not simply step onto the pad," Ehrig said. "Take several rapid steps as you approach. With your final step, plant your foot in the middle of the square, and then spring forward like you are about to leap over a fence. Holding your arms straight out from your sides will help your balance."

Hawk walked up to, then around the square, eyeing it suspiciously. "Then what happens?"

"You jump," Ehrig replied curtly. "You have jumped before, haven't you?"

Hawk walked up to Ehrig, looking him square in the eyes, and queried matter of factly, "This is another of your surprises, isn't it?"

Again Ehrig's broad grin greeted Hawk. "Of course. Now let us be on our way. Remember to hold your arms out to your sides for balance."

"We should walk. I didn't like the last thing you pushed me through, and I have a feeling I'm going to like this even less."

"Shall I toss you on it?" Ehrig countered even toned.

Looking into the man's eyes for a long moment convinced Hawk to attempt it under his own power. Again he circled the square glistening pad, inspecting it carefully. He was not sure what he expected to see or discover and wasn't surprised when nothing new was revealed to him. "From which direction should I approach it?" he finally asked.

Ehrig pointed down the street indicating that they would continue in the same direction they had been walking. Hawk moved half a dozen paces back up the street, stopped, looked at the object for a long while, and then held out his arms to the side, parallel to the ground. "I feel silly," he said, nervously.

"Go. No one is grading you."

With a small hop, Hawk started his approach. He veered off just as he reached the mark.

"You were doing fine," Ehrig opined. "Try it again. Place one foot into the middle with a spring forward."

Hawk gathered his courage and with a little less hesitation, took the short jog to the shining pad, sprung forward, and was instantly launched into the air. His initial reaction was to flail his arms, but it only took moments for his body to realize that his flight was stable in spite of the great speed and dizzying height to which he had been propelled. His arms felt strange as he held them out, like they were stabilizing him. Hawk could not bring himself to turn his head to look at any of the scenery that passed below him. Were the loose sleeves of his garment helping? Like the wings of a bird?

Suddenly something flashed in his peripheral vision. Then, there in front of him, traveling backward so as to face Hawk was Ehrig. "You are doing great for a beginner! Almost as if you were born for flight! Your father named you well!" He had to shout to be heard. Hawk did not have words to express how he was feeling. The look on his face told Ehrig all the information he needed without having to ask.

"You will find that as you approach the ground you will not be going as fast as you think you should be. Land as you took off: one foot, then the other, and run. You will see another pad about a dozen paces in front of you when you land. Do not break your stride! Just continue a smooth run onto it. We will have to make three more jumps to reach our destination. This landing will be on the soft ground of a pasture, the next will be on a street, then a pasture again for the final jump," Ehrig instructed loudly. Hawk only nodded in return, still looking straight ahead, not wanting to take his eyes off the course he was heading.

Gracefully Ehrig rotated in the air to face the direction of their travel. After turning, he seemed to run on the air for a short while and increased the distance between them noticeably. Hawk could see the rolling hills in front of him getting larger. Just beyond a lining of trees was large grassy patch of land. *That must be the pasture he was talking about.* They were descending now, and Hawk watched as Ehrig demonstrated the landing and take off techniques he had described.

As Ehrig rose in the air again after hitting the second pad, he turned to face Hawk and watched a near perfect landing and takeoff. Rising once again into the air, Hawk quickly caught up to Ehrig, who backpedalled a bit and matched Hawk's speed. "Our landing this time will be more of a jolt. Don't anticipate it. Just do it the same as before. It will not be a problem. It would appear that your natural talents extend beyond those of hunting, which you demonstrated."

Hawk beamed with excitement but said nothing as he focused on the task at hand.

As they approached the street, Ehrig again accelerated ahead of Hawk and landed first; however, this time he moved off to the side and stopped. He called to Hawk, "Keep going! I'll be right behind you!"

The wide smile on Hawk's face said it all. Without breaking stride, Hawk launched himself into the air for the third time. *I could grow to like this too much,* he thought as he rose high into the sky. This time Ehrig did not catch up to him as before. He made the landing and the final take off with pure joy at being high above the earth on his own. It was like the dreams of his childhood when he would fly high above the ground like a giant bird. *I must learn Ehrig's secrets to this!* Though Hawk was anxious to do what Ehrig had done during flight, he did not try experimenting on his own.

Hawk eyed another pasture ahead and prepared himself as he began to descend. His final landing was as flawless as the others had been, only marred when his fifth step squished his foot into the middle of a fresh horse turd. With a couple more steps he pulled to a stop, cursing out loud. Stepping into the manure did not bother him. Getting it all over his new boot did. He pawed at the ground with his foot to wipe off what he could, then pulled some of the long, lush grass to clean the rest. It was somewhat sticky, and his efforts not working very well.

Still cursing as he worked, Hawk almost jumped out of the boots when...

"Sir! Your language is appalling. Does your mother know..." Hawk turned toward the feminine voice whose approach he had not heard. "...HAWK!" Deborah shrieked, putting down the large bowl of steaming water she was carrying and throwing her arms around him. "I am so glad you're here!" she said softly.

Hawk almost did not recognize the girl in the peasant garb with a scarf covering her hair. Her use of his name brought recognition of the voice and the face. "Deborah! What are *you* doing here?" Holding her, feeling her head pressed against his chest made him feel warm inside.

"I was told to come out here and offer refreshment to a traveler..." she said, not moving away from him. "Oh, Hawk!

It was so wonderful. No. It was terrible. The castle was so beautiful, and then they arrested Felix and me! They say we have to stand trial tomorrow."

"They what? Arrested! What for?" Hawk said releasing her from his embrace. His look became serious as he waited for her to explain.

"We were arrested at the castle gate. I…" Deborah said as she bent over to clean Hawk's boot. Looking around and obviously worried, she continued, "I have to clean you up." As Deborah lifted the water, she noticed the clothing he was wearing. "Where did you get those clothes? You look so strange," she said pausing for a moment.

"As for what happened, I don't know exactly. Felix had gone ahead and was talking to the guard at the gate…" Deborah relayed the conversation between Felix and the guard, the rope, and her own arrest. "The other guard, after he told me I was under arrest, never said another word. He just led me toward the strangest doorway inside the gate and pushed me through. There was some kind of swirling light, then a flash of green, and I was here…dressed like this."

"A…what did Ehrig call that thing?" Hawk murmured to himself realizing Ehrig never did give *it* a name. "How long have you been here? What have they told you?"

"There is no one here! Just me…and the horses at that stable," Deborah said, indicating past Hawk and over the hill.

"But you said that you were told to refresh a traveler. Who told you that?"

Deborah sat down in the grass at Hawk's feet and put the cloth draped on her arm into the water bowl and wrung it out. She continued her tale as she worked to clean the filth from the boot on his foot.

"I don't know. It's like I have lived here all my life. I knew what I was supposed to do...my place. I have been feeding and caring for the horses for almost a month now. I really wasn't told that someone had arrived. I just knew it. I knew I was to come out here to meet you just now. I just didn't know that it would be *you*," Deborah said as she placed Hawk's left foot down and picked at the right with the rag.

"A month! How could you have been here for a month? I arrived at the Keep only this morning. You two could not have been far behind. Certainly not a month! Where the hell is Ehrig?" Frustrated he bent over, lifting Deborah to her feet. "He said he would be right behind me. And get up! It is not your duty to clean my missteps."

"Ahh, but it is. Tomorrow at court it will be your duty to clean up after her missteps...and Felix's." The voice behind him gave Hawk a start. He wheeled, his hand moving to his waist.

"Ehrig!" Deborah shouted.

"Ehrig! What is going on here? Why was—"

"You have been appointed to represent the two miscreants before Court of the Throne tomorrow," Ehrig interrupted. "I assume that you have been consulting with your client over her defense?"

"Her defense?" Hawk barked. "I don't even know what she is charged with. She doesn't know what crime was committed! I am no legal counsel. I'm a hunter. How am I supposed to defend her?"

Ehrig shrugged, waving off Hawk's concerns. "Those trivialities are not terribly important. Hex knows the details of the crimes and their motivations. Since you have gathered all the information here, I would suggest that you retire to your study to plan your defense," Ehrig said, snapping his fingers.

Chapter Fifteen

Hawk regained consciousness to find himself green. Nothing but green. *That son of a bitch has a lot to answer for!*

Hawk attempted to return to the pasture, but nothing happened. *I want to return!*

"Which son of a bitch?" queried a youthful voice. "Usually that means either Hex or Sapient6."

There in the dense fog of green was the form of a child sitting as if with his legs crossed beneath him on the ground, his elbows resting on his knees, his head cradled in his hands. Hawk could barely make him out from his surroundings.

"Ehrig! Them, too, everybody! I've been toyed with enough!" Hawk snarled in reply.

The voice coalesced into the form of a young man. "Oh, I quite doubt that." He smiled. "...and you aren't dead, anyway."

"What? Is that why I cannot go back?"

"Nah. You can't go back because you don't want to." The form disappeared then reappeared behind Hawk and seemed to be floating as if resting with one leg draped over a perch.

Turning to face the young man, Hawk said, "Now you are toying with me! Who the hell are you?"

The youth smiled even more broadly. "I am called Old Man, and I'm doing no such thing. I just came to see the cause of all the commotion for myself. Hex is right. You are special. Not that anyone could tell from the way you act. You aren't as nice to look at as the girl, though." Tilting his head and grinning, he said, "It was lovely meeting you, sir," Old Man said sarcastically. "Good luck at the hearing tomorrow. It should be fun."

The youngster sat up from his splayed position and began to blend into the otherwise all-encompassing green.

"You little turd! You can't just leave me here like this. What do you mean I don't want to go back?"

"I should," Old Man said sharply as he presented himself again, this time standing right in front of Hawk. "But you amuse me." Sticking his tiny finger against Hawk's chest, he said, "If you wanted to go back, you would. That's what I mean. Ithaqua explained that to you, did he not?"

"Who? Ithaqua?" Hawk was dumbfounded. He found himself, at the moment, at a complete loss. His anger forgotten, he said, "Ehrig is Wind Walker of the legends?"

Old Man's tone was that of sarcasm mixed with annoyance. "Special you may be. Bright? Maybe not. Yes, Wind Walker: the devourer of lost souls, he who removes the hapless from the mortal plane," the boy said as if mocking not Hawk, but Ithaqua himself. "It seems that you qualify as hapless if he stuck you here to keep you out of further trouble. Well…maybe not…you do have to appear before Hex. Now *that* should qualify you for hapless.

"That is why you don't go back. As much as you may want to, more than that," Old Man's voice changed to falsetto, teasing Hawk, "you want to rescue the fair damsel." His voice shifted again to the tone of a parent, "And you cannot do that by rampaging through the keep."

Old Man's stare caught Hawk offguard. He looked at himself to try to grasp what Old Man was looking for. As before, he could not see himself; he again was just awareness within the Light. But his awareness told him that Old Man was doing more than gazing into the green.

"How long do I have to stay? What, exactly, am I supposed to be doing while I'm here?" he asked.

"Ithaqua told you that time has no meaning here. You have all of eternity at your disposal. He could have done you no better." The youth was gone.

The sparkling cleared before Hawk's eyes. He blinked a couple of times and saw that he was seated behind a long wooden table. A half dozen paces in front of him was a large green chair with a middle-aged man sitting in it. The man radiated a green glow that reflected off and through the crystalline material upon which he was seated. The man's face was scarred into a perpetual frown. The eyes glared at him. "You are late."

Hawk rose from the wooden chair upon which he had been seated. As he rose he observed that Deborah sat to his left, Felix next to her. He pushed his chair back and walked around to the front of the table.

Still without speaking he sidestepped until he stood in front of Deborah with his back to her, then placed both hands upon the table and boosted himself into a sitting position upon it. "You are Hex." It was not a question.

"I am. You are late."

"No. I am not. I am Hawk...and I arrived when *I* was ready." Hawk spoke confidently, his tone bordering on arrogance.

Three guards, swords drawn, converged around the hunter, one on each side, one in front. The two at Hawk's sides pressed the tips of their weapons into his throat. The third turned in front of him and faced Hex. "My Lord?" he asked.

"Kill him." A new voice, cold as steel, filled the chamber, though it was no louder than an audible whisper.

Deborah slumped from her chair to the floor. Felix's eyes opened wide as Deborah fainted for no apparent reason, and he then turned his attention back to the events unfolding before him.

At the sound behind him, Hawk started to turn. With his movement, the tip of the sword at the left side of his throat punctured the flesh of his neck; the sword on the right followed his movement and maintained its pressure. Hawk flinched backward, causing the second sword to also pierce the skin of his throat. Neither wound was deep, but neither guard withdrew. Hawk froze; both weapons still invaded his flesh. Blood trickled down his neck and soaked into his robe. The realization hit him just as quickly: This was real. And so was his dripping blood.

Hawk was unable to see that at the moment Deborah had struck the floor, the two attendants who had bathed him at the castle's entrance appeared out of thin air and knelt beside her. The girl placed a wet cloth on the back of Deborah's neck; the brute gently lifted her unconscious form into his arms. He carried Deborah to the side of the guard in front of Hawk and stopped, facing Hex. The girl followed and dabbed Deborah's brow with a second wet cloth.

"Revive her. Then kill him," the same voice intoned. Hawk caught a glimpse of a black-cowled figure standing slightly behind the throne, stepping from the heavy curtains draped behind Hex.

Everyone remained silent as Deborah slowly regained consciousness. She shook her head and realized she was being held. She was struggling to gain her release from the arms of the brute when her body went limp. Try as she may, Deborah was unable to force her limbs to move. "That voice!" she managed to murmur. "I know that voice! It was in the Light." The softness of her tone could not mask the awe, and perhaps the fear, in her words.

Hawk heard her statement as the two swords clashed from within his throat. All but decapitated, he slumped to the floor.

In a blink, the cowled figure crossed the distance between the curtains and the brute holding Deborah. She could not see his face inside the hood of his cloak. He looked down at her without so much as a glance at Hawk's lifeless body. As before, his voice seemed to fill the room. "Do not disrespect he who sits upon the emerald throne."

"You murdering bastard!" she tried to scream, but again her words came only as a whisper. Felix sat speechless.

"Hmph," the cowled figure bellowed disgustedly, turned and began to slowly walk back toward the throne. "Give her her feet," he said as he moved away, waving his hand with indifference.

Maintaining control of Deborah's torso, the brute removed his arm from beneath her legs, gently lowering her. As Deborah's feet touched the floor she found she had control of her body again. The girl assisted in steadying Deborah. When the aides were sure that Deborah could stand, she was released and they stepped back behind the chairs at the table. Deborah leaned a hand upon the table to balance herself, then sank to her knees into the pool of blood that surrounded the hunter. "Hawk!" she cried. "What have you done?" She sobbed. Looking up at Hex through her tears, she added, "Why has his body not faded as before?"

"A lawful execution," Hex stated without emotion.

Hex's movement commanded the attention of all within the courtroom. "In the absence of a defense by your representative, you are found guilty of the charges before this court and shall be returned to the stables. Your servant's execution shall proceed as scheduled. Remove them." His voice resonated from the throne.

Upon hearing the pronouncement, Felix jumped to his feet. "Execution? Servant?" he gasped. Two guards were instantly at Felix's sides and grasped him under the armpits, lifting him from the ground. He began kicking, but as he opened his mouth, the third guard pressed his sword into Felix's abdomen.

"I am not her servant. What have I done? I have harmed no one. What have I done to deserve death? I demand to be released!" Felix yelled.

"Not another sound," the guard with the sword said between gritted teeth. "Your deeds are well known here."

Hex's eyes bored through him.

Felix stood quiet, strangely quiet. Until now, his life of crime had been unknown to anyone but himself and his victims. Mainly a thief, Felix had killed only a few men—necessary killings he believed: two after he was discovered robbing their homes and another outside a tavern in Falkenwrath. Felix was sure he had left no clues to his actions. Except for a few trophies he had kept, there was no evidence. Now he stood accused in front of strangers. *How does this man know my past?* he thought.

Nervously, Felix responded, "Deeds? I have done nothing wrong."

Hex leaned forward in his chair, glaring. "Do you dare deny your past?"

"I have not harmed anyone here," Felix stuttered.

"Return his belongings and release him!" Hex commanded.

The girl who had revived Deborah moved to her. Reaching down she gently put her hand on Deborah's shoulder. "My lady," she said softly.

Deborah slowly rose to stand before Hex. She took one step forward and stopped.

"Why?" she sobbed.

Hex stood and stepped down from the dais upon which the emerald throne rested. "Your journey began because of that question. At each turn during your travels the question was repeated. Now you continue to ask it here.

"This corpse remains. He cannot come back from the Light. That which is already here cannot come back here."

Felix grabbed his pack and put it on. Without regard he turned and yelled, "What gave you the right to kill Hawk?"

"This coming from a murderer! Remove him! Allow him another two years. Perhaps we can revisit his demand then."

Hex wheeled and strode to the curtains behind the throne and disappeared.

Deborah's attention turned to Felix as he was being carried out of the courtroom. The guards moved carelessly down the aisle toward the doors, then stopped and began stripping Felix's gear from him. Felix's things were haphazardly tossed about the aisle. A guard tore the pack off of Felix's back and flung it over his shoulder, not looking at the direction of where he was throwing it or caring where it would land. Felix's tossed bag landed by Deborah's feet; the flap opening before her, its contents spread across the floor. There in the mouth of the sack was a dual mounted blade. It was the same blade that had caused the wound on Felix's side. The very blade Deborah had given her husband as a symbol of her love. It was meant to protect Robert from danger. It was meant to keep Robert safe.

The guards grabbed Felix by the arms and began dragging him down the aisle again. As Deborah watched Felix's back through the tears in her eyes, feelings of grief for her husband flooded her mind, her body, her soul. The emotions she had managed to bury were exhumed in an instant, intensified, rooting her in place. There, at that moment, she understood.

Deborah watched as the guards ushered Felix out the door. She hoped to find out what had happened to her husband but she never thought she would find out this way. The question of her husband's death had been answered. From the depths of her emotions a new question emerged: *Felix, why?*

* * *

"Hehehe."

Hawk stood in disbelief at this child mocking his circumstance.

"Did you really think you stood a chance by acting so bold?" Old Man asked, floating with his legs dangling as if sitting on a table.

"I thought I had the right to arrive as I saw fit. Ehrig told me that. You reminded me of that!"

"Do you mean Ithaqua? And just what were you trying to accomplish by challenging Hex in his courtroom?" the boy asked, still laughing. The humor was lost on Hawk.

"I was not trying to challenge anyone. I still don't understand why I was selected to represent them anyway. From what I could see, they have done nothing wrong. No one has actually charged them with anything."

"Maybe, maybe not. What's the difference anyway? Hehehe!" Old Man was having too much fun at Hawk's expense.

"What do you mean what's the difference? Their difference is obvious! Deborah is a good woman. Her heart is pure. She has been beside me since that night on the ridge. Since that time, I have seen nothing of her nature that would lead me to believe she would harm anyone."

"I see. But she travels with the other man. His heart is not so pure?" Old Man probed.

"He worries me. His heart I don't know, but mine tells me that he is not to be trusted. But that is also not of her doing. I would have to accept blame for that as well. When I left in the night, I got lost. So I continued on, hoping she would find her way. It wasn't until after I met her in the pasture that I knew she was safe. I don't know what is being expected of me, but I know Deborah. She is not a criminal."

"And what of the other? What do you know of him?"

"I know nothing of him. I know he came upon me in the woods." Hawk stopped short of explaining what occurred following the discovery of Felix.

"Hehehe, you are not telling me everything there is. Do you think I don't know?"

"I couldn't begin to tell you," Hawk replied.

"Perhaps then, I should tell you. It was an excellent kill! I had the pleasure of seeing this man after you sent him here to die. We all did. And he would have, if not for her. She found him and took pity. If it not for her, he would have faded."

"Why am I here?" Hawk asked.

"This is a good question, one that deserves an answer. Do you feel your heartbeat?"

"No."

"Do you draw breath?"

"No, I don't."

"Still your mind continues regardless, if you will it to do so. The answer is simple. Yet many fail to comprehend it." Old man giggled. "Your answer is 'time.'"

"Time?"

"Yes! Time! Time has no meaning here. No meaning because time does not exist!"

"I'm afraid I, too, don't understand. How can time not exist?"

Old Man smirked. "You wish to understand time? Time cannot be explained, only experienced. This place does not exist and experiences no time. There is no better place for you to explore this. You are the hunter. Hunt for time here."

"You're not making sense," Hawk retorted. "Hunt for time where it does not exist? I thought you were going to help me. What does this have to do with what I am supposed to do?"

"Since what has happened out of the Light cannot be changed, what has occurred is permanent. But! Since time has no meaning, no limits, no barriers, or confines, it can be used. Time is change. It is deviance from what is. The Light is Deviance itself. It does not change!"

"More riddles and contradictions." Hawk sneered.

Old Man sighed. "A hint. A hint is the best I can do for you: The Light is the window to the universe. From here all that has been, all that will be, all that could have been, all that could be, is accessible. Hunt for time here."

"You are telling me I can go back and do the trial again? How?"

"No, the trial cannot be changed, but yes, you can go back. Back to any point in time you like. And from that point, you may continue and the knowledge you have gained remains! Use your mind. Search for the details you wish to revisit. What do you see?" Old Man asked.

"Nothing."

"Nothing? Concentrate."

Hawk struggled. Visions of the events in the courtroom, Deborah and Felix, the voice in the chamber, Hex on the dais—everything cluttered his mind. He could not separate one from the other.

"You must concentrate!" Old Man insisted, his young voice becoming stern. "Focus on one thing, find a point that stands out in your mind and grasp it!"

Suddenly Hawk could see the trial as it occurred. He watched as the guards took his life. He felt the piercing of the blades and the shock of death. Then almost as quickly as it started, the image had faded.

"What just happened?" Hawk asked.

"You have taken a very large step. You are much closer now. Use what you have learned and go. You have to start over."

"I don't know what to say. I still do not know what my business here is."

"Don't worry, you will know. It will come to you."

Hawk remained in the Green. He wondered if he would know what to do if he could get back to the courtroom. Having explained everything he knew to Old Man helped order his thoughts. Now Hawk worried if he would be able to convey his feelings to Hex in a way that would clear Deborah and Felix of the charges against them.

Chapter Sixteen

The brute and the girl escorted Deborah to her seat. As she took her place, the doors in the rear of the courtroom were pushed open as two guards ushered Felix, shackled at the wrist and carrying his packs, toward the table and chairs where the defendants would make their pleas. The guards removed the chains from Felix's wrists, turned, and departed the courtroom. Deborah sat at the end of the table opposite Felix, the chair between them empty.

Ehrig sat in the back row. Except for the hunter's decapitated body that remained on the floor and the shifting of players, everything was as before. No one seemed to notice, much less care, about the corpse that lay before the table where Deborah and Felix sat.

Hawk emerged from the Light.

"You are late."

From between them, Hawk rose from his chair, walked around the table, stepped over the body on the floor, and stopped between the table and Deborah's view of the man on the emerald throne.

"I am Hawk...and I arrived when summoned."

A quiet voice filled the room seemingly coming from

everywhere. "A nice touch, mixing truth with death."

Deborah leaned forward and whispered to Hawk's back, "Hawk, that voice! That's the voice that spoke to me!"

Hawk turned around, a look of surprise on his face as their eyes met. Deborah nodded, confirming what was running through Hawk's mind. This was the voice she heard when she was in the Light. This was the voice that allowed her to save Felix after Hawk killed him. Felix sat quietly, his head turning slightly, his eyes searching to find the source of the voice.

The voice continued, "More truth." A black-cowled figure stepped from behind the throne and closed his distance to Hawk. "Your own deaths do not bother you. You bring them with you."

As the figure approached with Hawk intently staring at him, Hawk realized the cowled cloak was not black but the deepest green of the forest on a moonless night. The words that were being spoken did not emanate from the figure; they were much more like those that he heard while in the Light—he was not hearing them at all—they were part of his consciousness. But Deborah was aware of them, too. Hawk stole a glance at Felix. *What about Felix? Was he aware of what is being said?*

Felix sat unusually still, his stare frozen on the cloaked figure standing before the table.

The resonance of Hex's voice forced Hawk's attention forward once more. "You used the Light well, young hunter. Your defense of your two...*friends*...is effective. The charges against them have been dismissed. You are free to go," Hex said as he stood, turned, and disappeared behind the emerald throne.

The figure draped in the heavy, hooded cloak turned and started toward the exit behind the throne but stopped a foot in front of Hawk, facing him. Hawk stared into the cowl and could discern no features; looking into the cowl was like staring down a deep well. The intensity of the being in front of him caused a shiver down Hawk's spine.

At Hex's pronouncement of his freedom, Felix jumped to his feet. "What the hell was that all about?" he exclaimed. "What defense? What charges? I spent two years in that damned dungeon. For what?"

The cowl turned slightly in Felix's direction; the voice, no longer quiet, cut with cold iciness. "Find a god in which to believe. Pray that you are never in this court again." The figure rotated, and in a moment he, too, was gone.

From behind them came a familiar voice. "Come. It is time for you to see," Ehrig said.

Felix turned toward the new voice behind him. "Who the hell are you?" he demanded.

"Ehrig!" Deborah gushed, running up to him and embracing him in a hug. Crying, she said, "Thank you for bringing Hawk back. Hex said he couldn't come back."

Ehrig slowly disengaged himself from Deborah's arms and said to her, "I did not bring him back." He smiled at her and wiped her tears, then turned toward Hawk.

Felix gasped as the green engulfed him. He bent forward slightly and reached out with his hands. Not feeling the table, he bent further. He still did not touch it. Felix cautiously took a step forward, then a half dozen. He should have bumped into it; he did not. The green that enveloped him was all pervasive. He straightened and lifted his hands to his face but could not see them, even when he covered his eyes with his palms. Slowly he shuffled forward; his toe kicked the first step of the dais where Hex had sat upon the emerald throne. In his blindness he carefully raised his foot and took the first step up toward where he remembered the throne to be.

At the sound of Felix's sharp intake of breath Ehrig, Hawk, and Deborah turned in his direction. The Green Light surrounded them as well, but they could see Felix's shadowy form groping for something substantial. As Felix slowly made his way toward the dais, Deborah stole a glance around her. The table and the chairs were gone; the entire room was empty except for the dais and the throne upon it. At the far opposite end was the huge round table surround-ed by sixteen chairs, tipped forward with their backs leaning upon its edge. Her attention turned back to Felix just as he stubbed his toe on the lower step of the dais. Hawk had moved and was now standing beside Ehrig, his eyes moving from Ehrig's twisted grin to Felix and back again. Hawk's brow was furrowed in puzzlement.

"Come," Ehrig said quietly as Felix raised his other foot onto the dais and stood there trying to decide what to do next. Felix gave no indication that he had heard Ehrig's voice.

"Is he…" Hawk whispered.

"…stupid enough to continue up to the throne?" Ehrig finished for him with a chuckle. "If he is, he will need that god sooner than he expects. But no, he will sit on the step. Now come."

"Can't Felix see?" Deborah asked. "He is moving like a blind man."

"No," Ehrig replied, "nor can he hear. His senses per-ceive the world as you do when you are in the Light. Only the green exists for him. His test now is to see if he can survive the Light here on the mortal plane. This is the test I had initially planned for Hawk, until you followed."

Ehrig took their arms and turned them away from Felix, walking them toward a wall. As they approached, Ehrig dropped his grip on Hawk's elbow and reached his hand out to the wall. It began to glow an even brighter green than that which surrounded them. "You may step through here." Ehrig stepped back a pace and placed his hands between each of their shoulder blades. The slight pressure prompted them to take a step forward.

"Show her around. I must tend to Felix now," Ehrig said as the light they stepped into engulfed them. Then Ehrig was gone.

Now there was nothing to see except each other.

Deborah turned a full circle. "Show me around? There is something to see? Besides green?"

Hawk began to concentrate. Suddenly the Great Hall of Deviant Hold appeared before them. They were looking down from the ceiling. In front of them was the table where they had sat during the trial; further ahead was the dais with the throne. Hex sat on the throne; Deborah and Felix sat next to each other. There was an empty chair at the end of the table next to Deborah. Deborah seemed to be looking around the hall nervously. Deborah gasped when she saw herself being escorted by the brute and girl to the empty chair at the end of the table.

Deborah watched herself. She was sitting in both chairs now—the one at the end and the one in the middle.

A few moments later Hawk materialized into the scene. He, too, was sitting in both chairs. Not on Deborah's lap, nor she on his. They both occupied the chairs as if the other were not there.

Deborah gasped again. "How can that be?" she whispered, turning to Hawk and seeing his eyes closed and brow furrowed as he concentrated intently.

The scene faded. She and Hawk were alone in the green again.

"I couldn't hold it any longer. It showed what I wanted though," he said quietly.

"What was that?" Deborah asked again.

Her curiosity demanded answers. Hawk was beginning to explain when the green of the Light flared. When the flash subsided, the form of a man lay gasping in front of them, his left leg missing at the knee. Twenty paces from him was another hulk of a man, cut in half at the waist and his right arm severed just below the shoulder. The three pieces of his body lay a few paces apart. The first's lower leg was nowhere to be seen. Neither was bleeding.

Deborah shrieked in horror.

"What the hell!" Hawk exclaimed.

"Go to hell yourself," the first man sneered, raising an arm toward Hawk. "Help me up!"

Still in shock and without thinking, Hawk reached for the injured man, who grasped his wrist and pulled. The man hopped a time or two to get his balance on his remaining leg.

"Thanks." He smiled down at Hawk.

"You're hurt! What happened?" Deborah managed to blurt, staring at the large man before her. His frame was nearly twice the size of Hawk's.

"I'm okay," the man said. "Nice shot," the man called, yelling toward the second man in the distance. To Hawk, he said, "You can let go now. My leg will be whole in a moment."

Hawk and Deborah looked down and gaped again. The leg then foot of the man before them were restoring, first repairing the muscle and tissue torn or missing from the wound, and then covering itself with newly formed skin.

"I am okay," he repeated. "We have to get back to the arena."

He pulled his wrist from Hawk's grasp and trotted over to his companion, who himself had been restored and was getting to his feet. They could see now that the first wore some kind of armor that made him look much larger than he already was. They had never seen armor like this before.

"Not nice enough," the second snarled as the first man reached his side. "I should have been able to dodge that cannon. You ready?"

"Sure," came the reply as the first man slapped his companion's shoulder.

Hawk and Deborah had slowly followed behind them, their curiosity overcoming their shock at the sudden appearance of this strange pair. As they approached, the green of the Light beneath the men's feet suddenly darkened to almost black and began to swallow them before the eyes of the bewildered pair. Hawk broke into a trot to close the gap; Deborah followed his lead.

They stopped at the edge of the darkened area and peered into the blackness. As their eyes adjusted, they could see the man in the armor dodging through trees and without breaking stride snagging a weapon like the one Ehrig had used in the cave. Almost immediately he fired and a ring of gas began to expand as it quickly moved away from the slender barrel of the weapon. They could not see the target among the trees, but as the ring exploded into a flower shaped burst of energy, a shower of blood and chunks of flesh rained from behind a tree.

Hawk and Deborah turned and looked at each other for a moment, then, without a word, surveyed the area around them. There was no flare in the Light and nothing appeared within sight. They turned back to the scene of the forest, and then looked at each other.

Still without speaking, they each took a step in the direction of the darkened green.

"You really do not wish to go there." A familiar voice halted their advance. "Oberon will kill you without a thought."

Startled, they spun around. Ehrig was only a pace behind them. "The rules in the arena are unlike those of the world. Entering the arena uninvited is a sentence of true death. Your quest here is not yet complete and Oberon would only gain strength from killing you...not that he needs it."

"What were they doing?" Hawk asked as Deborah asked simultaneously "Who were they?"

"Honing their skills. Working toward a better outcome in their next match, though they are not half as good in the arena as you two will be."

"Arena? What arena?" asked Hawk.

"*The* Arena. It is the ultimate test of a being's abilities. It is in the arena where a man's heart and character are truly tested. That is the reason very few become Deviants. That is the reason why I search throughout time for proper candidates. It is the very reason you were brought here."

"Brought here?" responded Deborah. "How was I brought?"

"You searched for answers. You joined Hawk, not for his purpose so much as your own. No, child, it was not by accident you met him. You were brought as Hawk was brought." Turning to Hawk, he added, "It is the reason for your dreams as a child and why I observed you then."

"I knew it! I knew it at the first moment you walked into my room at The Rusted Lantern." Hawk recalled the stranger that had visited in his youth, the mysterious man whose stories kept the children of Rothersbucke captivated for hours.

Deborah stood there, not understanding the transaction between them. And not without her own questions, either. Deborah approached Ehrig intently, looked him straight in the eye. "Just who are you?" she asked.

"My name is Ithaqua."

Deborah fell back a step. Her eyes went wide with surprise and shock. Every hair on her body bristled at the revelation. "*The* Ithaqua? You…are the…Wind Walker? You are he that—"

Ithaqua smiled. "Yes, 'he that devours lost souls.' It is mine to search out those with potential for Deviance. And to remove those that fail. Most fail. It is the reason your father's friend Fredrick did not make it home."

"You killed Fredrick?" Deborah inquired in horror.

She was only a child when Fredrick departed on his own quest toward Deviant Hold. Deborah could not remember the details, but she would never forget the pain and anguish on her father's face when his best friend was discovered dead on the side of a mountain. She could still hear her father swearing that Fredrick was a fool to even try such a thing, but Fredrick was determined to see it through. Now, here she was standing beside the man she believed took his life.

Deborah became angry. "Why did you have to kill him? If he was not destined to become a Deviant, why allow him to make the journey!"

"I do not encourage or dissuade those who seek Deviance, Deborah. That is not my charge," Ehrig said passively.

"But did you have to kill him because of it?" Deborah said, her emotions getting the best of her.

"I didn't kill Fredrick. I removed him...as I do all who fail on their quest. There was no point in taking his life. His life was already coming to an end."

"What do you mean, Ehrig?"

"I can't predict a person's death any more than you can. Nor do I cause the failure of the quest or of the life."

Hawk did nothing but listen to the exchange. There was not anything he could add to Deborah's claim, but the anger in Deborah's tone took him by surprise.

"But you were there my whole life! You have been in my home since I was a child," she said choking back tears of anger and sorrow. "Yet you devoured his soul, you son of bitch!"

"I am Ithaqua...Deviant. You refer to Ithaqua...legend... based in fact, lost in details, a story told over and over. Fredrick's soul was his own to find—or lose. As was yours, and Hawk's, back in my home when you each went into the Light. Had either of you failed to return from the Light, your fate would have been similar to Fredrick's. You would have died the true death and your bodies dissipated, as you saw, in a shower of golden sparks. You would have been returned by me to your families—as was Fredrick."

"You? You brought him back? You said you removed him."

"Yes, this is true. I removed him from our plane back to yours."

"Why didn't you tell me then?"

"Because you were not prepared then as you are now."

"Prepared? Prepared for what?"

"To become Deviants, Deborah," Hawk said slowly, cautiously.

"I have brought you before Hex, and he has found favor in you both. Sapient6 agrees. But those are not the only eyes that have been watching you. Every Deviant has been watching! At the appropriate time, you will be brought before the group, and each will have his say. Find favor with all Deviants and you will be accepted. Failure to capture but one vote, and your quest will end," Ithaqua said. "You have come a long way. Do you wish to continue?"

As Ithaqua finished his question, both felt the cold chill of death pass through them.

Hawk and Deborah stood fast. Each could hear the loud thumping in their ears caused by the pounding in their chests. It was time to make a decision. A decision brought upon them unexpectedly but...

Ithaqua stood patiently, as he had for all the previous years of their lives, while Hawk and Deborah struggled within themselves with the weight and finality of their choices.

Deborah looked over to Hawk and caught him as his serious face began to melt. The corner of his mouth curled slightly as his mind was lost in thought. She turned and faced Ithaqua. "I wish to continue."

Hawk looked at Deborah and saw the seriousness that accompanied the tone. His eyes turned back to Ehrig.

"Yes," was all Hawk said.

"And what of Felix?" Deborah asked in the same dark voice.

"He, too, will have to answer the very question I've brought before you," Ithaqua answered. "Like your own, his path has not been etched, either."

Ithaqua roared with laughter, his belly jiggling above his belt. "Come, we have things to do."

The Green Light began to fade. Hex's voice resonated as they found themselves back in the courtroom.

"You used the Light well, young hunter. Your defense of your two...*friends*...is effective. The charges against them have been dismissed. You are free to go." Hex stood, turned, and disappeared behind the emerald throne.

The figure stopped a foot in front of Hawk and looked at him. Hawk stared into the cowl and could discern no features; looking into the cowl was like staring down a deep well.

At Hex's pronouncement of his freedom, Felix jumped to his feet. "What the hell was that all about?" he exclaimed. "What defense? What charges? I spent two years in that damned dungeon. For what?"

The cowl turned slightly in Felix's direction; the voice, no longer quiet, cut with cold iciness. "Find a god in which to believe. Pray that you are never in this court again." The figure turned and in a moment he, too, was gone.

Two guards approached Felix and tossed his bag at his feet. Felix angrily reached down and picked it up, swinging it over his shoulders.

As he stood upright, Deborah approached him. The intensity of her stare was enough to send a shiver down his spine. "I know now why I am here."

Felix glanced around but said nothing, not quite sure what Deborah was talking about.

"It is my understanding you wish to become a Deviant, Felix. Is that your intention?" Ithaqua asked.

"Yes, that has always been my intent."

"And with all that you have experienced, you wish to continue?"

"Without a doubt," Felix said.

"So be it."

* * *

The Great Hall, which served as the courtroom where they stood, had been standing for an eternity. Uncounted souls had faced Hex within the confines of these walls. Every piece that furnished its interior was built from the finest materials, not only from this world, but also of worlds scattered throughout galaxies, each item intricately detailed by hands convicted before the throne, serving sentences preferred to the alternative. The painstaking detail and craftsmanship dictated an eternity to learn the craft and another eternity to complete—the better to be served by those whose crimes disrupted the sanctity of Deviant Stronghold.

Ithaqua led the three down the aisle to a set of very large, immaculately crafted, double doors hinged on a solid frame of Narra. As in every feature and detail throughout the vast room, these doors were flawless. Even more surprising was what was waiting for them on the opposite side. Ithaqua reached out and opened the doors, pulling them inward.

The contrast was immediate. Unlike the Great Hall, here there was nothing to admire. Nothing was maintained or cared for in any fashion. The room was dirty. Cobwebs lined the corners of the walls and ceilings. A lone chair next to the doors they had just exited sat empty, cracked and worn. The foyer was dark and damp, broken only by dimly lit sconces that announced several exits.

"This way." Ithaqua walked toward an opening between two sconces. The doors behind them closed as they crossed the threshold, but no sound was emitted as they came together. Deborah looked back at the entrance. The lack of sound struck her as odd.

"Where are we going?" Felix whispered to Hawk. A shrug, shake of the head, and Hawk's furrowed brow was his only reply.

"Shhhhhhh! In these tunnels, the slightest voice can be heard for miles," Ithaqua scolded. Ithaqua's sudden scolding caused Felix to flinch and take a step back. The confusion in his eyes was shared in all their faces.

"Here…stand right here." Ithaqua guided Felix to another cavity between different sets of sconces, then walked back to the original opening he had approached, mouthing to all three in a barely audible voice, "Now pay attention."

Sticking his head slightly into the mouth of the tunnel, Ithaqua let out a whispered "Ha." Pulling out and snickering, he ran to the side of Felix, grabbed his arm, and crouched slightly behind him. Felix, unsure what was happening, stood his ground next to Ehrig. Hawk and Deborah maintained their places just forward of the now closed doors. No one knew what to expect.

At first there was nothing…nothing except Ithaqua's obvious excitement. Then a faint vibration began to tickle the bottoms of their feet. The ground in the decayed room began to tremble slightly. Hawk and Deborah huddled a little closer together. Felix started to step away from the opening but Ithaqua held him steady. Dust fell about them in the darkened space.

"Here it comes! Here it comes!" Ithaqua said. His eyes widened; the smile on his face was broad as he filled with anticipation.

The room began to shake violently as the earthquake hit. From in front of the tunnel, Felix grabbed onto Ithaqua. The force of the blast of wind that hit them was incredible with the thunderous "HA!" that accompanied it. Felix was knocked back, but Ithaqua held him up. Screaming, eyes bulging, Ithaqua was yelling along with the loud noise and staring at Felix right in the eyes within inches of his face.

The noise was so loud that Felix couldn't hear him. The explosion, coupled with the look on Ithaqua's face, caused Felix to scream out as well. Their hair and clothing were blown backward as if they were standing in a tornado. As the sound began to fade, Ithaqua's voice slowly began to emerge. "Hahahahahahahahaha!"

Felix fell to his knees.

"Hahaha! I love doing that!" Ithaqua exclaimed. Slowly regaining his composure with a big grin on his face and a finger to his mouth, he turned to them. "This way now."

The passage they walked through was lined in cobwebs and algae that shimmered green in the awkward and minimal lighting that marked the way. Their footprints followed them as they made their way through the damp dust carpeting the ground.

It was a maze of tunnels. The three followed closely behind Ithaqua as he led them from tunnel to tunnel. Smiling and with purpose, Ithaqua stepped haphazardly around the clutter upon the ground. Occasionally, the group passed a door, but Ithaqua paid no attention to it. The twists and turns of the passages left the three followers completely disoriented as Ithaqua navigated his way down through the bowels of Deviant Hold. No one whispered a word.

Finally stopping in front of a small door, Ithaqua pulled out a ring of keys and opened it. Waving his hand, he ushered the three inside a cramped room where another access awaited. Closing the entrance behind them, he turned saying "Ah...here we are. Are you ready?" The excitement in his voice caused the words to sound childlike. "In this room lies the start of your training. Pay close attention, and you will do fine."

Brushing past the group, Ithaqua pushed opened the second set of doors. A bright light blinded them as their eyes fought to adapt to the sudden assault. As they adjusted to their surroundings, a serene calm enveloped them. It was as if they had stepped back outside the confines of Deviant Stronghold, back out into the woods from where they came. The space they had entered was filled with trees and rock. Sounds of a nearby brook could be heard, birds chirped, and they could feel the caress of a light breeze on their faces.

Ithaqua escorted them into the new room and then retreated back through the door. "Remember, pay close attention, and you'll be fine," Ithaqua stressed, pointing out toward the trees. Then he closed the door behind him, exiting the room and leaving them standing alone.

They stood there, and for a moment no one moved. The sounds of the woods filled the air. Peaceful. Calm. Then the stillness broke.

Hawk's instincts caught the sounds first. He could hear brush moving in the distance. He tried to pinpoint the direction of the sound but couldn't. It was not much longer before all three could hear the noise. The rustling in the bushes was so quick that none could follow the sound or tell from which direction it came. Here! There! Surrounding them! The group huddled together as the noise got louder and louder...closer and closer. Then from out of nowhere, a flash overhead! The ground in front of them exploded! *Boom!*

The explosion was immense. Dust and debris covered them as they found themselves on the ground. Shaking his head, Felix looked up and saw her. She was tiny, frail, and wearing next to nothing. The clothing she did have on was tattered and worn, serving to cover only what was necessary.

The waif approached them, a large cannon propped against her shoulder. She looked at them one at a time, surveying each. "Hmph. Do you know where you are?"

Hawk and Deborah immediately recognized what she was holding. It was the same weapon Ithaqua used to introduce Deborah to the Light. The same she used to enter the Light alone. Felix had no clue what she was holding but could not take his eyes off it, either. No one said a word.

"This is a training ground...and a proving ground." Pointing out into nothing she continued. "I've been tasked as your instructor. We'll be covering everything you'll need to know about weapons, tactics, and maneuvers. Do what I tell you and your chances of survival in the arena will greatly improve." The waif turned away, walked a few paces, and then stopped. "I am Megan," she said still facing the trees. "There are many new toys out there. You will get the chance to spend time with each."

"What the hell is that thing?" Felix whispered to Hawk as she moved away from them.

"You have a lot to learn," she said. Turning her head, her gaze bore directly into Felix, "so I suggest you pay attention."

*   *   *

Their skills were progressing rapidly with each new technique and weapon Megan introduced.

At first Felix had been disdainful of being trained by a female. As the days passed, he started keeping his opinions to himself and began to apply each lesson in earnest. Hawk was not sure whether it was due to Megan's undeniable skill or to the fact that Deborah had clearly advanced beyond him. In any case, Hawk was happy to not have to listen to the other man's complaints. For her part, Megan seemed to be oblivious to Felix's attitude and progressed his training without change before and after he had begun to apply himself. Deborah merely noted that, while Felix had not fallen far behind, he quickly caught up.

The only difference between the trio was Felix's ability in dealing with the Light. He continued to have trouble returning after being eliminated in their mock battles. Twice he had to be rescued by Megan after she unceremoniously sent him there. Hawk and Deborah, however, were finding their use of the Light was becoming almost second nature.

Although time was meaningless in the Light, what was spent in training was anything but. Over the course of the training, all three had become more fluid in movement and accuracy. Hawk was amazed at how even his own body and agility, honed over the years of hunting and being a woodsman, hardened and sharpened under Megan's eye.

Their jumping and dodging skills, vital in these games, were all but learned. No longer were any of the students standing still to take a shot, which always earned them another trip into the Light from Megan's ruthless accuracy.

Deborah became convinced that Megan's aim was purposely off by the degree of skill that they demonstrated— she never seemed to miss completely, but the severity of their wounds, or a trip into the Light, always went hand in hand with the praise or criticism she bestowed.

*   *   *

Wounds. This introduction tore into Felix's mind much in the same fashion that Hawk and Deborah had theirs ripped. In the beginning, their training seemed unfathomable. *How can wounds, certainly mortal, heal?* But they did.

The lectures that Megan used to interrupt the physical training were, at first, a welcome respite for their bodies. It was not long before they realized that the information given during these lessons taxed their minds to the limits and left them even more exhausted.

It was during one such break, early in their training, that Felix challenged Megan on the role of the Light in the arena. Megan was kind enough to use herself as the example, although the way she did it was anything but kind. As she led the introductions to the various weapons that lay about the field, the group was sitting in a semicircle in front of her when the obvious question was asked. One she had apparently anticipated.

"What happens if you are actually shot by that?" Felix asked. "We get our bruises and scrapes. They hurt when they happen, but then they just go away within seconds."

Megan looked at him, expressionless, as if considering her answer. Suddenly a weapon they had not seen before appeared in her hand. Without hesitation she fired. What looked like a thick liquid landed between his feet. A very distinct popping and sizzling sound emitted from the glob as it flew through the air. Two drops, each the size of a small copper coin, splattered on his right boot.

Felix flinched and jumped to his feet. Looking down at his foot, he saw that it was not a liquid but a mass of very, very tiny worms, much smaller than the size of a gnat, crawling over each other. The popping and sizzling sound grew louder as twin wisps of gray smoke rose from beneath the corrosive material.

Felix looked up at Megan, back at his foot, and, falling to ground with a howl of agony, began ripping at the boot. The sizzling sound of the mass devouring and disintegrating the boot and flesh was unnerving...as was the popping of each tiny beast as they gorged themselves on their meal and died in their own corrosive waste. The effect was devastating to watch.

Deborah's and Hawk's eyes widened in horror as they witnessed the two spots on the man's foot widen, deepen, and merge into a single hole that, in a matter of a few more seconds, eroded away about a quarter of Felix's right foot and stopped.

Deborah's stomach emptied on the ground when she realized the destruction of Felix's foot was being caused by living creatures. "Worms!" she gagged, barely heard over Felix's howls of agony.

There was no blood. The edges and interior of the wound were cauterized black. Felix gripped his ankle with both hands trying to get his pain under control. He finally stopped screaming, but the expression of pain remained. Every muscle in his body was as tense as a tightly coiled spring as he attempted to cope with the injury.

"Not worms," Megan replied to Deborah, as if nothing were out of the ordinary, "the larvae of a small, biting, but otherwise harmless fly." Without pause, she turned to Felix. "Up until this point, here in training, the Light has tended your wounds. You were right in referring to bruises and scrapes. That is all any of you have received so far. Now you are a cripple—and without the Light you will remain that way."

As if to be more dramatic, Megan pulled her cannon, stepped back, and fired into her own leg. The explosion was loud, causing the three already sitting on the ground to fall backward. The leg was mangled, blood spewing from the open wound. The grimace on her face was real. Other than Felix, who was dealing with his own wound, the others felt the pain that shot through Megan as she fell to the ground.

Using her arms and good leg, Megan dragged herself the short distance to a sack she had placed near the front of the class prior to starting today's lessons. Out of it, she produced a large stone. It was a green stone about the size of Hawk's fist. It was covered in dirt, but there were spots that had been rubbed clean by the leather of the bag. The light that it emitted was brilliant and blinding. Megan pulled the stone into her chest. And then it happened.

The leg, mangled and bleeding profusely, simply stopped oozing. Right before their eyes, the damage was slowly repairing itself. Megan sat quietly and let the transformation continue. The pain in her eyes began to fade; relief indicated on her face as the tension in her body relaxed. No one could say a word. Hawk and Deborah could not take their eyes off the miracle that was happening in front of them. Even Felix was mesmerized, briefly forgetting his own pain. As her limb slowly became whole, the stone's brilliance began to fade. It was not long before the stone had become nothing more than a rock, indistinguishable from any other rock. But Megan's leg was healed without a trace of the havoc that had been wrought upon it only minutes before.

"It's a *'Buchedd chan 'r Gwyrdd Chyneua'* but most call it 'The Life of the Green Light' or simply a Healing Stone," Megan said looking at her fresh leg. "It is the only use of the Green Light that Sapient6 allows to be used in the arena. If you find one of these, grab it! Use it to heal yourself as necessary and as time permits. But remember, these stones work rather slowly, as you just saw. You can still lose a battle and cost yourself the match."

"My foot," gasped Felix, "is not healing!"

"The Light is alive," Megan continued, "an entity within itself. It shows itself as it chooses. It can be in front of your eyes and without prior knowledge of its existence, you would never know it was there." Megan tossed the stone on the ground as if it never had any value and she had never touched it in the first place.

Felix scrambled over and grabbed the rock from where it landed. When clutching the stone to his chest had no immediate effect, he rubbed it over his crippled foot. Other than new pains emanating from his injury and up his leg, nothing happened. He howled anew as he dropped the rock and looked up at Megan. She reached into the bag and tossed him a different stone. Then she passed the other students stones of their own.

Felix caught the stone midair and hugged it to his chest.

As the brilliance of the healing stone began to fade, so too did the injury on his foot. Just as the wound healed, the light suddenly ceased, leaving another ordinary rock. Hawk and Deborah were as amazed at this power of the Light as Felix was thankful.

"And in the Light?" Hawk asked.

Felix's gaze focused. He wanted to hear this answer. He needed to hear the answer to the riddle of what was the Light.

*   *   *

Although Felix struggled within the Light, the development of his skill as a marksman was undeniable. His abilities were proving at times to rival, if not eclipse, those of Hawk. More than once during their frequent clashes in the arenas Felix had bested both Hawk and Deborah.

Deborah's skills had also improved. But her desire to remain competitive was driven for a much different reason. She had not forgotten what she had learned during the course of the trials. The image of her husband's knife in Felix's bag as it landed on the floor in front of her was etched in her memory, burning. It was this image that made her clashes on the field more and more driven, more and more aggressive, more and more violent. Deborah was changing.

Each pupil's skill level had matured as they had as individuals. They had become familiar with all the various "toys," as Megan first called them within the arena. No longer were any of them too timid to try out a new weapon. Their maneuvering had improved greatly, and the tactics they employed one on one had impressed Megan enough for her to come to her next conclusion: It was time to push them further.

As with every step she took to press a new lesson, Megan wasted no time. She gathered them together at the start of the new day. "There will be matches where you must learn to work with a partner. You must quickly learn his weakness and strengths just as you must learn those of your opponents. To succeed in battle, you must become flexible in your strategies, adapt and adjust," she explained.

Forming teams of two, she said, "Hawk, you fight by my side. Deborah, Felix...you will be our opponents."

Not waiting for a response, Megan sprinted off, Hawk right behind her. Felix and Deborah departed in the opposite direction. With the sound of the now familiar cannon's grenade exploding, the match had begun.

Felix and Deborah located a cannon and Gatling Gun wedged under some brush. Felix kept the cannon as Deborah collected the ammo for her weapon that was scattered close by. They headed through the trees separately but within sight of each other. Slightly staggered in position, Deborah followed behind Felix as he made his way through the course, keeping a watchful eye and ear to any sudden changes in their surroundings.

With the weapon in his left hand, Felix came to a stop and then crouched down. Deborah followed suit and watched as he turned to signal that he had heard something in front of them. *Hmmm, what was that?* she thought. Deborah watched as Felix switched the weapon from his left to right hand. Although the shift was fluid, Felix had a look of awkwardness and discomfort about him. Deborah, attempting to move closer, took a step toward him when...*Boom!*

From the corner of her eye, Deborah saw the movement and dodged away from where the round had landed. As she leapt, Deborah turned, returning fire. Dodging, weaving, Felix and Deborah counterattacked as Hawk and Megan made their assault. From the right, Deborah saw Felix raise his cannon firing, covering her shifts in position. Both could hear the rattling of a handheld Gatling Gun. From behind, Deborah felt the stippling of bullets as they pierced her body.

Deborah tried to fire back but felt her strength rapidly waning. Making one last attempt to retaliate, she turned and jumped into the incoming torrent of bullets. With everything she had, Deborah fired as many rounds as she could toward Megan's position. Megan, anticipating the response, quickly dodged away from the rounds' deadly path. Without remorse, Megan finished the task at hand. Green.

Alone in the Light, Deborah thought for a moment about what she had just witnessed. But the thought was quickly disrupted as Hawk had finished off Felix in their clash.

"Damn!" Felix made his presence known.

"We better get back," Deborah responded.

Felix knew his weaknesses. The pain in his left side was from a wound he had received the day he disposed of a drunk outside of the tavern in Falkenwrath years back. Although the wound had healed, the discomfort that lingered was a constant reminder. He had hoped the Light would heal that long ago, but he was wrong. It hadn't.

More than that, Felix feared the Light. He struggled to grasp the ability to return. He understood the concept of the Light, and from Megan's teachings, Felix became stronger in it. What he could not understand was why he had to some-times fight to find his way back.

"Give me a second." Felix felt for Deborah's presence in the Light. Deborah could feel Felix reaching for her but said nothing.

"Are you coming?" Deborah asked finally, frustrated.

After a brief pause, he said, "Yes, of course I'm coming. Let's go." Sensing her, Felix followed Deborah out of the Light.

As they emerged from the Green Light, both Megan and Hawk were waiting. Other than some slight shrapnel damage, Hawk was unscathed, smiling as the two returned. Deborah tossed him a distasteful smirk. "Yeah. Like you had anything to do with it."

Megan gathered them around. "You should have learned something out there today."

As Megan emphasized the lessons to be gleaned from the last battle in the arena, Deborah's mind was elsewhere. She had discovered something today, but it had nothing to do with the arena. It had nothing to do with the weapons. What she had learned was Felix was weaker on his left side than he let on. *But more important than that,* she realized, *Felix feared the Light!*

Chapter Seventeen

From time to time, a Deviant would drop in to see the new recruits. Some visited out of morbid curiosity, others from boredom, and others still for the target practice. This was not one of those trips. For the brothers, this visit was for preparation.

Oberon and Dagger had been brought into the fold of Deviants long ago. Found in a remote part of the galaxy, the brothers were plucked from a life of violence deep within the caves of Fenirene, a small mining planet whose only resources required the difficult task of excavating the iron ore that kept the fires burning—that and fighting. Forced into the second trade by birth, Oberon and Dagger were feared by even the most skilled of fighters.

They had a unique connection that allowed for them to prosper in their world. Early in their childhood, long before their days of digging in the tunnels, long before their first of many mine-hollow bouts that followed, the brothers realized each could sense what the other was feeling, seeing, and thinking.

They were too young to understand how these capabilities would protect them back then; their gift was not discovered in the ring, but out in the woods behind their home. The fashion in which their discovery took place could have served as an indication of how their future would unfold, but it did not. This was because their secret was not revealed in the heat of battle; it was discovered in fear.

The secret was kept from everyone—even their parents had no knowledge of the gift they shared. At first it was a game to them, using it to get what they wanted from their parents. Then it became a tool they used in school, both in the classroom and out in the schoolyard when a bully would try to push his way upon them. As the brothers grew, they practiced and honed and eventually became fluent in their gift.

Their fighting skills also improved. The children of Fenirene knew of life in the tunnels. Often in the schoolyard, challenges were made and accepted along the lines of that life. Alone in the ring, the brothers were formidable foes. Coupled with the use of their gift, it did not take long until the school toughs stopped challenging Oberon or Dagger altogether.

In the tunnels of Fenirene, it was only a matter of time before a conflict would occur. Conflict, no matter how trivial, almost always led to the ring where disputes were certainly settled for good. The brothers used their abilities to fend off or defeat those who opposed them. But in the process, Oberon, the older of the two, realized that there was more to what they knew. It was not long after their names became notorious in the ring that Ithaqua made his presence known. Sapient6 chose well in sending Ithaqua to bring them to the Hold. They were a perfect fit.

Each brother was ferocious in the arena. Both had an innate sense that allowed them to determine where an opponent would be long before he thought about getting there. But for the brothers, destroying a target was not as exciting as the hunt. Like a cat toying with its prey, they would find, follow, then add to the frustration when least expecting it before sending their victim into the Light. The abilities they both possessed, coupled with their natural instincts as fighters, more than qualified them for their eventual position within the Deviant Stronghold.

Each being acted differently when pushed into a corner, when outnumbered or overwhelmed. It was this reaction the Deviants wished to see. There was only one way to ascertain this information and that was to witness it, to force the circumstance. At the time deemed appropriate, the Deviants would see to it that the prospect was tested. This test was designed with only one purpose, to mentally rip the person to shreds. This was the response that would determine final acceptance into the world of Deviance. Skills were important, but those could be improved over time. But the survival instinct is innate and very few beings are ever forced into this mental state. The responsibility of pushing the prospect to his wit's end, to break him, to compel action upon the last nerve belonged to an overseer. Oberon and Dagger were overseers. And both were experts at retrieving that response. Every student eventually faced one, or both, of the overseers.

*   *   *

The tavern was empty at this early hour of the morning and except for the couple at the table in the far back corner, Ithaqua and Megan were alone. The sun would not rise for another two hours. The torch next to them had been extinguished and the serving maid could hardly see that the table was occupied as she approached with two tankards of ale. As she drew near, the voice that reached her ears was saying, "I believe we are starting to see the warrior Hex sent you to bring us."

Megan stopped short at the girl's approach, looked up at her, and flipped a silver coin onto the tray she was carrying even before the girl had removed the first tankard. "Thank you," Megan said with a smile. The silver coin, rather than the usual copper, told the girl with certainty there was no point to lingering. Deftly placing the drinks before the pair, she retreated. "Rizon should have beaten Hawk this afternoon," was lost to the girl's ears as Megan watched her return to the bar.

Ithaqua grinned. "Hawk's ten to three win was impressive, indeed."

"Deborah and Felix have also come along well," she said. She turned her attention back to Ithaqua. "It won't be long now."

*   *   *

Not long after meeting, it was Ithaqua who arrived at the proving ground one morning and gathered Hawk, Deborah, and Felix together. In a serious tone he spoke, "It's been a long journey for all of you. You have each been through much training and have been given an incredible understanding. Megan was very thorough in her teachings."

Looking at all three, he continued. "You have all been charged!"

"Charged? Charged with what?" asked Hawk.

"You are all suspected of Deviance," he said with a wry smile. "Therefore, you shall all face trial."

"Court?" Felix said recoiling. "Again?" Sapient6's admonishment had not been forgotten.

"Yes...you shall go to court once more," Ithaqua said, ignoring the man's reaction. "But you have been given your defense. You will represent yourself and will have only one soul to hold accountable for your failure or success! Now go, rest. Your dates with destiny have been set."

At that moment, the door to the training ground opened and three guards holding long spears followed a lead guard toward the group. The lead guard acknowledged Ithaqua with a curt nod. With a silent signal, each junior guard took a place at the side of his charge. Hawk's face was stoic, the muscles in his jaw flexing. Deborah looked at Hawk to see if he was as nervous as she. If he was, she couldn't tell. Felix showed no emotion, either, when she glanced in his direction. The charged were ushered through the doorway back into the room before the tunnel. The three were lined one behind the other before the lead guard moved to close the training ground door, leaving Ithaqua behind, and opened the tunnel doorway.

Hawk's mind was reeling. He did not know if this was the last time he'd see Deborah, and the thought of saying goodbye in this way bothered him. *I've got to talk to her. I need to tell her goodbye.*

All three were led through the tunnels out of the bowels of Deviant Hold to a different part of the stronghold, one where they had not been before. When they reached the entrance to the chamber quarters, the lead guard opened the door and stepped aside. The three junior guards cleared the way allowing Hawk, Deborah, and Felix to cross into the foyer unescorted.

Hawk crossed the doorway into the entrance hall first.

He realized that a chance to get Deborah alone was not going to happen. Stepping aside to allow room for everyone else, Hawk paused, allowing himself a moment to look at Deborah as she entered behind him. The message in his eyes matched all that Deborah was feeling. She fell into Hawk, pressing her head against his chest, wrapping her arms around him. Hawk took her in his arms and held her close. For a few moments neither spoke.

Felix stepped uneasily around them, careful not to interrupt. He watched as his traveling companions found each other, unsure of what to think about this revelation.

Neither the lead, nor junior guards moved to interfere with the pair.

Deborah's embrace loosened slightly as she looked into Hawk's eyes.

Hawk leaned in to kiss her. Deborah raised her head to meet him as their lips touched tenderly. As they embraced, Hawk said, "Me, too."

After a few moments, the lead guard made his presence known, and Hawk released Deborah from his hold, taking her hands in his.

The junior guards took places by their charges once again. With another silent order, each defendant was led away down the corridor toward his or her chamber. Deborah's was first in the row, followed by Felix's. Hawk's was the third. With the three defendants positioned in front of their respective doors, the lead guard stomped his boot. Simultaneously, each entrance opened. The guards stepped aside as the three entered their respective rooms.

The rooms were comfortable, each with a four-poster bed ringed in curtains. All would find a large mirror rested above a dresser filled with everything they would need for an extended stay. A chaise lined one wall along windows that allowed a view into the courtyard.

Though the furnishings were warm and comforting, none would sleep. Each would wrestle with Ithaqua's words over and over as the night passed. But in the morning, nobody came for them. Alone in their rooms, all day they waited. Another night passed, yet when the next morning arrived, nothing. A week had come and gone, but still no one was approached. Although they weren't afforded the opportunity to see each other, Hawk, Deborah, and Felix had begun to relax.

* * *

Deborah was awakened by the sounds of people walking down the corridor. As the steps drew nearer, her heart pounded harder and harder. But they were not coming for her. No, those footsteps only slowed as they passed, then continued on to the next door. Felix's door.

The pounding was silenced by the creak of hinges, revealing Felix had answered. Muffled voices seeped through the door as Deborah pressed her ear to it, trying to understand what was being said. Deborah closed her eyes and concentrated on what was beyond the other side. *Nothing.*

* * *

Bam! Bam! Bam! came the shudder of her door. Deborah was so startled that she tripped backward and fell hard. *Bam! Bam! Bam!* followed again. Recovering, Deborah picked herself up off the floor and reached for the handle, opening it slowly. Two guards stood there before her. One guard reached out and handed her a rolled parchment as the other stepped back to allow Deborah the space she needed to exit her room. "It's time."

She quickly made herself ready, grabbed her things, and followed the guards down the corridor. As they made their way through the poorly lit passageways, Deborah attempted to read the ornate calligraphy written in archaic prose upon the scroll.

~Summons~
Deviance Has Been Accused.
You Are Hereby Summoned To Your Defense.

Deborah managed to contain her nervousness, showing no emotion. Inside she was terrified.

*   *   *

Sapient6 and Hex had taken their places of honor, sitting high above the multiple arenas as Deborah was led through a dark passage and stopped in front of two large wooden doors.

The lead guard spoke up. "Here, once you enter, the trial begins. The others are waiting. You will face Oberon and UY. Are you ready?"

"Yes," Deborah said. Inside she trembled.

The silent guard turned and pushed the doors open. The bright light blinded her as she stepped through the entrance and into the arena.

*   *   *

The door slammed behind Felix. He looked around to try and familiarize himself with his surroundings as his eyes adjusted. River and rock, trees lining a clearing, he hadn't been here before. Felix's heart was racing. *This isn't a courtroom,* he thought. *This is the arena! Face trial, go to court, Ithaqua had said. This is my chance!* Nervousness filled him as his eyes scanned the field. *There!* Resting next to a large stone in the middle of the clearing, he spotted the butt of a Gatling Gun. He raced to the spot and armed himself, taking the extra ammo next to it. Feeling a little bit more relaxed now that he was holding a weapon, Felix cautiously moved toward the treeline.

Dagger and Old Man had already separated. With the sound of the slamming doors signifying the trial had commenced, Dagger, quick to familiarize himself with his surroundings, gathered several weapons—a hand cannon, a Gatling Gun, and rocket launcher. He loved the rocket launcher. Unlike Old Man, Dagger loved to toy with his prey. Dagger enjoyed tracking, locating, and frustrating his opponents before sending them into the Light. He never tired of that little game.

Old Man was a patient warrior. Having been a Deviant for many, many years, he grew tired of "chasing" the targets. Although he would venture out now and again to face his opponents, he preferred to allow them to come to him. His weapon of choice was the long-range sniper rifle. His "cane," as it was affectionately known to his fellow Deviants. Old Man made his way above the trees, found a vantage point where most of the field was in view and calmly prepared. In fact, as he settled in, Old Man spotted Felix making his way toward the treeline. He smiled.

Felix had no clue where he was.

*   *   *

Deborah stood still for a moment. The doors behind her disappeared as they slammed shut. A long bridge crossing a moat leading to a castle was before her. A weapon lay on each side of a bridge's mouth. Ithaqua's words came flooding back into her mind as she realized that the court he was referring to was not going to be within four structured walls as had happened before. For all she was feeling inside, Deborah knew the best approach for her was not stay there in front of the now closed doors. Moving quickly, she grabbed the hand cannon and the Larvae gun, along with the extra ammunition.

Quickly surveying the area again and seeing that there were no extra shells nearby for the hand cannon, Deborah made her way across the bridge. Looking down, she noticed the river under the bridge seemed to be teeming with the larvae that filled the canisters in her hand. Deborah shivered at the thought of falling. As she completed the crossing, the entrance to the castle began to creak open.

She watched as the large doors slowly opened. Cautiously, she took the hand cannon, checked to find it was loaded with one full magazine, and passed the doorway. Deborah was taken aback by the serenity of the garden courtyard she had entered. Neatly trimmed shrubs and bushes lined the gracefully curved walkways that wound through the flowers. Statues of heroic looking figures stood guard. For an arena, she was expecting to see more darkness and turmoil or evidence of fighting, not the peacefulness and tranquility that was before her.

A path of stone led to a landing up ahead. Deborah moved to her left, careful not to stray into an obvious open line of fire. The statues were lined in two evenly spaced rows. The figures depicted were of none she had ever seen before. Another set of large doors was already opened beyond the large landing. Deborah dodged between the sculptures, hoping they provided some cover from an opponent's eyes, closing the distance between her and the doors. Just before she reached the landing, she tripped upon a stone. The bright green light radiating from the stone revealed its importance. Deborah quickly unearthed the stone and placed it into the sack holding the spare ammunition.

Oberon and UY were waiting, as both knew the layout of the fortress very well. As well they should, it was Deviant Stronghold. Deborah was given the same entrance Hawk had used upon his arrival. The twisting tunnels and wrapped around passages were perfect for testing the wits of a young recruit in her final trial.

*   *   *

Felix's head jerked back and forth. He had heard something behind him but couldn't see anything. Dagger had been watching him for some time now.

The woods that lined the clearing were thick, making it hard to discern shapes among the shadows. Dagger decided to play his favorite game. "Left or Right" he called it. Stepping left would earn you a warning as "I left you alone." Stepping right meant you stepped "Right into the Light!" He'd laugh as he retold these tales at the Deviant Round Table.

Felix stood still for a moment longer. He knew someone was out there. Looking left, he started to step when behind him again he heard a twig snap. He jumped right. The roaring whine of the projectiles flying in his direction grew louder. Before Felix could react, the rockets exploded at his feet. Dirt and debris of tree erupted in all directions. Felix fared no better and woke in the Light.

"Damn!" Felix muttered.

*   *   *

From within the shadows of the doorway, Deborah could see a foyer dimly lit by sconces lined along the walls. She saw the picture frames but did not take time to admire any. Her focus at the moment was what lay before her. Ahead, at what seemed to be the middle of the passage, was an opening in the wall. As she neared, Deborah saw split ramps that spiraled downward to another large hall. At the very bottom level were large crates stacked upon each other, but randomly spread. In between was another launcher—rockets. Cautiously, Deborah made her way down the ramps, careful not to make too much noise as she did.

UY was already there waiting. Armed to the teeth, he watched as Deborah walked right past him. It was dark in his little cutout in the wall, but he could see her clearly. He waited as she cautiously made her way down the ramp.

As Deborah reached the bottom level, she armed herself with the rocket launcher, then watchfully made her way into another hall. There was a shadow at the other end of the corridor. *Oberon?* Deborah pressed up against the wall as she carefully took aim. Suddenly, a feeling overcame her. She was not sure if she should fire. The shadow was not moving and seemed more to be relaxing! *Relaxing? Had the trial started?* she wondered.

Above Deborah's head, a fan turned, causing a slight hum from the motor and blades. She crept a little closer to the shadow and then stopped. She had gotten as close as she wanted for the moment. Concentrating intently upon her intended target, she pondered what do. *The overseers would not be so careless,* she told herself.

Still unsure, Deborah decided perhaps it would be better to make sure the trial had begun. "Hello! Can we fire yet?"

There was no response.

"Hello? Can we fire yet?"

Still no response but this time she saw movement from the shadow. *What the hell is he doing?*

Deborah stood, still not facing the direction from which she had come. Thinking it was the sound of the fan's noise overhead, she yelled louder, "Can we fire yet?"

"YUUUUUUUP!" UY yelled with glee from only five paces behind her. Deborah turned in shock as UY pulled his trigger. The cannon shell exploded directly into Deborah's chest. Bits and pieces of Deborah flew everywhere. She awoke in the Light.

*　　*　　*

Felix had made his way out of the Light and into the field of battle once more after falling victim to Dagger's little game. Felix vowed to not get caught like that again. Recalling what Megan had taught him, he kept moving. Being careful to pay attention to the signs around him, Felix decided to stay just inside the treeline as he made his way between the clearings, picking up whatever weapons he could find.

Old Man lay waiting. He watched as Dagger closed the distance that separated himself from Felix. Dagger was relentless. He would send Felix into the Light a thousand times if he could. Old Man was not to be cheated out of his fun. Taking careful aim between two trees that lay ahead of Felix's path, Old Man relaxed. His breathing became so calmed it was as if he didn't need to breathe at all.

Felix made his way through the trees, bouncing back and forth randomly. Pausing just long enough to get a bearing before he would move again, this time he was ready. Feeling better about his actions, Felix stepped between the two trees Old Man had selected. The crack of the rifle echoed throughout the arena, catching Dagger's attention. In mock frustration and a smile, Dagger started his tracking all over again. Felix never heard a thing as his head became a bright pink mist. Old Man pulled the bolt back and reloaded his cane, smiling as he did so.

"Damn!" Felix said, irritated.

*   *   *

Just like a damn man! Deborah was angry. *The shadow, Oberon, he never spoke. He just sat there!*

Deborah reentered the arena. She was not frustrated. She was pissed. She made her way up the stairs and through the hallway again. This time, before she stepped toward the ramps, she took a good look around. She saw UY's hiding place. With her hand cannon, she fired two rounds into the hole in the wall. The explosions were loud, but nothing. No matter, she knew now. This game was on.

Instead of continuing down the ramps as before, Deborah decided to traverse the remainder of the hall. She discovered there was a rifle sitting at the other end. Deborah took the rifle along with the extra cartridges and pushed forward, deeper into the Hall. Oberon waited. He knew Deborah was not going to fall for the same trick twice.

Deborah continued around the corner and down another wide, sloping ramp. The bottom of the corridor opened into a larger room with more boxes, weapons, and two openings to more darkened passages. Taking what she could carry, behind one set of boxes just before an opening, Deborah saw the shadow again.

Not wasting time, she pulled the trigger of her rocket launcher. The tightly grouped missiles flew toward the shadow. The explosion was loud and the damage impressive, but there was no evidence that anyone was destroyed by the blast.

Oberon was quick. He jumped out from within the opening where Deborah's failed attack had destroyed his cover. Firing his Gatling Gun, the rounds stippled her across her chest and back along her legs. Deborah fell. Without saying a word, Oberon finished her off. Her body faded as she woke in the Light.

*   *   *

The deaths were adding up. Both Felix and Deborah were finding themselves defeated and sent into the Light over and over. Felix's frustration was mounting. So much so that he was having a harder and harder time focusing. Deborah's emotions were also having an effect on her. Every time she felt she was close to the win, UY or Oberon would somehow find a way to kill her.

"Deborah! Are you in here?"

"Yes! Again...but I'm not staying long."

"Wait!" Felix said, but it was too late, Deborah had already entered her arena again.

Felix sat for a very long moment to try and regroup. Then he made his way back to his arena where he saw Old Man was adjusting his position. Felix ran into the woods.

*   *   *

Deborah had made her way deeper into Deviant Hall. The corridors were all becoming familiar now. She realized that one hall would wind itself into another that she left behind. The maze was becoming clear to her. She made her way through the network of tunnels and passages, gathering weapons along the way.

*   *   *

Felix found what he was looking for. Grabbing the sniper rifle, he made his way and took cover behind a large stone that rested near the cover of trees. So wrapped up in finding a Deviant before he was spotted, he neglected to arm himself with any other weapon.

Staring through the sights, Felix poised himself for a shot. He found Old Man still moving, climbing the rocks of the side of a hill above the trees. Old Man was close to a small plateau, preparing himself for his next attempt. Felix felt the jubilation in his chest as his heart pounded. "Stay still," Felix said as Old Man took his final stage.

Dagger overheard Felix's whispered words and saw the weapon he was holding. His reaction was instantaneous.

Three blades flew through the air. Each found their mark. The first penetrated Felix's hand causing him to flinch as he pulled the trigger. The second and third penetrated his neck and skull, but not before Felix's round found its mark. The force of the bullet in his shoulder spun Old Man around. Felix's body began to fade.

"Ha! I got you! One for me!" Felix screamed. "Where are you?"

Old Man did not answer.

"Old Man!" Felix repeated. The green that surrounded Felix was dense. "Old Man? I got you! Are you here?"

Felix called out louder and louder, his frustration getting the better of him. His anger grew more and more intense as the realization set in that Old Man was not in the Light. The loss of control over his senses pushed Felix over the edge.

Chapter Eighteen

As the trial proceeded, Deborah found herself becoming more and more determined. She realized she was not going to win this trial. And what would come of it, she had no clue. But the decision was made; she was not going to allow them to see her squirm on account of it. No. If anything, she would show just the opposite. She was determined to make her mark regardless of the outcome. Entering the arena once more, Deborah gathered every weapon she could find.

Deborah heard the rounds of the Gatling Gun hitting the walls behind her as they stippled their way around, and through, her position. Not knowing who was doing the firing, she jumped out of the way and lobbed her own volley of cannon in the direction of the attack. It was UY. The fight was on. Deborah's rounds fell close to UY's position and exploded. She could tell she hurt him this time. She was not fairing well either as her strength was slowly evaporating. *The stone!* Crawling behind a crate, she pulled it out and held it to her chest. Slowly, the bright light faded as her wounds began to heal.

Deborah lifted herself out of her hiding position in time to see Oberon had made his way into the room where she and UY had been fighting. Oberon and UY both had weapons drawn. Deborah had pulled out two weapons of her own, the Larvae gun and the rocket launcher. Without hesitating, she fired both. UY could hear the familiar crackling of the larvae in flight. Deborah emptied the weapon, splattering the ground with misshapen balls of larvae. UY's agility was sorely tested to dodge the incoming rounds. Simultaneously, missiles exploded near the position Oberon had just vacated.

Oberon released his own rockets as UY fired a burst of Gatling Gun rounds at Deborah's position. She jumped. She jumped high. And she jumped quickly! The move surprised both UY and Oberon as Deborah kicked off the brick wall and landed above a crate.

Rockets flew in UY's direction as Deborah did her best to eliminate the pair. UY fired back as he evaded her incoming volley. Oberon took the opportunity to pull his favorite weapon.

Deborah knew time was running out...and so was the ammunition for the launcher. Firing the last round, she threw the launcher at UY, buying herself a brief second from his sight. She leapt from the crate she was on to another, doing the best she could to use whatever cover available while she pulled out the cannon.

It was too little, too late. Oberon had already fired the Flur rifle. The large vaporous fluorine gas ring expanded into a lethal sphere of energy as Oberon fired the second, detonating hydrogen shot into it. Deborah was caught in its deadly explosion.

*   *   *

Deborah awoke in the Light. She took a moment to gather her senses when she heard crying. *What the hell is that?* She followed the sounds until her senses found the source. It was Felix.

"Felix?" she found him huddled in a ball in the dense green of the Light.

"Help me."

Deborah watched as he writhed on the floor. "Help you?"

"Help me, Deborah…get me out of here."

Deborah's first instinct was to reach out for Felix as she had when she first found him lying on the floor of the Light. Suddenly, she stopped.

"Deborah! Get me out of here. I can't make it on my own," Felix said. The expression sounded to Deborah as if he was exhausted.

"No." Her reply was calm.

"What? Help me!" Felix said angrily.

"No. I won't."

Felix tried to right himself with what little strength he had, reaching out for Deborah.

She could feel him get closer so she moved away.

"Deborah! Why won't you help me?" Felix pleaded, the desperation in his voice increasing.

"It was you," Deborah said, her passive tone morphing to anger.

"What are you talking about?" Felix gasped.

"You killed him." Deborah's voice was filling with vengeance.

"I didn't kill anyone…what are you talking about? Help me…please!" Felix's voice was wavering.

"The scars on your side, where did you get them?" Deborah demanded.

"It's been so long…I don't remember."

"What of that blade you have in your bag? The dual blade! How did you come to own that?" Deborah's voice was filled with emotion, filled with anger and hate, with sadness and sorrow.

Felix was scared now. "My blade? I've had that for years now…why? Deborah, please!"

"That blade belonged to my husband," Deborah stated. Her voice was choked with tears. "You killed my husband."

Deborah's mind flashed back into the courtroom to the moment when she discovered Felix's secret. An image came into view from within the denseness of the green. Felix saw what Deborah was projecting. The sight of the open bag on the floor revealing the unmistakable handle of the sheath-covered blade was still fresh in her mind. How Deborah wished she could get her hands on that knife now! Then, as if she had summoned it, his pack appeared between them. It was all too real! She grabbed the sheath and pulled the blade. Looking at it, Deborah yelled, "This is NOT your knife!"

That realization caused Felix to panic. He lunged toward Deborah only to find she avoided him, preventing their touch. "Help me!"

"Not this time, Felix. Had I known it was you who killed my husband when I first found you here in the Light, I would have listened to Sapient6's words. I would have let you die in the beginning." Her words stung.

"It was you? You pulled me from this place the first time? Please, Deborah, I didn't know. How was I to know! I didn't mean to kill him!"

Deborah's anger overwhelmed her. Her presence in the Light was shifting from point to point with no true direction.

The form of Felix was lying on the ground, arm extended, reaching out for something but touching nothing.

"You didn't mean to kill him? You killed him with the very weapon you took from him. The knife I gave him!" Deborah was crying. "You're a thief. You're a liar. You're a murderer!"

"Help me, please." Felix's words were fading. The differentiation between his body and the Light was diminishing, being enveloped by the Light, vanishing along with his words. "Deborah...please," Felix pleaded as he heard Deborah's final words.

"And now...you're dead." Deborah stood back and watched as the final image of what was Felix faded into the Light.

Deborah took a moment to herself, shaking within the Light. She attempted to compose herself before going back to the trial but failed. She began to sob. As she cried, her body emerged from the Light, back into the garden near the foot of the landing. She was still holding the knife and sheath in her hands, the tattered straps draped along her side. Deborah's mind reeled. For a moment she forgot where she was and what she was doing. The flood of memories of Robert overshadowed everything.

Those feelings did not last long. She heard echoes of movement coming from down the corridor. Deborah had had enough. Attempting to regain her composure, she tied the sheath straps around her waist and leg. Not caring what danger could be in the garden, she exited the castle and crossed the bridge. Deborah armed herself with the hand cannon and made her way to face her opponents. Deborah was finished running.

Her first round landed by Oberon's feet. UY had circled behind her, but Deborah wasn't being fooled. She turned and fired again. The round fell short. She fired again. And again. And again. And again. All the while, the Deviants were making short play of her futile offensive attempts.

Then *click, click, click.*

Deborah was out of ammunition. With the little resolve that still burned inside her, Deborah discarded the cannon and pulled the dual blade from its sheath. She extended her arm toward the Deviants, prepared to defend herself. Both Oberon and UY studied her carefully. But her resolve did not last long. Deborah knew it was over. With nothing left within, Deborah bowed her head and lowered her weapon. Through watershed eyes, she looked up at them, expecting to be painfully sent into the Light yet again.

UY's youthful, strong, able body bent over. His face aged in seconds as Timothy emerged. Reaching within his cloak, Timothy pulled out his walking staff as he slowly turned away and walked back into Deviant Hold, the doors shutting behind him. Oberon's body lifted off the ground and became engulfed in a blue flame. With an approving smile and a nod, he vanished.

The trial had ended.

Deborah dropped to one knee, mentally and physically exhausted, still holding the knife, tears streaming down her face. Calm and serenity had returned to the courtyard when the breeze around her began to slowly swirl. Her long, flow-ing, golden brown hair began to dance as the wind circled harder and harder. Slowly lifting off the ground as if a hand had reached down to raise her, Deborah's arms and legs were pulled gently spread as the clothes she wore, tattered and filthy from the trial, mended and transformed into a long, flowing, sheer gown. Deborah's deep blue eyes be-came radiant, emitting a bright light as her skin became clean and pure. Previously unseen glyphs decorated the now new leather of the sheath strapped to her waist and thigh; still in her hand, the precious blade glistened.

As the wind died down, Deborah was lowered to her feet. The castle doors suddenly opened wide. The girl quickly entered the courtyard. The brute followed behind, his head lowered. Taking the lead and reaching for her hand, the look in the servant girl's eyes reassured Deborah. Gently, she guided Deborah to slip the knife into its place. Taking hold of the now empty hand, stroking her hair as she did, the servant girl led Deborah out of the arena.

The brute followed closely behind.

Chapter Nineteen

Hawk waited in his room. Some time had passed since the pounding on the doors had awakened him. The long silence that followed was making him drowsy and soon sleep overcame Hawk once more. The visions in his mind flashed. He heard the screams again. He heard the loud sounds and explosions that scared him so as a child. The detonations in his dreams materialized at the pounding of the door. *Boom! Boom! Bam! Bam! Bam!* The door shuddered as the guards beat on the door, yanking Hawk from sleep.

Hawk rose from the bed, gathered his things and walked over to the door. *Bam! Bam! Bam!* He opened the door, stepping out without saying a word. The guards formed a circle around him as they had around Felix and Deborah. The lead sentinel glared his orders at Hawk, handed him the scroll, and then turned abruptly. Hawk opened and read the notice, and then nodded his head acknowledging the summons. Without hesitation, the guards started walking forward. Hawk followed the leader, his escorts in tow.

The corridor through which they traveled was as dark as the tunnels they had traversed when he was being led to the training fields. No one said a word or made a sound. Hawk knew better than to break with the code.

The lead sentinel stopped in front of what looked like a wall of stone. Hawk could feel his heart starting to race as the adrenaline pumped through his veins. The guard posted alongside Hawk and said in a deep, gravelly voice, "Once you enter beyond this wall, the trial begins. All you see oppose you. Are you ready?"

Hawk's chest rose deeply then slowly fell as he nodded. The lead sentinel lifted his staff and slammed it to the ground. The brick wall before them became semi-transparent. The escorts fell away, their backs against the tunnel walls. Hawk stepped forward and through the barrier. Nothing changed. It looked like a continuation of the dark tunnel he was already occupying. Hawk looked back, but no one was standing behind him, nor was there a wall.

Cautiously Hawk stepped forward. He came upon a chamber that opened up to three doors. Studying them, cautiously, he approached the one on the left, trying to listen for what was on the other side. Turning his head sideways, placing his ear against the door was when he noticed the weapon that had appeared behind him in the center of the buried room. It was a rocket launcher.

Hawk moved toward the gun, but it disappeared, stopping him in his tracks. Stepping back toward the door caused it to reappear once more. *Hmmm…*Hawk stepped toward the middle door. Again he could not hear a thing, but when he turned around he saw the Flur rifle. Moving in front of the third revealed the Gatling Gun.

Hawk had shown promise with all three weapons during training. He really enjoyed the rapid firing of the Gatling Gun and the heavy push of the rocket launcher.

But in his mind, nothing compared to the Flur rifle. When Ithaqua used it to send him into the Light the first time, the weapon scared the hell out of him. But after being given a chance to use it during practice, he came to understand the effectiveness and deadly efficiency of it.

Hawk stepped back in front of the second door. The Flur rifle sat there with extra ammunition on the ground next to it. He reached out and cautiously opened the door. A blast of rushing wind hit him in the face, forcing him backward a step. He saw the weapon was still there. Hawk armed himself and stepped through the door.

*   *   *

Trees and hedgerows at their edges forming the arena's boundaries surrounded steep rolling hills. An old bridge linked two of the biggest hills over a dry creek bed that led to a low open field overran with tall brush and weeds, splitting the large cemetery. Crosses and headstones lined the tops of both hills like a perfect permanent crop planted by a morbid farmer. A barn sat as a cornerstone separating the field from an old dilapidated farmhouse in the corner opposite the bridge. The house was partially surrounded by tall old trees with large thick branches that reached out in all directions. Old wooden planks squared the lot connecting the barn and the house, forming a makeshift fence.

Within the confines of the farmhouse yard laid Flur rifle ammunition alongside a rocket launcher, no spare ammo for the launcher was allotted in that position. In the center of the bridge connecting the mass graveyard was a Flur rifle with no spare ammunition but with cartridges intended for the rocket launcher. Hawk would find ammo for the Gatling Gun sprinkled throughout the arena…if he was lucky. The Gatling Gun was located in the thick brush at the bottom of the dry creek bed. Within the barn laid a hand cannon. It was the only weapon with the correct ammunition cartridges next to it.

Hawk surveyed the landscape from across the field opposite the farmhouse. He gave himself a moment to gather his surroundings, allowing his instincts to take their proper place in his decision making before setting out. He saw nothing to cause alarm. It was the "nothing" that worried him. Hawk decided to avoid being out in the open so soon and set out along the treeline.

Dagger had chosen to wait near the farmhouse where the trees could give him the advantage of a clear line of sight and plenty of cover. There was no predicting where the defendant would enter the arena and he was hoping to be the first to engage but that honor would befall Oberon.

Oberon was waiting and watching as Hawk entered the arena. Tucked away in a hedgerow, Oberon patiently allowed Hawk to close the distance between them. Once he felt the objective was met, Oberon brought a rocket launcher to bear in the direction of Hawk, waiting for the signal that the launcher had acquired its target.

Hawk stopped. Pausing in his tracks, he scanned the field. Nothing. *Something's not right*, he thought.

The rocket departed the launcher clean. The trail of smoke behind the speeding projectile caught Hawk's attention from the corner of his eye. Hawk ran a few steps toward the trees, but the rocket's line changed with him. Without thinking, he ran toward the incoming missile, closing the gap, dodging as he moved closer. The missile wove side to side, countering every move.

Hawk's timing was perfect. At the last possible moment, he jumped out of the path of the rocket, rolling to his side on the ground while keeping an eye on the missile as it flew by and exploded. What Hawk did not see was the second rocket that followed in the smoke trail of the first. The impact was hard at his feet. Hawk was in the Green Light before the smoke cleared.

*   *   *

Hawk didn't waste time. He emerged in the arena this time near the mouth of the bridge connecting the cemetery hills on the side closest to the farmhouse. Hawk's smile at seeing his weapon of choice faded when he discovered that the only extra ammunition in the area was for a rocket launcher. Hawk stashed those away knowing he'd eventually have to find that weapon. Hawk also knew he had to get out of the middle of the field.

Hawk crawled on his belly, trying to keep as low as possible between the rows of headstones as he made his way toward the barn. As he neared the barn fence, he looked into the farmhouse yard and saw the rocket launcher. Not wanting to rush to the launcher, Hawk took a moment to survey the area when he noticed something peculiar above it. At first Hawk thought his eyes were deceiving him but no, there it was, hanging in the tall trees, directly over the launcher was the sack that had been taken from him. *How long has it been?* flashed through his mind as he glanced around.

Dagger was also waiting within the confines of the barn fence. Dagger, like his brother, was patiently waiting to spring his trap. Armed with a hand cannon and prepared for a close engagement, he waited to see if Hawk would go for the sack. What greeted Dagger was not what he expected.

Hawk knew the sack was a trap. He had set many of them himself in his time as a hunter. Instead, Hawk back-tracked and moved to the barn, then around it where he saw Dagger waiting for him. Taking a deep breath, Hawk sprang to action, pulling the trigger from his hip, sending a growing ring of fluorine vapor toward Dagger. Time slowed and his heart pounded as Hawk held his breath waiting for the seemingly slow moving ring of gas to reach a position where the hydrogen plasma of the second shot would complete the deadly combination.

Oberon had seen Hawk jump from his position, but it was too late to warn his brother. Not that it mattered. Dagger was much quicker than Hawk had expected. The vaporous ring had barely left the barrel when, in a single continuous motion that made Megan's feline grace seem clumsy, Dagger dodged left in a leaping cartwheel motion, switched his weapon from the hand cannon to a Flur of his own, and fired.

It all happened too fast and too late for Hawk to react. Dagger fired a hydrogen round that pierced into the center of Hawk's own fluorine shot causing a massive explosion that engulfed the area surrounding it—Hawk included.

*   *   *

Hawk's senses returned in the Light. He was sitting on a bench before an open portal that looked down upon the field from which he had just been removed. Sitting next to him was Old Man, putting down a tankard of ale from his mouth. Old Man smiled. "That was terrible. You are going to have to do better than that."

Hawk did not know what to say and just stared down at the scene of the arena.

Continuing, Old Man asked, "So, are you just going to sit here? An interesting approach to one's trial...sitting in the bleachers, cheering for himself, waiting to see how it turns out. Wish I'd thought of that during mine. It would have been less painful." Old Man's smile was broad behind the irony of his words.

"How in the hell did he do that?" Hawk demanded. "He was three feet in the air and upside down!"

The smile disappeared. "Get your ass back down there!" The Deviant's usual friendly countenance had turned to a snarl.

Confused, Hawk took a deep breath, concentrated, and reappeared just below his bag and where Oberon's cannon grenade exploded in the back of his neck a mere moment after he got his bearings. The portal, the bench, and Old Man were nowhere in sight this time.

The number of kills began to mount, and Hawk was feeling every one. His frustration was beginning to mount as well. After one particular encounter with Dagger, he took his time getting back. Hawk took a moment to figure out what he was doing wrong. Each engagement, with either Oberon or Dagger, led to another trip back into the Light. There was a pattern to this...something was there...but he could not figure it out. And what the hell was his bag doing there in the tree!

That's it! Hawk thought, *What did the voice say? All that is kept is gained in peace. What is lost in war shall be no more. The voice wasn't talking about the bag. It was talking about ME! Be at peace. Release yourself. Release your mind!*

Déjà vu—Hawk entered the arena near the Gatling Gun buried in the thick brush of the dry creek bed. He searched the area for extra ammunition but found none. He needed more than what was loaded in the weapon. Taking a look around caused his head to swirl. His heart began to race. *I've been here before. I know this place!* Hawk had a flashback. Every night Hawk dreaded going to sleep for fear of the hell that ensued in his mind after his eyes closed. And now here he was, actually living the torment that had plagued him as a child. Hawk was in the cemetery he saw in his first vision. Hawk froze.

Oberon and Dagger had set up across the open field of headstones in perfect position for a crossfire ambush. Using their innate ability to see, think and feel what the other was experiencing, the two had covered what they thought would send Hawk into the Light again, pushing him further into his personal hell.

Hawk began thinking like the hunter he was. He climbed the side of the hill that led to the center of the graveyard. *I've seen what happens next. Let's change the outcome!* he thought. Instead of continuing up the hill he backtracked and traversed the creek bed back toward the barn. There, he crept his way and armed himself with the rocket launcher and ammo for the Flur rifle. *Good.* He knew they were out there in the field. Now it was time to turn the tables into his favor.

Hawk took another look around, this time truly studying the arena as a hunter in the middle of a strange forest. He wanted to know everything he could about the terrain that surrounded him. Hawk had to focus but there in the grass, close to the beginning row of headstones, was a sparkle. *Is that a...it is!* came the realization as his eyes focused on the launching pad buried in the grass.

Hawk made his way into the barn where he found the hand cannon waiting. This is it. Gathering all the ammunition he could carry, he exited the barn. Completely out of character, Hawk began firing blindly, lobbing round after round of grenades over the crest of the hill as he ran toward the gravestones. The rounds landed closer than Oberon appreciated. The fight was on!

Oberon rose up from his place of concealment and fired in return. A Gatling Gun at his hip, Oberon stitched the ground leading up to his target. Hawk dodged to his left. Dagger did not waste any time. Closing the distance that separated him from his brother, he too fired his Gatling Gun in the direction of Hawk.

Anticipating the entrance of Dagger into the fray, Hawk leapt forward, firing the cannon in Dagger's direction as he did, all the while crossing directly in front of Oberon. Dagger's crossfire rounds found their mark into the side of Oberon's leg. Dagger jumped to the side, but not before the grenade exploded at his feet, propelling him further in the direction of his leap.

Dagger and Oberon linked in the field, briefly communicating through their minds. Hawk saw the confusion he had created. He shifted his guns, pulling out the Flur rifle. Letting loose a volley, the expanding ball of vapor made its way toward the center of his two opponents. But it did not get there in time. Oberon and Dagger reacted quickly, safely exiting the ring's effective circumference and avoiding the deadly explosion that followed.

Oberon decided to change tactics. Talking to his brother,

Dagger agreed and moved opposite, circling behind Hawk. Holding a cannon of his own, Oberon fired to Hawk's left, pushing him down the hill and into Dagger's snare. Dagger, anticipating Hawk, allowed his launcher to wind up with multiple rounds. Clearing the crest of the hill, Hawk came into full view. Not waiting for the signal that the launcher had locked onto the target, Dagger released his projectiles, dropped the launcher and pulled out his Gatling Gun.

Hawk saw the rockets leave their perch and made to run. As he turned, his foot snagged and he fell forward, landing on his belly. The rockets zipped past harmlessly, exploding in the distance. Hawk looked to see what he tripped over and saw a magazine of Gatling Gun ammunition. He reached down, quickly retrieving the case and sprinted toward the bottom row of headstones.

Oberon and Dagger closed the gap between Hawk, who was running out of room fast. Oberon, having shifted again, pulled his Flur out and aimed. Bullets from Dagger's Gatling Gun reached Hawk as he neared the field's end of headstones. Hawk felt every piece of hot metal rip into his back and shoulders.

Without thinking, Hawk pulled out his rocket launcher and began allowing the rounds to spin. Holding his finger tightly on the trigger, he leapt forward as hard as he could toward the launching pad. Using the downward slope as he landed, he shifted his momentum and pushed backward with all his might—backward toward Oberon and Dagger!

Hawk was propelled high above the two Overseers. Reversing his position in flight, Hawk released the volley of rockets whining in the chambers of his launcher, and then continued firing individual shots with reckless abandon. Oberon, witnessing the feat, wasted no time. He fired into the air ahead of Hawk. As Hawk and the now expanded ball of energy met, the rockets he had fired made their marks.

Hawk awoke in the Light…along with Oberon and Dagger.

*   *   *

Dagger could be heard from within the dense green that surrounded them saying, "Damn! I can't believe it. I can't believe he took us out like that!" Oberon, for his part, had found an admiration for the newcomer but said nothing in response. Hawk knew he should be excited, but in reality he was too exhausted to respond to anything he was hearing.

Many distant voices began ringing in Hawk's mind, arguing and yelling. Hawk could hear his name mentioned within the faint cacophony. Still in the green, he could barely hear the conversation about him taking place. Hawk tried to concentrate on the voices of Dagger and Oberon as the dissonance grew louder, trying desperately to understand what else was being said. But before he could make sense of the chorus, the voices instantly ceased. The silence was as piercing as the noise. Hawk realized both Oberon and Dagger were gone. Hawk figured the two had left back to the arena and it was about time he did as well.

But Hawk was wrong. When he reentered the arena, it was not Oberon and Dagger that he came upon. What he encountered was a bright green glow. At first he was taken aback, but it was not long before he recognized the brilliant force of light that he had faced upon the hill. It was the very glow that he had charged so long ago but failed to assail, the glow that took his bag and staff from him after speaking the words that echoed in his mind not moments before. It was Hex himself.

There Hawk stood. Near the center of the hill of crosses, he didn't move as the glow drew nearer to him. From deep within his mind the voices reappeared. Hawk could hear the words of conversations happening about him. He could see the persons who argued for and against him. The arguments of voices shouting over others permeated his head. Visions of Deborah, Dagger and Oberon flashed through his mind. The extreme echoes bouncing off the inside of his skull forced him to his knees. Hawk grabbed both his ears as the shouting became louder and grew louder still. Deeper in his mind, he could see Hex, gavel in hand, reacting to the wild yelling and shouts of those who surrounded the round table. Unable to find relief from the terrible noise, Hawk's eyes opened wildly, letting out a scream as Hex's gavel fell, landing hard upon the table's surface.

Silence.

Then a vision—surrounding the large round table were many, though Hawk recognized only a few. All wore the dark green cloaks favored by the Deviants, the hoods cast back off their heads. All except for two whose hoods obscured their faces. One to Hex's right whose cloak appeared darker than the others, almost black. The other to his left wore cloak that was a lighter green.

Hex gazed about the table, raising the gavel once more, silently demanding each raise a fist high so all may see. Respectfully bowing his head, Hex started at his right, allowing the most senior his voice first. The fist of Sapient6 fell hard upon the table causing a thunderous crash—and there the hand stood. With his vote cast, Hex glared. Circling the table, each Deviant dropped his fist, pounding the table, as did the person before, resonating in a deafening roar.

Hawk's mind, trapped, was forced to witness the spectacle when the slightest hesitation caused his heart to stop.

As Hex came full circle, Hawk watched as his glare came to a halt on the person in the light-green robe, fist still held high. Hawk watched as this mysterious entity raised a second hand. The hands paused. Then, slowly, the hood was removed revealing the person underneath.

Deborah? Hawk was stunned.

From a slightly tilted head, Deborah's gaze reached out and locked upon Hawk. The instant their stare met, her tightly clenched fist landed hard upon the table. Hex's gavel came crashing down immediately behind it. For acceptance unanimity was required. The vote had been cast.

Hawk's mind ripped back to reality. Still in the arena and still on his knees, he attempted to stand but felt as if he were being lifted to his feet. Then, without pause, he continued to rise. From out of nowhere, a large gust of wind hit, lifting him higher and higher to the heights of the trees. Hawk's head hung slightly, his arms and legs separated outward as if pulled by two opposing forces. The sky that surrounded Hawk became electric. He felt a surge of power boiling deep within him; the heat and shock coursed through his veins. As the strength of the power intensified, Hawk was encased in a brilliant light. He let out a loud yell as thunder and lightning discharged from the core.

Hawk's arms flailed as he felt his weight fall out from under him. Instinctively, he pushed downward, attempting to counter the fall. To his surprise, Hawk found himself slowing his descent. Another gust of wind pounded into his chest as he was tossed higher into the sky. Thunder roared and lightning continued to flash.

Again he fell and with all his might, Hawk pushed against the sudden plunge. The energy within him burned. Hawk could feel himself becoming stronger. With each blast of wind that hurled him into the sky, the effect of falling became weaker and with it, the energy that surrounded him diminished.

The lightning's brilliance slowly dissipated and the rumble of the thunder faded in the distance. When it was over…silence reigned.

Whoosh, whoosh, whoosh—Hawk, the clan's newest Deviant, lowered himself to the ground.

The Tale Ends.

The Book of Deviance
18,966:14-28

The prophet, as was his wont, lay upon the great table in the Throne Room of Deviant Hall. Upon his back, all four feet extended to the heavens, brain-dead by any evidence obtainable by any practitioner of medical arts throughout time or space, a half-drunk flagon of ale clenched in the grip of rigor mortis.

The west wall of the Hall, engulfed in the Glow that is Green, held the Throne of Legend and, from the throne, in the depths of the Glow, Hex spoke unto the Deviants assembled:

"Heed thee now and turn thy attentions to the prophet!"

Hex called upon Scorpion, who did thereby climb upon the table and the corpse. Sitting on its chest, staring into the gapping nostrils, the bug did arch forth his tail and plunge the lethal stinger into the tip of the prophet's nose.

An explosion of purple over the prophet's face, that touched it not, sent entrails of the ten-legged one in all directions. As one, the Deviants wiped ochre from their faces and availed themselves of the services of he called

Soapy. UY slipped the weapon back under the table and
Scorpion smiled from his seat at the table of honor.

Eyes again clear beheld the familiar column of Green
Light, seemingly suspending the now erect Ithaqua above
the assemblage. The eyes of the Wind Walker glowed emerald as his mouth articulated:

"Verily I say unto thee, thy story shall be told. Thou
knowest the book called Deviance chronicles thy glory.
Thou knowest the unwashed devourers of the by-products
of meat, which thou findest to be indigestible, clamor for
thy deeds. Thou knowest the minds uncleansed by the
Light comprehendeth not the Book wherein tales of thee
and the wisdom of the Light reside.

"I say unto thee that not Hex, nor Six, nor Light itself
canst longer abide the piteous whines of the unwashed and
they shall have thy story.

"Know thee this: thou shalt not read the story as told
unto the unwashed, for thou wilt recognize it not as being
from the Book. In thy grief of seeing not thy name again in
writing, thou mayst piss up the rope of despair, but
moaneth thou shalt not.

"Know that thy story, told in terms thou couldst comprehend from within the womb, confoundeth the
unwashed. Were Deviance understandable to them, he
would not march upon the Keep in which thee dwell with
his torches, pitchforks and chants. Thou wouldst be de-
prived of thy sport.

"He shall have thy story for which he clamors, but understand it, he will not. In his wallowings of ignorance,
thou shalt be subjected to learned analysis of the prose,
laughable in expectations revealed and assumptions clung
to as a mother's teat.

"But the devourers of indigestible by-products of meat shall have thy story."

The column of Light over the table winked out; the prophet dropped into his preferred countenance and the flower burst from UY's rifle again splattered innards of Bug over the Deviants assembled. Scorpion giggled.

About the Author

Gustavo was born in Los Angeles, CA. After graduating from Rancho High in North Las Vegas, NV, he joined the US Navy, retiring from service in 2005. Gustavo took a position with a major uninterruptible power system company as a Field Service Technician, eventually becoming a Technical Product Trainer.

Though the idea of writing The Green Glow "Hawk's Arrival" sprouted in 2000, the work didn't start until 2005. Whether this story continues has yet to be determined. But then again, no one knows what lurks in the Green Glow.

Gustavo enjoys playing guitar, song writing, singing, and of course, telling stories. He currently resides in the state of Washington.